REQUIEM

Darcy hugged the Electrostun to her cheek, aimed, and squeezed the trigger. Electricity crackled as a white arc of fire surged from the insulated barrel of the weapon and snapped through Mozart, its point of contact directly below the jawline.

Mozart screamed as he had never screamed before. Emotions that made no sense whiplashed through Darcy's mind: panic, flight, *guilt*. And hate, too, directed at this creature to which she had devoted so much of herself for so long.

There was an undercurrent to the alien's shriek that she had never heard before. He was her savage and innocent child, and she had betrayed him.

Now she would have to face the consequences. . . .

Don't miss any of these exciting *Aliens*, *Aliens vs. Predator* and *Predator* adventures from Bantam Books!

Aliens: Earth Hive by Steve Perry
Aliens: Nightmare Asylum by Steve Perry
Aliens: The Female War by Steve Perry and Stephani Perry
Aliens: Genocide by David Bischoff
Aliens: Alien Harvest by Robert Sheckley
Aliens: Rogue by Sandy Schofield
Aliens: Labyrinth by S. D. Perry
Aliens vs. Predator: Prey by Steve Perry and Stephani Perry
Aliens vs. Predator: Hunter's Planet by David Bischoff
Predator: Concrete Jungle by Nathan Archer

ALIENS™

MUSIC OF THE SPEARS

Yvonne Navarro

Based on the Twentieth Century Fox motion pictures, the designs of H. R. Giger; and the Dark Horse graphic novel Aliens: Music of the Spears *by Chet Williamson, Tim Hamilton, Timothy Bradstreet*

BANTAM BOOKS
New York • Toronto • London • Sydney • Auckland

ALIENS: MUSIC OF THE SPEARS
A Bantam Spectra Book / October 1996

ISBN 0-553-57492-2

Published simultaneously in the United States and Canada

Bantam Books are published by Bantam Books, a division of Bantam Doubleday Dell Publishing Group, Inc. Its trademark, consisting of the words "Bantam Books" and the portrayal of a rooster, is Registered in U.S. Patent and Trademark Office and in other countries. Marca Registrada. Bantam Books, 1540 Broadway, New York, New York 10036.

PRINTED IN THE UNITED STATES OF AMERICA

OPM 10 9 8 7 6 5 4 3 2 1

In memory of Patty Wold,
and music ended far too soon.

"Miz Von, do you have time?"

Acknowledgments

Thanks to Howard Morhaim for finding another project for me to see to completion, and to Anne Groell for helping me to get it there.

My gratitude to Chet Williamson for a great story, and to Jeff Osier for a lesson in the fine art of appreciating dark music and sending examples to go with it.

Paula Guran, Stephen Spruill, Beth Massie, Don Kinney, Alexa deMonterice, and John Platt: In your own way, each of you has held my hand and helped me dance a little through life in this fall of 1995. Words do not exist that are big enough to express my love and gratitude, and that would make you understand how special each of you are.

As time passes and I move into my second year in cyberspace, I learn more and more that the "GEnie gang" is a wellspring of ongoing friendship, support, and humor. You guys are all different, and all great.

Special appreciation and love, always, to Don VanderSluis.

Prologue

He couldn't believe she wouldn't turn on the lights.

For this occasion, Jarlath Keene had dressed in the best of his well-appointed wardrobe. He'd wanted to convey all the most important attributes—money, power, influence—and the brushed technosilk Paoletti suit he wore expressed all of that and more—as well it should for the fifty-five hundred credits it had cost him. In that respect, Keene's strategy had proved disappointingly ineffective; while the room he stepped into was completely without light, there was a feeling of expansiveness to it that Keene had never encountered in an apartment or condominium before, especially in the small and hard to find buildings in overcrowded Manhattan. He felt immediately and utterly dwarfed.

Illuminated only by the smoggy night sky shining through the penthouse's floor-to-ceiling windows, the lightlessness of the interior made no difference; there was an undercurrent of opulence in the place, of *decadence*, that could not be disguised. Keene was drenched in it with every sense but sight: the carpet beneath his fine Italian pseudo-leather loafers was thick and springy, the air laden with expensive perfume. He wished he didn't have to grope his way across the room—it made him feel awkward and put him at a distinct bargaining disadvantage—but when he did, his fingertips sped across genuine silk and leather upholstery on the plush furniture. His desire to see made him check all the switches and lamps, but none of them worked. The frantic, faraway city lights did little to illuminate the condominium, but they would have to do. Obviously, the woman had the switches wired to some master control to which only she had access. It seemed he would have no choice but to conduct his business in the shadows.

"Mr. Keene."

Her voice was soft and absolutely feminine, a whisper in the dark as delicate as a filmy scarf falling through the air. Keene caught himself before he whirled, turned instead with as much dignity as he could muster given the fact that he was standing in the dark and talking to a woman who seemed no more than a specter from across the room. He cleared his throat. "Yes, Miss—uh . . ."

"Mina."

"Mina, then. Thank you for agreeing to see me." Something about that sensuous voice made the perfectly tailored suit seem suddenly too small, too hot, despite the meticulously filtered and cooled air in the penthouse. "I know it was short notice—"

"My time is quite valuable, Mr. Keene. What do you require?"

Now she was only ten feet away from him, with her back to the row of huge windows. The silver-and-gold sprinkled expanse of Manhattan outside the glass faded to darkness behind her, outclassed by her inky silhouette. Only the woman's eyes were visible, glitter-black, indescribably mysterious. Her hair, unbound in defiance of Japanese tradition, fell to her hips in a straight line broken only by its own muted shine. Mina was a legend among the highest echelon men on earth—those with fortunes numbering in the billions—and a speculative fantasy to everyone else. Why had she agreed to see him?

"I . . . have a proposal," he managed. She said nothing but Keene imagined her raising an eyebrow in doubt—it would be finely shaped and the color of a midnight ocean over eyes like oil. "Of a business nature, of course. Regarding a . . . *mutual* acquaintance." Keene twisted his neck, the collar of his custom-made shirt suddenly uncomfortable. "I would compensate you more than generously for your efforts."

Mina didn't have to laugh for Keene to sense she was more than slightly amused at his clumsy verbiage. Like the scent of her perfume, his words hung in the air between them, though not nearly as pleasant as the fragrance of Charielle. "*'Efforts?' What an interesting choice of words, Mr. Keene.*" She sank onto a chair in front of the window, her descent very much like the smooth, flowing dip of a snake dancer's rope . . . or maybe the cobra itself. Oddly, the condominium was completely silent, as though it had been thoroughly soundproofed. For some reason, Keene had expected soft background music, something romantic and hard to come by . . . a harp, perhaps.

"Maybe," Keene suggested silkily, "the . . . ah, *gentleman* with whom you are associated is not attending to your needs. There are more complexities than wealth that impact upon the liaison between a man and a woman, and I have sources who tell me that there is another gentleman of means who greatly desires your company." Not bad, he thought. The lines were rehearsed and delivered almost flawlessly; only the *gentleman* part tripped over his tongue—no surprise there considering his personal feelings regarding the man in question. "I am prepared to grant you a substantial bonus for your consideration."

"*I see.*" Mina turned her face toward the window and now Keene could see her profile, barely: high forehead, small straight nose, the rounded line of lips above a classic chin. *"And what of the man I leave behind, Mr. Keene? What of him?"*

Now Keene was thankful the telltale lamps were off, glad that there was nothing but moonlight to show the foxlike grin that tried to play across his face. He fought and won the struggle to keep any hint of glibness out of his tone. "Life sometimes deals unfortunate hands, does it not? One must learn to deal with the twists and turns of fate. Many people believe their destiny is preordained from the moment of birth."

"And you—what do you believe?"

That voice, so sensual and sweet, like warmed dark chocolate flowing from a spoon. In itself it was dangerously distracting. "I-I believe a person controls their own life," he said. "Everyone's existence is unique, formed by the billions of experiences that happen to them and no one else."

"Really." Mina was silent for so long that Keene had begun to think she'd lost interest, the allure of the deal just hadn't done it for her. What would it take? he wondered. Drugs? More credits? He hadn't quite drained himself dry for tonight, but it wouldn't take much more to do it.

"All right," she said suddenly. *"I'll do it. But absolutely no one must know of our conversation tonight. If our meeting tonight became public knowledge, there would be . . . severe repercussions for both of us."*

"You can trust me comple—"

"And," she interrupted, *"you will have the bonus you mentioned converted into straight currency. But you will hold this currency until I call for it after I make the appropriate arrangements. Do not deceive me, Mr. Keene, or you will see an entirely different outcome to your wishes. It will not be pleasant."*

"I assure you—"

"You may leave now, Mr. Keene."

He opened his mouth to speak but a door opened somewhere behind him, sending his heart into a double set of jumping jacks within his chest. White light spilled into the room and stopped abruptly, as if it didn't dare go beyond the stretch of its own three-foot rectangle.

"My assistant will show you out. I will contact you when the time is right. Good night, Mr. Keene."

He wanted to protest, to demand the right to see her face-to-face. Hundreds of thousands of credits—his lifetime accumulation—were on the line here. Did he not have the right to look into her eyes and see exactly who she was?

In the end, Jarlath Keene walked out of Mina's apartment with his head held as high as he could, a proud duelist bested but not killed by the opponent. The feeling gave credence to his thirst for vengeance, and that was all the better. To him, Mina was the hairline crack in the foundation, the kind that worked its way at a level far deeper than the trappings of mere money and business. He would sleep well tonight knowing that his hand had initiated that tiniest of fractures.

With enough care and patience, a crack could become a chasm.

1

Manhattan, 2123

Jarlath Keene's office at Synsound Corporation was in "the Tower," which was the generally accepted term for the offices of the vice presidents. While Manhattan was its home—and thus most lavish—office, Synsound was a huge company with bases around the world. There were thirty-four other vice presidents in this building alone, and Keene felt a lot like one old goat in a herd of younger ones; that he was fifth or sixth from the top of the ladder, depending on whose head was on the hierarchy chopping block at any given time, rankled him constantly. As far as he was concerned, his title of Vice President of Music Development meant nothing more than the fancy brass nameplate on the wall outside his office door and the private secretary who sat at a desk nearby. Every important decision that cost over two thousand credits still had to be submitted to someone else for approval.

Dusk had fallen early tonight, brought on by a

denser than normal layer of smog that mixed with the low-lying, dirty-looking clouds that spit a constant, gritty drizzle onto the miserable people stuck on the streets far below. Two more stories up and the floor-to-ceiling windows in Keene's office would have been blocked by the sickly mist that signaled the first of the clouds. As it happened, Keene could still see—lucky him—the MedTech Building three miles away, the air encircling it cleared of vapor by the constant spikes of electricity that zapped through its private airspace, generated by a MedTech patented device that sterilized the air around the building's intake vents before it ever reached the precious lungs of its employees. When MedTech had first put their little toy into operation six years ago, the electrical noise and static feedback generated sound spikes on every master syndisc in the recording studios at midlevel in the Synsound Building during the first hour and damned near wiped Synsound out; only an emergency injunction had halted the Atmosterilyzer. The court battles had been hot, heavy, and expensive, and the outcome a split: MedTech could continue using its Atmosterilyzer—after all, it was only looking out for the health of its employees and the cleanliness of its medical testing facilities—but it was required to pay damages to Synsound for the re-recordings that were necessary, and before it could put its device back in use, it had to develop and install a force field system that would limit the electrical spikes that were output to its own grounds. Now the two companies were bitter rivals, and that suited Keene just fine. He hated them both.

A knock and the sound of the oak-paneled door that led into his office being opened made him turn. "Yes?"

"Damon Eddington is here to see you," his secretary Marceena said stiffly. A stout woman in her early forties, she'd undergone a drastic change in her appearance last week. The previous reddish-brown pageboy hairstyle was gone, replaced by a style that was shaved and dyed black on the sides, then crowned with a mop of spring-tight orange curls. She might have had the skin on her face tightened and she'd definitely revamped her wardrobe; today's new outfit was a tailor-waisted, short-sleeved green suit that looked as if the clothes had shrunk a few sizes while she was wearing them. Completing the ensemble was a purple scarf tied around her pudgy neck and tucked into the collar of the jacket. The whole thing was atrocious.

Thinking back, Keene was sure she'd done it to look more attractive, perhaps thinking that he would finally afford her more than his work-related attention. Not a very pretty woman to begin with, Keene thought that Marceena now looked like one of those antique squashed-face dolls that had recently become popular again and were now soaring in price. The idea that this had been her goal all along nearly made him chuckle aloud. In any event, when he hadn't commented on her new look, Marceena's demeanor had gone from polite to cool, edging on frosty. What did she expect—that he would ask her for a date? Not likely; Keene was a fit and healthy fifty-two going on thirty. He tried to feel pity for her but couldn't; the truth was, he had more female companions than he knew what to do with already, and not one of them was over twenty-five. Did she really think she could compete? Her constant attempts were annoying.

With Marceena standing in his office door as the go-between for him and Damon Eddington, it seemed like the perfect time to give her a reintroduction as to who gave the directives around here.

"I'll be with him as soon as I can." He purposely turned his back on her and went back to gazing out the window.

"He's . . . quite upset," Marceena said, a note of uncertainty creeping into her voice.

Keene wanted to grin but didn't; the reflection might give him away. "I *said*, I'll be with him as soon as I can." He intentionally let a note of nastiness cut through his words.

Another moment of hesitation, then he heard the door close and let the smile flow over his mouth. Let her deal with Damon Eddington for a quarter hour, he thought. She wasn't a stupid woman and she'd know it was Keene's way of chastising her. Still smiling, Keene walked to his desk and began clearing it of the Duplidroids, Incorporated contract and acquisition proposal form—it wouldn't do to have Damon glance down and see that Synsound was paying a single mutadroid manufacturer more than a million credits to re-create a band called Jane's Addiction in time for the quarter-century mark in two years. With the evidence cleanly swept into the top drawer, he spent a few minutes tidying the contents of the other drawers in his desk, then finally sat back on his chair to wait. The minutes ticked by and Keene fought the urge to laugh aloud; he could well imagine what was going on in the secretarial suite outside his office.

"What's taking so long?" Damon Eddington demanded. He leaned on the secretary's desk, seeing her pull back nervously. "I thought the purpose of an appointment was to schedule time to talk to someone, and Keene said he would *see* me, damn it!"

"And so he will, Mr. Eddington." The woman's voice was honey smooth, utterly professional. "Please, just wait. I'm sure he'll be ready any minute."

"Fine." Damon spun and strode back to the fake leather couch, resisting the urge to kick at the fancy coffee table in front of it. The thing was metal and glass, and he could picture the surface shattering and magazines flying everywhere, another temper tantrum traceable to the not-so-legendary Damon Eddington. Instead of lashing out, he flounced onto the couch, watching the secretary for any sign that Keene was calling for him.

When nothing happened after another ten minutes, Damon dug his flask out of one of the pockets of his vest and took a small swig of sweet blackberry brandy, let it roll over his tongue and momentarily take his mind off how insulted he felt. This was a game to Keene, he was sure, but for what purpose?

Synsound—with Jarlath Keene at the reins—already led him around by the proverbial nose; as far as Damon was concerned, forcing him to sit out here like a fool showed that among other things Keene was possessed of a deep and despicable streak of meanness. The secretary—he couldn't remember her name—had probably been told to stall him for as long as she could. For all Damon knew, she might have been told to keep him out here until he gave up and went away. His lip curled; not likely.

Damon took another swig of brandy and screwed the top back on the plastic flask, then tucked it back into his pocket and forced himself to relax against the softness of the couch. As always, his mind was full of music, a dark composition of his own making that had been in the process of a slow and painful birth since the reviews of his last small concert had been printed on the newsdiscs. After a few more minutes he dug inside another pocket and pulled out his portable recorder; if Keene was going to waste Damon's entire day by making him wait outside his office door, then Damon would try to use the time as best he could. After all, the secretary was a built-in audience.

He hummed a few notes, then a few bars, letting them swirl like discordant shadows in the air as he warmed up his vocal cords. Already the woman was frowning at him but he paid her no attention; what did her opinion matter when the rest of the world seemed to hate his creativity more? In the scheme of Damon's life, Keene's secretary was nothing.

"Hm-mm-Mm-mM-mm—" Stretching his voice and losing himself in the sounds and tones, the pitch of his voice rising and falling until it flowered in full song, not words, but a sort of drawn-out vibration that was as true as he could make it to the original source, the dying wails of jelly junkies in detox centers. Now the secretary's face was scrunched up in revulsion, her head sinking low on her shoulders like a turtle trying to escape an attacker. As Damon's voice, a decent baritone in itself, grated the next experimental lyric into the microphone embedded in the recorder, he saw her snatch up the telephone receiver on her desk and punch repeatedly at a button on the intercom. He smiled to himself; he didn't have to stop singing to know what she was saying. When she got up and came over to where he sat on the couch, her back was rigid and there were beads of perspiration high on her forehead, just under the line of burnt orange curls. Damon was pleased that his music had affected her; it didn't matter that she didn't like it. He'd take whatever results he could get.

"Mr. Keene will see you now," she snapped as Damon paused and looked at her questioningly. "You know the way."

That made Damon grin outright. The *way?* Oh, yes—he sure did. Keene's way, Synsound's way . . . the way of *trash* as far as Damon was concerned. But it was useless to argue, especially with this nothing little woman, so he nodded and stood, putting away his recorder and ignoring her audible sigh of relief. She didn't bother leading him to Keene's door, and Damon didn't expect her to.

Keene's office was expansive and as tastefully furnished as the man himself was dressed. Damon didn't follow fashion much, but the Ricci Matté suit Keene wore was impossible to disregard, and no doubt the matching shoes were just as expensive. His glistening, steel-gray hair was impeccably styled, his exquisite hand-painted tie an insult to Damon's own well-cared-for but only moderately expensive Danforth padded vest. The man was obviously bathing in credits—Synsound was clearly making more money than it knew what to do with. Why then did they fight for every credit on his contracts and make it so hard for Damon to draw a simple advance?

Keene sat behind an immense maroon Plexiglas desk cleared of almost everything, but there were too many gold and platinum soundiscs framed on the walls to maintain an illusion of a man with a multitude of leisure time on his hands. Row after row hung in expensive teak frames, with one wall almost covered. And Keene himself: smug, sleek, and ever-patient, he had the look of a man who had resigned himself to the tedious chore of dealing with another annoyance in his life and had dubbed himself a martyr for his tolerance. Even his voice was carefully modulated, without the slightest hint of inflection. "What is it now, Damon?"

The old Damon Eddington, the man he'd been before being suffocated by Synsound for so many years, would have turned and walked out . . . *after* telling Keene to sit on it and spin. No—the old Damon Eddington would have walked out of the waiting room three quarters of an hour ago.

The present Damon Eddington walked in with his head bowed as if deep in thought with his hands crammed into the loose-fitting blue jeans that were his everyday uniform, watching his feet work their way across the perfect carpet as though the sight were the most important thing in the world. He sat on the chair in front of Keene's desk without comment, and when he finally looked up, his dark eyes were soft, his vision focused on something faraway that only he could see.

"I want . . . an *alien.*"

The double take Damon expected never came; Keene didn't even blink. The executive's hands remained folded calmly on the desk's highly polished surface, the reflection below his fingers making him look like some double-handed android built to play a newly invented hellrock instrument. "You want an alien," Keene repeated. Damon squelched the impulse to remind Keene that this wasn't a psychiatric bull session where the doctor repeated everything the patient said to make sure he had understood it clearly. "Let's see," Keene continued. "You're not into weapons, so that's out. You're not into medicine or drugs, either. That puts those out of the picture. So exactly what do you need an alien *for*, Damon?"

Damon spread his hands, unconsciously willing Keene to understand, to show the slightest trace of empathy. "For the *sound.*" The last word carried on the filtered air of the office like a drawn-out whisper, a sibilant floating in the air that teased both of them.

Finally, a reluctant crack in Keene's disposition as the older man unwillingly bonded with Damon's dreams for an instant, hearing as the eccentric artist did the alien singing from its steel throat and screaming with a tongue of acidic flame.

Damon's words faded away as he and Keene stared at each other.

Bitter memories flash-danced in Damon's head as he waited for Keene's decree, and he remembered the first time an alien's screams had ever found its way into his ears. It had been on a vidscreen in a store window, a NewsVid item from Channel 86 about an infestation in the Long Island Incarceration Colony, sensationalist crap designed solely to grab the passersby and glue them to a vidscreen. And it had worked on Damon, though not for the reasons the media planners might have anticipated. The footage had shown a clot of aliens bunched in a subbasement of the LIIC's main prison, on the defensive against an army troop wearing suits constructed of the same material labs used to store acid and bearing flamethrowers loaded with long-burning jellied napalm. To Damon the creatures' screams had translated to one thing, unadulterated or diluted: *hate.*

And Damon *hated* so very, very much . . .

How many reviewers had slammed his work as "tiresome," or "obscure," or, worst of all, "boring"? The reviewers detested him, the public ignored him, Synsound humored him. All the while he struggled on, trying desperately to reach a public that seemed to want only hellrock or bloodrock, or—God help them—android singers and performers so mutated that they had four arms, multiple heads, and mouths coming out of their mouths in a twisted parody of aliens. The closest John Q. Public came to exposure to the gentler sounds of the past was, again, in re-created androids; before dwindling into ambiguity, Elvis Presley's duplicate had piqued enough interest to gain a hall named after it, and Caruso's fabricated double sang for the upper class every night at the NewMet Opera House. A steady trickle of credits from the older generation supported Synsound projects like "Buddy Holly Sings Garth Brooks III" and thousands of other re-recordings of centuries-dead artists—androids of Jim Morrison, Jimi Hendrix, Janis Joplin, Kurt Cobain, Charlie Parker, Clifford Brown, Richie Valens, Dwayne Allman, John Lennon, Patsy Cline, and others regularly belted out new hits.

And Synsound, owner of practically every piece of music and musician in the world—including Damon—sat above it all with people at its helm like Jarlath Keene, a man with virtually no imagination, no *vision*. As far as Damon was concerned, the stages of Presley Hall were the Manhattan home of hell on earth, filled with appalling reengineered mutadroids that were half android, half mutated instrument, surrounded by the dregs of humanity who flocked to listen to the groups. Few people appreciated Damon's careful live recordings of serious music, the darker blends from wonderful classic composers like Beethoven, Paganini, Mozart, Vivaldi, Bach, so much beautiful music recorded on rare twentieth-century instruments—violins, harps, dulcimers—all expensive and a struggle to come by. Synsound again, indulging him, *using* him as a pawn to show the world how it sponsored and supported what remained of the "arts" while it survived—*prospered*—on the ridiculous, discordant trash for which the people of this century constantly clamored. He hated Synsound almost as much as he detested the concertgoers who appreciated only torture and terror, responded only to the grotesque, frightening androids cavorting and screaming on the stage. If what they wanted was hate, and pain, and the repulsive, Damon decided, *he would give them exactly that.*

The press conference he'd called was only a stage for him to announce to the country and every place the NewsVid would carry the story how much he *hated*—John Q. Public, Synsound, *everything*. His tirade against Synsound and its customers had gone on for as long as he dared before he feared the media would turn away in boredom. "*For you all, for Synsound,*" he'd railed into their microphones, "*I will write the ultimate composition . . . a Symphony of Hate!*" Afterward, his employer smiled its corporate face and nodded, pleased at the attention its pet artiste had generated and shrugging off Damon's anger with a humorous attitude. He was an artist after all; they were supposed to be temperamental, angry, excitable. It was those very feelings that made them *creative.*

Damon's work on his masterpiece had carried him everywhere. No place was too dark or dangerous: he visited madhouses, prison wards, even execution chambers where he watched killers leave this world shrieking in rage. A favorite haunt was the downtown government detox center where the screams of jelly junkies bruised the eardrums and forced the workers to wear hearing protection.

But it was the news item that made Damon search the sound library for VidDiscs from the Homeworld War of ten years ago. The poor quality and low fidelity of the military recording devices didn't matter; the screams of the aliens as they fought and were destroyed blasted through Damon's senses like electricity, burning his mind, stealing his breath. No one and nothing else in the world sounded like an alien, *nothing.* And nowhere else did the creatures' shrieks of malevolence belong more than in Damon Eddington's Symphony of Hate.

And here Damon sat, once again at the mercy of Synsound's whim.

"Why don't you use the sound from the VidDiscs? It's the obvious answer." Keene sat back and studied Damon Eddington. While he was tall and medium built instead of skinny and starving, Damon still unwittingly fit Synsound's policy of how one of their stable of unorthodox musicians should look. His receding hair was as black as crude oil and pulled back from his high forehead into a thin ponytail. Dark eyebrows arched sharply over darker eyes and his long face ended in a double-cut goatee that grew to a good two inches beyond the end of his chin. Keene already knew what the musician's answer would be and he kept his expression carefully bland while he waited for Damon's words.

"Because it's *crap,*" Damon said in disgust. "Don't you realize what the army battalions were using? We're talking about the government here—they had handheld recorders, for God's sake. Obsolete magnetic tape and microphones with plastic screens over them to keep the battleground dirt out of the electronics, plus every recording is undercut with tank and weapons fire, explosions that muddy up everything. I can't re-record that rubbish—I need clear, crisp sound. *Presence*, Jarlath. I want it to sound like the alien itself is standing in front of the mike and roaring at it."

Keene rubbed his cheek and tried to look thoughtful. Damon was such an easy toy, up and down, like those ancient yo-yos twentieth-century children had played with. "Then we'll synthesize it for you." As he'd expected, Damon looked horrified.

Up and down.

"You've got to be joking!" Damon balled his fist and held it up. "You know I hate synthesis. It's *got* to be live. I won't put any of that electronic mishmash into my music!" He looked at his fist and relaxed his fingers, as if just discovering his own hand. Keene could see the composer visibly trying to calm down. "Listen, Jarlath. This is my *masterpiece*, the epitome of everything I've ever done. I want to do it all myself, even down to recording the alien screams. And for that I need one of those creatures alive, a *real* alien."

"I . . . see." Keene let Damon dangle for a moment, then gave him a narrow-eyed stare. "What you're telling me, Damon, is that you want Synsound to spend vast amounts of money to illegally procure an alien for you so that you can use that same creature to create a musical work that will show the world how much you hate us."

Damon wasn't fazed. "Exactly. But you'll do it anyway, won't you?" He folded his arms and leaned back.

"You have to admit that I'm a constant source of advertising even if you and your company don't appreciate my hard work."

Ah, such smugness from a man who was too arrogant to realize he was nothing more than a child under Synsound's disciplinary lash. Keene leaned back himself and waved a hand. "Spend vast amounts, Damon? Hardly. As a reminder, we have an advertising department with budgets and corporate mandates, remember? Forgive me for pointing out that they can handle publicity far more pleasantly than you can. In the end, I'm afraid you're a low-priority item. I'm limited as to how much I can spend to indulge your inventive aspirations, no matter how far-reaching you . . . *believe* they will be. The methods by which we can obtain for our little pet—you—his *own* little pet are severely curtailed by budget factors." He was rewarded by the insulted scowl that spread across the musician's face. "Funding an expedition to Homeworld is certainly out of the question," Keene continued, ignoring Damon's offended expression. "Bribing the military is always possible, but again, far too expensive—too many hands in the financial pie would have to be filled. Still," he said slowly as the image of a taller building surrounded by the bright beauty of jagged electrical flashes a few miles away filled his mind, "there may be a way." He smiled for the first time since Damon had come into his office. "I'll see what I can do."

Knowing the meeting was over, Damon stood and spread his hands. "It just won't work otherwise. I *need* it, Jarlath. The Symphony, it will be a big hit. You'll see."

"Good-*bye*, Damon." Keene folded his hands on the desktop again, a clear signal that his patience was at the breaking point. For a second he thought Damon would protest—would he actually *beg* this time? But no, while the musician looked like he wanted to, eventually he turned his back and walked out, his angry footsteps making muffled *thunks* against the carpeting.

As soon as the office door closed behind Damon,

Keene swung to the VidPhone on his desk. He gave it about thirty seconds—enough time for Damon to walk through his secretary's area and turn into the hallway leading to the elevators—then buzzed Marceena.

"Yes?"

She sounded as worried as she looked on the monitor, as though he might send her after Damon with instructions to bring him back. Keene liked to hear the note of anxiety in her voice; it kept her respectful. "Get me Yoriku," he said simply. He didn't wait for a reply before snapping off the connection.

Twelve minutes. Keene tapped his fingers on the desk and counted each movement of the LED clock display, one by one, as they flashed by. Amazing. How could he forget the time he failed to answer a summons from Yoriku's assistant for a half hour? Keene had been in the midst of a delicate contract negotiation with one of the country's hottest new stars and felt it was unwise to give the woman and her agent time alone to pick through the contract undisturbed. Everything he'd done back then had been for the good of Synsound, every waking hour was spent contemplating ways to better the company and his position in it, and increase those corporate profits to the parent. How bewildered he'd been to subsequently find himself with instructions to proceed to a tiny city called Black Lake in the Canadian province of Saskatchewan. Once there, he was ordered to personally supervise the relocation of a Canadian lyric writer to Manhattan—Keene, a so-called high-level vice president, was being used by Yoriku as a damned travel escort!

Finally the private incoming light on the VidPhone flashed. *"What is it, Keene?"* Yoriku's face filled the screen, wavering with static. Despite MedTech's force field, the phones had done that intermittently since the Atmosterilyzer was put into use, something in which Keene took secret, perverse pleasure.

"It's about Damon Eddington, sir."

On the screen, a corner of Yoriku's mouth turned up slightly. *"He is an amusing man."* The emotion disappeared as quickly as it had come, and Yoriku's broad face smoothed out again.

Keene made himself smile in return. "Yes, sir. He *is* funny, very funny. In fact, after our conversation you may think he's even funnier. It seems that Eddington has come up with an . . . unusual idea concerning the project he's working on. You remember that, I'm sure—his 'Symphony of Hate'? He visited me a short while ago with a request. It's quite original—I don't believe anyone else has ever asked for this." And Keene recounted everything about his conversation with Damon, embellishing where he felt it was necessary to ensure he maintained Yoriku's attention.

At the end of Keene's narrative, Yoriku shook his head. His voice grated through the VidPhone speaker, like old rust being wire-scrubbed off a steel beam. He had been in the United States for decades, but his words still carried a heavy Japanese accent. *"It is impossible to get Eddington this alien for what I am willing to spend on him."*

Keene let himself grin widely. He was quite pleased with the scheme he had come up with practically as Damon had been speaking. Not many people would have been so quick on their mental feet. "Not necessarily, sir. I believe I have a solution. It will be risky, but . . ." Yoriku started to shake his head again and Keene risked interrupting him, trusting that his next words would instantly smother any annoyance his poor manners raised. "Of course, it would involve . . . ah . . . MedTech."

Yoriku's image froze for a moment. *"In what way?"* His voice, not particularly pleasant to begin with, dropped lower as his thin eyes narrowed all the way to slits.

So Keene told him his plan, in all its exquisite, deceitful detail: setting times and listing the equipment required, what other things and who would be needed to see it through, fine-tuning the details as he went. "So that's it," Keene finished a short while later. "What do you think, sir? Are we in a position to . . . *humiliate* MedTech?"

The answer was obvious as Yoriku's mouth spread in a smile that reminded Keene of the dangerous, toothy grin of a hyena. Keene had heard the rumors but hadn't dared call attention to himself by acknowledging the stories or asking anyone else in the company if they were true. Now Yoriku's black expression confirmed them all: one of the most powerful men in the world, yet he had lost the thing most precious to him . . . his exquisite, legendary lover. It had taken so long to happen that Keene had begun to believe that the woman had lied to him, but, *finally*, the whispered stories said that Mina now graced the bed of a younger, high-powered executive at MedTech.

"We are indeed in such a position, Keene." Yoriku unexpectedly pushed his face close to his vidscreen; on Keene's end, it looked as if the man had snatched up the phone and pressed his nose against it. Keene could see the pores in the man's skin; it was totally disgusting. *"And I want them to know it was Synsound. Not right away, but eventually. Is that clear?"*

"They will, sir." Keene tried to make his voice as soothing as possible. "When Eddington's Symphony of Hate is released, there will be no mistaking the origin of the sound." Yoriku backed away from the screen, looking pleased. As the Japanese man leaned back and rested his hands on the arms of a chair that was no doubt *real* leather, Keene was again reminded of the hyena, this time with a full belly. "I will need assistance," Keene hinted slyly. "Someone to—"

"You may send for Ahiro. I will instruct him to be at your disposal in all respects."

"Excel—" But Yoriku had already disconnected, leaving Keene to glare at the static on the vidscreen and grit his teeth for a moment before he buzzed Marceena again. Up and down, he thought. We all play the game. Problem was, he hated being the one spinning on the end of Yoriku's yo-yo.

"Yes, Mr. Keene?"

"Find Ahiro and send him up." He didn't give her a chance to question the order, taking his cue from the way Yoriku had cut off their own conversation. He didn't want to listen to her whine anyway. Perhaps she'd been with him too long, with Synsound too long. All she did was complain about having to do things she didn't like or thought were beneath her job duties. Did she think he should hire an assistant to work for her as well? Not likely.

More waiting, but at least when he got here, Ahiro would be much more respectful than Keene's secretary was. Keene didn't like working with the man and would have preferred to find someone else, but he had to admit that he'd never encountered anyone like Ahiro, who damned near treated Keene's words as God's own. Well . . . not really; the top command, of course, was Yoriku. There was a connection between Yoriku and Ahiro about which Keene remained utterly clueless, and all his careful inquiries had dead-ended. The inquiries themselves had been dangerous, and he'd been meticulous in his efforts to make them appear nothing more than a healthy curiosity about the man who headed—well—*owned* the company for which Keene worked. Useless effort, wasted time. The slender Japanese man with the grave expression slipped around the corporate headquarters with barely a word to anyone and free access to anywhere in the building, and whatever the tie between Yoriku and Ahiro was, it would not be shared with Keene or anyone of his ilk.

Keene stood and cracked his knuckles thoughtfully as he stepped to the window and stared out. Secrets, secrets—everywhere around him. They made him nervous, curious, *crazy* with wanting to know them all. He'd have to work harder on this thing between Yoriku and Ahiro later on . . . perhaps next summer, after his first round of questions had been forgotten and a new staff was settled in place inside Yoriku's private offices. Turnover was a constant in a company this size, especially after the raises and disappointments each spring. There were those inside who could not be bought, true—the ones like Yoriku's personal executive assistant and file manager, who had been with him for something like fifteen years. Unlike

Marceena, however, that woman had an assistant—several, in fact. When Keene had built his savings back up to speed, he would go to work on those two, as he had on Mina.

Keene didn't know how, but the next time he glanced away from the window—a mere three minutes later—the mysterious Japanese man with the ragged scar across his right eye was standing in front of the desk.

2

Christmas Eve

It was a warm and miserable holiday in Manhattan, the worst that Ahiro could remember spending in this hellhole. In his own home country there would be clean, crisp snow on the mountaintops if not the streets themselves, and the sidewalks and buildings would be just as crowded as they were here but cleaner. Ahiro had not been to Japan in many years, but he could still remember the sweet smells of evening meals drifting from the paper-screened windows of the freshly scrubbed tenement houses that had grown like mushrooms in the neighborhood where his childhood home had once stood. Scents of sake and green tea, hot rice and fried vegetables; clean, comforting, *welcoming*. Not like here, where the smells of aircycle exhaust and trash rotting on heated sidewalks overwhelmed everything, ignorant of the barriers of class and property value as it drifted on the air currents.

Tonight multicolored lights blinked in the show

windows of the department stores while hundreds of miniature androids in festive costumes obediently followed the commands of their loop programs to dance and make merry in the displays. In the window of the Manhattan branch of Macy's, a four-foot-high Santa Claus belted out three-syllable rounds of "Ho-ho-ho!" as he checked off names on a list spewing continuously from a computer in a room that was supposed to be a replication of his office at the North Pole. Across the street, the Montgomery & Sears conglomerate had its own presentation going in blatant competition for the shoppers' eyes—a full dance troupe of twenty-four-inch ballerinas and brightly dressed soldiers performing *The Nutcracker Suite*, complete with a synthesized version of the original musical score blaring from high fidelity speakers.

It didn't seem to matter to anyone that it was after ten o'clock, the end of the preholiday shopping season, and the weather was wretched; there were plenty of people on the overlit streets to hear the blasting music. Most, huddled under umbrellas or inside rainslickers dripping crud-filled water and clutching their plastic-wrapped gifts as close to themselves as possible, paid little attention. Spurred by a slight and carefully timed upswing in the country's economy, the crowds this year had been enormous; millions of people, cars, and aircycles choked every shopping district in the city and quickly resulted in the worst smog storm Manhattan had endured in half a decade. Now the streets were filled with the debris left by the shopping sprees of the masses, the air was clogged with dust and pollution, and Ahiro and his men were forced to wait patiently as the last of the die-hard patrons bought their wares and scuttled along the sidewalks like common mutant cockroaches in the muck.

Finally, with only a quarter hour left before midnight, they slipped out of a smelly alcove in the back entrance of the decrepit building at 103rd and Manhattan Avenue and headed into the heart of Central Park. The last refuge of grass and pigeons in the area, it was still open to the public only because of MedTech's public relations policy; the corporation had pulled the City of New York out of yet another bankruptcy in 2075 by leasing Central Park for the next half a millennium. While they continued to allow the general public to roam its patrolled walkways during the day, the nightly rapes, muggings, and murders had ended abruptly at 12:01 A.M. on January 1, 2076, when MedTech's Elite Security Force powered up the newly installed wireless fence at its boundaries and loosed several thousand GuardTech Robots within the park's limits. Manufactured to look like Doberman pinschers and rottweilers, the robotic dogs ran on internal solar timers that followed the daylight hours from season to season. They were virtually indestructible and attacked anything that moved on two legs and weighed over thirty pounds—unless you wore a MedTech identification transmitter that was accepted by the program currently powering the internal computer in the GuardTech dogs . . . the key word being *currently*. Elite Security changed the program regularly, and MedTech employees were accustomed to reporting to their supervisors to pick up newly programmed transmitters at unpredictable times.

Tonight, Ahiro and his team were at once surrounded by a dozen GuardTechs drawn by their movement, red crystal eyes gleaming and metal mouths yawning wide . . . before they turned away and trotted off. Silent, the men crouched in the darkness and watched them go, and only the youngest showed his nervousness by fingering the transmitter Ahiro had given him earlier. Another few minutes and they continued on their way, sliding through the shadows like night mist until they reached the park's center and the pride of MedTech—its home office building. The chromed steel and glass tower gleamed even in the midnight smog, stretching one hundred twenty-three stories into the sky to show the upper research laboratories eternally surrounded by a halo of electricity.

Ahiro did not need words to tell his ninjas what to do; handpicked, personally trained, the tiniest of nods said it all and was instantly obeyed. Entering the building was nothing, like passing through dry water for all the difficulty it gave them. Likewise were MedTech's carefully placed security cameras useless; Ahiro knew the location of every one, the direction in which it would point at what time, which way to duck and how long to do it. So easy . . . but not a setup; Ahiro had a nose for those and tonight every one of his instincts was saying *"Go!"* Unlike the often dispassionate regime at Synsound, MedTech was a jealous employer and it guarded its employees like a mother lioness watching over her cubs. Someone was always unfortunate enough to draw holiday duty, but never would MedTech have sacrificed two of its night watchmen to the razor-edged swords of Ahiro and Yosako as it did tonight. The corporation's choice would have been to substitute a battalion of heavily armed soldiers with instructions to shoot on sight to kill.

The descent was short and swift, through clean corridors that smelled of disinfectant and were lined floor to ceiling with easily sanitized stainless steel. Ahiro found the surroundings pleasing and infinitely more preferable than Synsound's overused hallways. Down here it was clear that a limited number of people were granted access, whereas Synsound was overrun with people and dirt—performers, stagehands, marketing, sales—thousands of people went everywhere. Had his circumstances been different, Ahiro would have liked a position where he could work in an environment like this one. But life was as it was, and wanting what could never be was a waste of time.

As they moved on, effortlessly avoiding the cameras, overhead sprinklers began to regularly mark their passage. Shortly after the appearance of the sprinklers, flame nozzles began jutting ominously from the walls at random heights starting at floor level. Staggered every twelve feet on each side of the passageway were fireproof safety chambers protected by hardened steel doors and locking mechanisms that engaged automatically when the door was opened and shut a single time. After that, only a MedTech computer program would release the titanium tumblers and free the person who had shut him or herself inside.

Five levels underground, Ahiro and his men stopped in front of the final door. The massive piece of metal was three times wider than any of the escape hatches and weighed at least a ton, and this morning the card reader embedded in the wall next to it would have accepted the cardkeys of only a half-dozen people at MedTech. Tonight one of those six would be used to gain entry, and tomorrow its owner would discover in his pocket a useless plastic substitute.

Without a second thought, Ahiro slid the cardkey from the waistband of his black suit and slipped it into the slot. A breathless moment as they waited for the red warning light to come on and an alarm to go off; instead there was a hum that was felt more than heard and the green light on the opposite side of the mechanism blinked. They heard a dull clang as the massive internal bolts slid free of the door and retracted into the wall. Ahiro slipped the cardkey back into his inner pocket with deliberation. Like the doors to the chambers that lined the corridor, this one would also relock automatically; without the cardkey, they would be trapped inside the inner chamber. He gave a moment's consideration to intentionally dropping it on the way out, then changed his mind. There was no sense in destroying that connection . . . yet.

When the door slid quietly to the side, the seven of them spun through without a sound, swords ready. Behind them, the laser sensors in the door waited for a beat of five, then triggered the auto-close. In the space of a heartbeat, they were cut off completely from the rest of the MedTech Building. From the *world.*

Knees bent, weapons raised, they crept forward. They were in another corridor, wider than the one outside and made of a series of huge pipes joined to each other, like the sewer mains that ran under the city. The surfaces here were strangely slippery, not steel like the outer passageway, but coated instead with some sort of beige industrial plastic. The rounded ceiling was higher and held a tangled mass of steel-encased tubes—water, electricity, coolant, perhaps flammable gas. Barely visible behind the tubing were heavily screened air ventilation grates, each no bigger than six inches square.

As the antechamber widened again—still with those same odd sections and alcoves—Ahiro saw three, then four titanium-barred enclosures branching off the main passage—*feeders.* Closed now, empty of the animals that were probably periodically loaded into them. Beyond that . . . nothing. No robotic watchmen, no androids, no *security.*

This is wrong, Ahiro thought as they moved quickly toward another door at the far end. There should be guards, men with guns—

Ten feet behind him, Higuchi gave a strangled cry and Ahiro heard the man's sword fall to the plasticized surface of the floor. He whirled and his breath caught in his throat. Higuchi had lost his balance, slipped in a puddle of something greasy; always the slowest of Ahiro's ninjas, now he cowered, frozen, as something huge and multisegmented bent over him.

Defense meant something different in this lab.

Shades of black cut by pools of slime the color of translucent green leaves, the alien was over seven feet tall and impossibly fast—far too fast for Higuchi. For a moment that nearly cost him his life, Ahiro saw in his mind's eye what Higuchi saw, heard what the already dead man heard—

A mouth full of teeth like white swords, and another within that one, snapping wetly as the creature's thick, ceaseless saliva swirled in the air. The noise of the beast blotted out everything but the gnashing of its teeth as they sank greedily through Higuchi's skull as though it were nothing, and Ahiro thought not of swords but of spears—long and deadly and dripping with the blood of multitudes on the music of its battle cry, the sound of huge and angry gods screaming out the symphony of their rage.

There were three aliens, and now only six men. They charged out of the alcoves where they'd been wrapped around reinforced water pipes like giant snakes. Ahiro had never fought an alien before—few civilians had—but he was a quick learner and amazingly swift with his sword. Not so for Yoshi, Ahiro's second in command, and a detached part of Ahiro watched the battle as if he were outside himself and studying it for the future, then was surprised that his prized pupil would be so clumsy with his blade when the weapon was expected to be another appendage, a *part* of the warrior. But Yoshi was too slow and the alien was monstrously quick, its armored black claws slicing away the front of Yoshi's nightsuit and taking half his chest with it, then finishing the job with those terrible, glistening teeth.

Now it was down to Ahiro and four men. Ahiro felt like he was circling an enormous praying mantis, and the feeling was intensified when Matsuo took the offensive with one of the creatures and struck—the tempered steel of his ancient sword, passed from generation to generation in his family and said to bring tremendous luck—slicing his foe from neck to hip in a single lethal cut. Matsuo paid dearly for his exuberance when the alien gave a death shriek and acid blood splashed from the gaping wound and bathed his face. His mask disappeared instantaneously . . . as did his lips, the skin on his face and neck, even the cartilage of his nose. He might have screamed, but no one would ever know; he had sucked in a mouthful of alien blood and burned away his tongue and vocal cords.

Four men to two aliens now, and the remaining ninjas had learned a valuable lesson. Swords flashing, they changed tactics and aimed for the joints of the legs and arms, crippling their enemies as blow after blow separated the gangly limbs and split the ridged black shells that cupped the creatures' equivalent of elbows and knees. Even the tails whipping in the air fell victims to the merciless blades, their sharp-spaded ends twitching uselessly on the gore-splattered floor. It wasn't long before Ahiro and his three remaining men stood over the spasming, maimed aliens, dismissing the claw-tipped fingers that clutched uselessly at the floor in agony. To Ahiro, these were nothing more than overgrown insects, not worth the measure of his time that it would take to put them out of their misery. The only thing that mattered was . . .

The nest.

It was beyond the doorway at the far end, and when Ahiro and his men stepped through it was like entering a place unlike anything he'd seen on this earth. As with the previous chamber, the ceiling was high and lined with industrial tubes and cables, the same ones that fed through the wall from the outer room. In here, however, they were no longer accessible, buried as they were under layer after layer of shimmering resin. Strands of it twisted and turned overhead and around the walls, forming into hundreds of knobs that looked more like human vertebrae than anything else. Miles of the stuff, encircling the room and looping back over itself to spill onto the floor until it bunched into little hills at irregular intervals. Atop each small hill, perched like an immense, obscenely bloated and elongated lump of flesh, was an unhatched alien egg.

Ahiro moved as rapidly as he dared. His men hung back, their wide, terrified eyes searching the shadows of the outer chamber for movement and flicking back to him and the half-dozen ovals of living death that faced them. Ahiro didn't blame them; just the scent of a human within six feet of an alien's egg was enough to make the knobby cross etched deep into its top split and fold back like the flowers of a poisonous flower. He chose as his target the closest one and sprinted over to it; on the way, he pulled a specially designed locking clamp from his belt. By the time he reached the egg, Ahiro had it unfolded and ready, and he jammed the four prongs of the clamp over the "X" in the egg's surface and pushed the white button on the device's top. Spikes shot from each side of the four extensions and buried themselves on either side of each slit, digging deep and holding like prehensile teeth; ready to be born or not, the egg could not hatch until the proper code was punched into the clamp's miniature keypad.

Ahiro nodded to his men, then gritted his teeth and slipped his arms around the egg's slimy surface. A hard tug and the egg broke free of the resin with a sound like brittle plastic being torn; around Ahiro, a few of the eggs began to quiver, the smell of the nearby humans triggering their instincts. They had to leave *now*, before they were overrun by the scuttling, eight-legged creatures that looked vaguely like spiders but could catch a man in less time than it took to scream.

Another five seconds and they were out of the nest, stepping nimbly among the shattered limbs of the still living and hissing aliens and the bloodied, melting bodies of their comrades. Half of his men would never leave this room, but Ahiro did not stop to consider if the prize had been worth the price. Keene had told him that an egg must be obtained, and then mapped out the strategy by which Ahiro could do it; Keene was allowed to order Ahiro to do these things because Yoriku decreed that Synsound needed the alien egg and he himself wished that it be done.

The men who had died here today had died for a great cause. Ahiro would honor their memory, and he would forgive them the stupidity that had led to their wasteful demise, but only because they had died for Synsound, and in so doing, they had died for Yoriku.

And Ahiro would do anything for Yoriku.

3

Christmas Day

"This is a helluva way to celebrate Christmas morning, Phil."

MedTech Elite Security's Chief of Operations Phillip Rice leaned against the locked door of the Alien Resources Lab and waited for his men to catch up. "If you men would pick up your pace," he retorted, "we could get this over with and go on about our lives." The man who'd first spoken, Eddie McGarrity, gave him a sullen look but didn't answer. "Open it," Rice said.

"Don't you have your cardkey?" McGarrity asked.

"I left it in my office," Rice answered. "You have yours, don't you?"

"I've got mine." Ricardo Morez, the third man on Rice's team, began working his hand past the outer layers of his heavy security suit.

"Forget it," McGarrity growled. "Mine's right here." He yanked the piece of white plastic from the breast pocket of his suit and double-flipped it around his fingers smartly, as though it were a playing card. In an uncannily swift move, he snapped it forward and rammed it into the card reader on the wall.

In response, the mechanism's red light began to blink rapidly and a short, shrill alarm went off somewhere over their heads. McGarrity jumped and yanked the card back out. "What the hell!" he exclaimed.

Rice stared at him. "What's the matter with it?"

McGarrity peered at the cardkey. "Beats me. Maybe it's got something on the surface—"

"Sometimes they demagnetize if you put 'em next to your cash card," Morez offered. "I did that to the cardkey to my house once."

"Yeah, well, I don't exactly keep *this* one in my wallet, if you know what I mean." McGarrity scowled and shoved the cardkey into the reader slot a second time. This time as the red light blinked, the alarm gave a longer, more pronounced ring.

Rice's eyes were dark. "Don't do it again or the alarm will stay on. It thinks you're someone unauthorized trying to get into the lab. We'll use Ricky's to get inside." He held out his hand. "Let me see that thing."

McGarrity handed it over as Ricky found his cardkey and inserted it into the reader. A half second to process the information, and the reader's light glowed green. There was a hum of electronics and hydraulics as the bolts moved and the door slid open.

The smell was atrocious . . . *enormous*. Blood, human waste, the scent of acidic alien decomposition; Rice was glad for the temporary delay this cardkey business would give them. Intentionally diverting his gaze, he reached around the door to a small keypad on the wall inside and punched in a code to disable the automatic timer that would shut the door in five seconds. Then he turned his attention back to the cardkey. "Look again, Eddie," he said after a moment. His voice was sharp as he held up the square of white plastic. "This isn't a cardkey—it isn't *anything.*"

"What the hell are you talking about?" McGarrity demanded.

"Just what I said. It's not your cardkey." Rice gave his man a steely look. *"So where is it?"*

McGarrity's mouth opened and closed. "I-I guess I don't know, boss. I had it the last time I looked—"

"Which was when?"

"Well, I guess it was when we got the clean uniforms. I . . . maybe I didn't look close," he admitted. "I just, you know, emptied the pockets of the dirty one into the clean one. I didn't inspect every single thing in there."

"Good job," Rice said sourly. "Let's go see the fruits of it."

"Just a damned minute," McGarrity protested. "I don't see your cardkey readily available either."

"I know where it is."

"Yeah?" McGarrity's face was nearly as red as his hair. Morez looked like he wanted to say something, then wisely decided to stay out of it.

"You got a problem with me, Mr. McGarrity?" Rice asked. His tone was low and calm, vaguely ominous. "If so, tell me now. The three of us will go up and I'll get it. On the way back down, we'll stop and clean out your locker. In case you haven't figured it out, we've got a major security breach here and it seems to be directly traceable to *your* careless loss of a highly classified cardkey."

All the anger seemed to drain out of the Irishman's face. "Nah—I'm sorry, Phil." He looked pained. "I guess coming down here's just got me on edge, that's all."

"Fine." Rice turned on his heel and motioned at the doorway. "Let's go in."

Without looking up, Rice pulled a scalpel from a pocket of his security suit and began cleaning his fingernails as though he were using nothing sharper than a nail file. The other two men were still moving through the carnage in the lab, casting occasional quick glances across the room to the door at the far end. Rice didn't blame them for being nervous, but he wished they'd get past it—after all, they'd been down here for almost three hours. While he had disabled the door to the lab when they'd first arrived this morning, after a quick glance inside to make sure there were no bodies lying around with face-huggers on them and no empty eggshells, Rice had made damned certain that the entrance to the nest was closed and locked; only the personal password of the head of the Bioscience Division would open it now. Finally, he'd ordered that the remaining cardkeys that allowed access to the Alien Resources Lab be canceled and new ones issued.

"Three dead watchdogs and three dead dirtbags," McGarrity growled. They were five sublevels down and the air should have been naturally cold; instead it was heated to nearly ninety degrees and saturated with moisture from the in-ceiling humidifiers because the eggs did better in a tropical climate. The temperature and muggy air were doing wonderful things to the corpses scattered around and Rice could hear the nasal tone Eddie's voice had taken on as he breathed only through his mouth. The other man grimaced and shoved aside a stiff tangle of alien limbs, probing underneath the rigid remains for anything that might give them a clue.

Rice looked up. He was a big African-American with bulging muscles and the lower half of his hair dyed a stylish pure white. Most people avoided making him angry, and for good reason. Right now his face was calm, but his eyes were hooded and nearly as dark as the top part of his coal-black hair. No one else knew that fury was making the washboard muscles of his stomach ripple beneath the fabric of his shirt. "Hardly seems like a fair trade."

"No shit." Ricky flipped another sheet on his clipboard, then let it drop back and began rapidly pressing buttons on the MedLink Port he pulled from his utility belt. "Especially since they got an egg."

"Don't remind me," Rice retorted. The scalpel disappeared and he plucked a pair of heavy rubber gloves from the tool bag his team had brought in and set by the main door. He snapped them on, then bent and locked his oversize hands on the shoulders of the body nearest him, the only one with any semblance of a face remaining. He hauled it up easily and held it in front of him, scowling as he studied the dead man's lolling head. Another trained Japanese ninja; whoever he'd been, his martial arts instruction hadn't gotten him squat in here. "Who are you, you bastard?" Rice hissed into the slack face of the corpse. "And where the hell's my *egg*?" No answer—obviously—and after a moment he shook the body once, then turned and tossed it atop the heap in the center of the room with the remains of the two others that had been scraped off the floor.

"Nice try, Chief." Eddie sounded amused and Rice dearly wanted to belt him. That man had the strangest sense of humor he'd ever come across. "Did he whisper his secrets in your ear?"

"Up yours, McGarrity. One way or another, we'll find the sons a bitches. And when we do, they'll think fighting these aliens was a picnic compared to what I'm going to do to 'em." Rice glanced around the chamber again and saw Ricky still peering at the Med-Link Port; abruptly the olive-skinned man's mouth turned down and he snapped the Port off-line and clipped it back onto his belt. Rice already knew what the answer would be, but he had to ask anyway. "You get anything at all from the prelim checks?"

Morez gave a negative shake of his head. "Not a thing. No identification on the bodies, of course, but we knew that. It shows a serious desire to hide when you have your fingerprints lasered off, but I was still sure we'd pick up something from the CityWide computers, a physical for grammar school, *something.* Shows what I know—the DNA checks are coming up stone empty. As far as MedTech knows, these guys don't *exist.*" Morez stared at the three cadavers curiously. "You think we missed something?"

"No, and the odds are the rest of the tests won't find anything either. I figured these guys would be ghosts." Rice waved a hand at the bodies of the ninjas, then carefully nudged one of the alien carcasses. "We'll go for the usual, just for giggles—retina scans, WorldWeb DNA searches, palm and footprints, whatever. This is a pro job though. We're not going to find anything."

Morez looked doubtful. "I don't know, Chief. Once the research department taps into the main network in Washington, then moves onto the WorldWeb—"

Rice's shrug cut him off. "Suit yourself, Ricky, but look at these guys. I'd bet my next paycheck that all three are illegal imports. Hell, chances are that when they were alive, they probably didn't even speak English."

"What makes you so sure of that?" McGarrity reached a gloved hand down and lifted a bottom jaw clear of the puddle of melted flesh and blood around it. "Can't exactly tell what language courses the guy took from his dental records." He gave the other two men a dark grin, then glanced at Morez just to be sure. "You pick this up on the Port's scanner?"

Morez pointed to the MedLink Port. "Yeah, I got 'em, safe and snug."

"These ninja types almost always come from out of the country," Rice told them. "Completely untraceable, usually government or corporate. A government job doesn't make sense in this instance, though. We would've gladly donated an egg to keep the grants flowing. It's got to be corporate. But who?"

"This is as much cleanup as I'm doing," McGarrity announced. "I'm not a friggin' housekeeper. Sanitation can pick up the rest of this crap. For this, they ought to bring in a mini-plow." He shoved the last severed alien limb to the edge of the pile of dead flesh, then straightened with a groan, eyeing his handiwork with disgust. "I dunno, Chief. You sure it's not junkies?"

Rice motioned to his men and they followed him out of the chamber gratefully, stripping off the soiled gloves and dropping them in a moist pile inside the lab door. "I doubt it. The only thing that would do druggies any good would be a queen—that's the only place they'd get the jelly. Dealing with a queen is impossible for a layman—the diet and the environment's got to be just right, plus the jelly around the eggs isn't any good unless the eggs are fertilized. That means they'd also need at least one drone. We're not exactly talking about a hobby you can keep in a basement somewhere. By itself, an egg is nothing but death." Rice's expression turned thoughtful. "Unless that's exactly what they're looking for." They passed a couple of men dressed in SaniSuits and Rice nodded his permission for them to go in and do the final mop-up and disposal.

"What do you mean?" Morez asked. "Seems like a lot to go through for suicide. Hell, why not just walk in front of a monorail? At least that would be quicker." He grimaced. "I can't imagine having something like one of those things growing inside of me, then chewing its way out. When I go, I want to do it in my sleep."

"Coward," McGarrity said flippantly. Morez shot him an astonished look and the larger man laughed. "Just kidding, you fool."

"Who knows why these religious fanatics do what they do?" Rice asked. "But the queen freaks are almost always junkies, way too buzzed out to pull a job like this. Those people don't have resources—they pour everything into getting more jelly and drink it as soon as they get their hands on it. This *had* to be a professional job—how they'd get into the Alien Research Lab itself, huh?"

"I think we've got an idea," McGarrity said.

Rice smacked a fist into his palm. "Exactly—the bastards got their paws on your cardkey. Isn't it just too fucking convenient that all the bioscientists have ironclad alibis for themselves *and* their security keys, yet one of ours turns out to be missing?"

"That is pretty snaky," McGarrity agreed as they left the subcorridor behind. "I don't know what to say about mine, Chief. I know I had it the last time I changed suits and I can't explain where it went." In front of them was the elevator door on the left, and the staircase on the right; they headed for the elevator by unspoken agreement. None of them wanted to climb five flights of stairs after sweating in the re-created tropical air of the lab for nearly three hours. After a couple of minutes of silence, McGarrity spoke up again, his tone of voice less cavalier. "Phil, do you . . . do you think I'm going to be canned for this? I guess I'd understand if you had to, it being your responsibility and all."

When Rice hesitated before answering, McGarrity swallowed. "I don't think so, Eddie," Rice finally said as they boarded the elevator. They were all large men, and their combined weight made the elevator bounce appreciably. "Since you can trace the cardkey back to the locker room, I think that shows it could have been any one of our cardkeys that turned up stolen. That'll be my position, and I won't take it further unless I'm backed against the wall. If that happens, I'll try to give you as much advance notice as possible. But I'll do my best to pull for you, and as things stand now, I'll think you'll be all right."

For a moment the big redhead's face looked as relieved as a lost little boy's after being reunited with his parents. "Thanks. I really appreciate it."

"Ricky, I want you to keep on top of MedLink," Rice said as the car began its ascent. "Help the research department go as deep as they can, rattle some suits in City Hall if necessary. Put the fear of God in whomever you have to without actually breaking anyone's toes. Step on 'em a little, but *I want these bastards.*" The three of them stood silently, drinking in the cooler, filtered air of the elevator as it carried them to the seventieth-floor Security Center. As it stopped, Rice spoke again. The tension in his voice made it clear he wasn't in the mood for arguing. "If I can't get what I want from the DataSystems," he said darkly, "we'll put the bloodhound on their trail."

"The alien?" Morez said in surprise.

Rice's black eyes glittered in the crystallized beams thrown by the reception lights as they stepped into the stark black and white decorating of the Security Center's lobby. "Your alien," he said softly.

"My bloodhound."

Damon Eddington thought there couldn't be a drearier time or place in the world than Manhattan at dawn on the day after Christmas.

It made him think of his long-dead grandmother. At first he didn't know why, as it'd been years since he thought of her or his parents. Then memories from decades earlier surfaced, and he recalled that for a few years when he was a kid, before his grandmother died, his parents had shipped him off to her for the holidays. He'd thought he would hate it—she was a dried-up old woman who lived in a four-room apartment in the Bronx, a convenient holiday baby-sitter for his mother—but after the first year he'd *wanted* to go. Christmas itself was always a disappointment, a flashy holiday that held no religious implications for him or his family, and certainly less gratification from the childish viewpoint of gifts. His grandmother had little money to buy toys or soundiscs for her strange grandson, and Damon's mother and father seldom troubled themselves with anything other than the necessary clothes. A couple of pairs of socks and some underwear usually, once a small gift certificate to the Synsound Circle Store that made his mouth drop open in surprise. That pretty much summed up the history of Christmas gifts during the childhood of Damon Eddington.

But at Grandma Sheridan's he'd felt . . . *okay.* Not as though he belonged—never that—but that it was all right with her if he was different. She wasn't trying to hide him from her friends or coworkers, and if she had someone else against whom she was comparing him, the grandchild of someone in her building or perhaps a card-playing companion, she never showed it or mentioned anything. He had worked enough odd jobs to buy himself an inexpensive disc player and a decent set of headphones a long time ago—headphones were the only way his parents would tolerate his music—but Grandma Sheridan waved the headphones away and told Damon he ought to be listening to the music the way it was meant to be heard—floating on the air in front of his ears, not reduced to a bunch of unseen electrical impulses forced through wires. "Damon, my boy," she'd said in her shaky, ancient voice, "I'm half-deaf anyway. Unless you turn it up so loud it puts cracks in the walls, I probably won't pay any attention."

Dawn on Christmas morning . . . that's what had brought the memories back. Looking out the soot-smeared window of his sixth-floor loft, he could see the rooftops of a few smaller buildings scattered down the block, like crumbling mushrooms struggling amid the high-rises that were inexorably infringing on the neighborhood. Post-Christmas then had looked pretty much the same as it did now—gray, damp, sometimes with dirty snow piled against the curbs from the plows. About the only things that made it visually any different now that Damon was an adult were that there were more high-rises—always—and no cars around here, because nobody drove the old clankers in the poor neighborhoods anymore. Everyone around here stuck to aircycles and express rides on the monorails.

If Damon closed his eyes and concentrated, he could still bring the sounds and smells back clearly in his mind: on December 26 and with barely enough light to see by, his grandmother would get up, make a pot of strong coffee for herself, and, as she did every year, pull from the refrigerator the carcass of the small turkey she'd cooked the day before. With a full-length apron in place to protect her housedress, Grandmother Sheridan would sit at the table and patiently poke and prod the bones of the turkey until they were stripped clean of meat. That done, she would carefully divide the leftovers into small piles, wrap and label them in her unsteady, spidery script, and store them in her freezer. She always set one packet aside to be made into a tried and true recipe of homemade turkey tetrazzini for dinner that night. How many times had Damon spent the day after Christmas just listening to his favorite music on the disc player and waiting for that wonderful dinner, not to mention the creamy, semisweet chocolate pie that always followed?

Only three. Damon hadn't smiled much when he was growing up, but he remembered being twelve years old and smiling at Grandmother Sheridan the morning his parents came to pick him up from her place the final time. He could still *feel* the smile on his lips as he waved good-bye to her the last time he saw her alive, a stretch of his mouth as it adjusted to something odd and poorly fitted but still so very special. *"See you next year!"* That's what he had said, and she had smiled in return, her sagging, wrinkled face pulling up as she nodded. Standing at his window now, three decades and some odd years later, Damon wondered if the old woman had possessed any inkling that there wouldn't *be* a next year for her. Had she known that late on a rainy night in March of the following year her lungs would simply get too tired to work? Sometimes Damon thought about the look on her face and wondered.

She was the only person he'd ever loved, and he still missed her.

Damon turned away from the window. His home was a room in a warehouse-turned-apartment building off West Thirty-eighth, something the artists and musicians down in Greenwich Village insisted on calling a loft. In reality it was cold, crawling with the smaller breed of building cockroaches that did everything but carry off his sheet music, and had four leaky spots in the roof and the decrepit outer brick wall. He couldn't decide if the biting cold of winter was worse, or the dampness of spring when he had buckets all over the apartment to catch the water that dripped from the ceiling. Each spring was a crap shoot of trying to guess where the leaks would turn up and if more would appear, plus there was always the question of whether or not this would be the season that the rotting ceiling would finally give way. Getting his cheap-ass landlord to send up heat in the winter was likewise a constant battle, and as far as the summer months went . . . in a word, Damon *cooked.* Personally, he was disgusted with the idea of being a "starving musician." He was tired of being hungry for better food than vegetables from the Five Boroughs Genetic Hothouse and the soyburgers that the manufacturers swore tasted just like beef—he thought they tasted like dry, mashed beans with beef-flavored salt; he wanted to taste the real vegetables that were still freshly grown in pockets of South America and try the experimental fruits that were coming out of the irrigated portion of the Mojave Desert. Somehow he doubted that Jarlath Keene ate soyburgers and tuna meat farmed from aquatic clones four nights a week like Damon did; the executive looked far too well satisfied for that.

Damon shivered and stepped away from the multipaned window and its profusion of drafts. This is it, he thought bitterly as he wandered back to the unfolded futon that served as both his couch and bed and lowered his shivering body onto it. *My life.* After a few moments he crossed his legs and pulled the blankets around his shoulders, watching vacantly as his breath misted in front of him in the nearly frigid air. His landlord lived in the larger apartment two stories down, and if nothing else, today was still part of the holiday weekend; in a couple of hours the greedy bastard would be up and moving around, and Damon would get some heat—*if* the old man hadn't gone out of town to visit relatives. Occasionally he pulled that shit and no one could get in touch with him for days. Heat generally rose, and by all rights Damon's apartment should have been the warmest in this piece of crap called a building; that it was always freezing fed Damon's suspicion that the landlord had run electric baseboard heaters in his own place to cut down on the overall bill for the building. Damon had considered buying his own but ultimately couldn't afford it or the higher electric bills that would result.

Speakers and crude recording equipment surrounded Damon's futon, stacked against the walls in a jumble of wires, plastic cases, labeled and unlabeled soundiscs, and old cassette tape machines, his testing ground for new music and a self-critic's hell for the old. None of the electronic equipment he had here was good enough to generate recording-quality stuff, of course, but he could work with it enough to start projects, even output a few demo tapes to offer to Synsound. Beyond that was Synsound's own lab and the state-of-the-art mixer, digital recorder, and signal processor that the corporation let him have constant access to, *flaunted* at him at every opportunity. Someday, he thought, I'll be able to—

"Knock it off," Damon said out loud.

So far this morning nothing else had broken the silence and his voice was shockingly loud in the chilly loft. He *hated* that word. *Someday.* Someday I'll do *this*, and someday I'll do *that.* As a boy, he'd always thought like that, in terms of that elusive something that was going to happen at any time, as though all those things, those wonderful accomplishments, were close enough to reach if he only managed to stretch enough. It wasn't as though there was anyplace but Synsound to which he could offer his creative output; the company had swallowed up its competition long before Damon was born. New music companies popped up, of course, but Synsound's business plan worked—quite aptly—on the greed factor: when a tiny new competitor popped up, the megacorporation bought them out by offering them too much money to refuse, under-the-table deals made to avoid the federal monopolization laws.

Someday . . . always that.

Someday I'll make my parents proud of me had, over the course of a decade and a half, evolved into *someday I'll make them notice me.* But they'd never done either, and it didn't matter that his music grew more despondent or dark or strange. Nothing Damon did made him anything to his parents but what he was: a nuisance, a slipup in birth control that they were bound by governmental laws to look after for eighteen years, a continuing, quiet embarrassment because of his strangeness. They probably hated him all the more because of his unpredictability: he hadn't acted like a "normal" teenager, hadn't been into whatever syndrugs happened to be on the street at the time—and there was always something available—hadn't even gotten into the usual adolescent trouble with girls and VR gangs and bloodrock music. He was a shadow in their lives, a shadow *over* their lives.

Damon had started working longer hours as soon as he could. Unemployment be damned; there were plenty of shit jobs available if you were willing to wash dishes, bus tables, and haul trash—plenty of dirty and usually illegally run restaurants tucked between buildings in the neighborhoods. As a teenager he'd scrubbed trash bins, gutted fish, and scraped thousands of layers of grease off stoves and griddles to pay for his guitars. As much of an outcast as he was, he'd still met others like himself during high school, music lovers and rockers, pickers, a few singers. He'd come a long way from being a zit-faced, gangly kid with dark hair, white skin, and a guitar that seemed as much a part of him as one of his arms.

And look at him now. He'd advanced into manhood determined to make his mark on the world with his music, convinced he could reintroduce forgotten classical forms to a public saturated with industrial discord, mutated androids, and screaming synthesizers. Back then, he'd even had a partner and friend, although that relationship had died when Damon had gone in his own direction. What a fool he'd been, and his continued failures turned ultimately into depression, and *that* turned into still darker tunes. All those years passing by, listening to bleak and brooding music and feeling a kinship with it that gradually evolved into a fierce and undeniable loyalty, letting those emotions bleed soft, inescapable blackness into his work. Now that music, his work, had surrounded him and forced out everything else in his life, had *enslaved* him.

No friends, male or female, anymore. For a short while in his early twenties there'd been a woman in his life, a six-month period during which he'd tried, unsuccessfully as it turned out, to devote some of his time and life to something other than composition. That he could no longer remember her name shamed him; he had loved her and told her so, but his feelings were absentminded and weak, unnourished by the attention a relationship like that needed and deserved. She'd had red hair and hazel eyes . . . or was it strawberry-blond hair and green eyes? More useless remorse and self-reproach.

So today, in the here and now of his life, what was left?

Obsession.

Rage.

And hate, of course. Damon hated the public, hated Synsound, hated Keene . . . but most of all, he hated *himself*, for his undeniable love of this most obscure subgenre of music to the exclusion of everything sane, everything normal. So many wasted hours spent in supreme self-loathing, asking that most treacherous of questions . . .

Why could he not have loved something more . . . *marketable*?

5

Ahiro checked on the egg once every quarter hour.

He knew the workmen on the apiary project thought he was obsessive, but that did not concern him. Yoriku's apiary was going to be completely different from the Alien Research Laboratory at MedTech from which he and his men had stolen the alien egg, and Ahiro was amazed at the variations and committed to seeing that it was built correctly. While it was true that the end goals were nothing alike, there were a few essential things they would—or should—always have in common. Containment was the prime factor, with safety following as an equal second. Depending on your point of view, it might even be the other way around.

At the MedTech lab, everything had been made of steel coated in acid-resistant plastic. MedTech's bioscientists must have watched their creatures with hidden video cameras; here at Presley Hall the preferred viewing method was going to be an eighteen-foot length of double-paned quartz windows that started at the floor and went two thirds of the way to the twenty-foot ceiling. Steel I-beams reinforced the glass halfway up and at six-foot vertical intervals. Beyond the glass wall extended a huge cage of titanium bars sheathed both inside and out with that same laboratory quality plastic, pushing back a good thirty feet into an unused portion of the empty third-sublevel warehouse. The only way in was a switch-controlled door in the middle section of the glass. Soon an alien, a creature uncontrollable by humans, would pace within that windowed space. What would it think as it did so? Thoughts of freedom, no doubt, much like the dreams that Ahiro didn't dare let multiply in his own mind.

In the meantime, within the larger cage the unhatched egg was encased in a glass case of its own that was barely large enough to contain it. With the computer clamp still closing it off and the two Synsound bioscientists monitoring it constantly, the sealed egg was again kept safely within a temperature-controlled environment anyway, *incubated.* There it waited, motionless inside its tiny, quiet world, lulled into dormancy by two layers of sound-insulated glass and the intensely filtered, scentless air surrounding it. *Anticipating.*

Work on the apiary proceeded at a steady pace, well within the schedule that Keene had outlined in his final two-hour teleconference with Ahiro and Yoriku. Technically Ahiro was on the site as a supervisor, although he wouldn't have known a metric bolt from a piece of soldering material if any of the workers had asked him. His presence there was vital on a more subjective level: whether the laborers who hammered and bolted and welded knew it or not, it was Ahiro's instinct that guided everything, his opinion that mattered after looking at a completed section as to whether it would serve its purpose in safely holding a fully grown alien. A single shake of his head and the entire project would grind to a halt until the problem was corrected and they could move on.

The work was completed on December 31. Only one other person in the world knew that it was Ahiro's birthday, and other than a telephone call, no one acknowledged it. That was fine by him, and he thought the completion of the apiary was a fine gift. Ahiro did not think of it so much as a gift from Yoriku that he would be allowed to work with this off-world creature, or with the eccentric musician called Damon Eddington; Ahiro cared nothing about either. The gift was that he, Ahiro, was to be allowed to do this *for* Yoriku, in service to the man who had saved not only his life, but that of his infant sister's two decades ago and cared for them both ever since.

Most people thought that the fabled Yakuza had ceased to exist in Japan in the last years of the twenty-first century, when the sixteen largest finance and manufacturing corporations in Japan had merged into a single megacorporation. The resulting entity had narrowly missed going to war with the Japanese government over the right to self-control, avoiding a military confrontation only by neatly strangling almost all of the illegal import/export and drug operations in their country as a show of supposed honesty and good faith. Caught in the conflict because of their father—a high-powered man who trafficked in cocaine, opium, and the rarer forms of synthetic Ice—Ahiro was ten years old when he held his eleven-month-old sister and saw their father nearly cut in half by a spray of bullets. When the man wielding the machine pistol turned toward Ahiro, whose face was already split across his right eye by exploding glass, the boy hugged his baby sister tightly and stared the masked assassin full in the eye, refusing to look away from the man about to murder them.

Yoriku had saved them. There was nothing flashy about Ahiro's memory of the man or his actions; a single soft word—*"No"*—and the soldier had lowered the barrel of his weapon and stepped aside. Twenty years ago Yoriku had been thin and fit, and had boasted a thick head of gray hair where now there was only thinning white. To this day, Ahiro could still hear the man's voice and the words that had changed the course of his life and that of his sister's forever.

"You are both too young to die."

Ahiro had never seen her again, but he spoke to her often and knew she was treated well. Sometimes he wondered what she looked like; she never told him that or any of the finer details of her life, nor did she ask about his. It would be inappropriate for Ahiro to ask; like him, she owed Yoriku everything. In life their father had been a criminal and a drug dealer, but he had also been a traditionalist—and as was customary with ancient Japanese heritage, honor was everything. Yoriku had asked for and received a sworn oath of lifelong loyalty in return for their lives; at ten years old, Ahiro had fully understood the magnitude of what he gave. Neither he nor his sister had ever seen their mother again, and both assumed she'd been killed. That was another thing that Ahiro did not bring up; to do so would be to tarnish his promise, disgrace his word. Such a thing was unthinkable.

Brought to America soon after his father's death, Yoriku had seen to it that Ahiro was privately tutored in those areas that the older man believed would be the most useful to him and to the boy in the future. English, reading and writing of course, basic mathematics. Beyond that the schooling turned to more down-to-earth subjects; Yoriku was not raising a corporate executive—those were available by the hundreds. Instead he wanted someone who could do nearly anything that might be required in a day-to-day world filled with jealous and dangerous competitors—work with his hands, defend him, obtain things for him that might be difficult for someone else. Ahiro learned to work with wood and metal and plaster, and how to supervise those who could construct the things he did not know how to construct himself, such as electrical and mechanical systems. Above all, he learned to be that ultimate of Japanese servants for Yoriku: a ninja.

In the years since then, Ahiro had never questioned the things he did for his savior. Again, it simply wasn't done. Nothing mattered but Yoriku's wishes—legal or illegal, fair or unfair—those were concepts that applied only insofar as Yoriku chose to apply them. The training Ahiro had received in the years after his father's demise had irrevocably reinforced this thinking. He had become Yoriku's personal soldier, and nothing could distract him from his duties. As part of a most unorthodox teaching method, his martial arts instructor had insured that the one thing that held so much danger for any developing warrior—women—would remain forever out of Ahiro's reach; at age twelve, just after his voice had deepened, Ahiro's manhood was irreversibly eliminated.

Now he was an adult, and all that remained for Ahiro was Yoriku. He had no friends and, for the most part, no family. He lived in an expansive but sparsely furnished apartment above a dojo in the East Village that was owned by but untraceable to Yoriku. He spent the majority of his time there, training constantly and always ready to walk out the door; no matter what he was doing, Ahiro could be dressed, if necessary, and headed down the back stairs of the dojo in under three minutes.

Next to Yoriku, the dojo was the only thing to which Ahiro devoted any attention, and over the years he had made sure that his dojo gained a reputation for being among the best in the city but also the most selective and difficult. The students who applied were always illegal immigrants, honorable young men who had trained in Japan from down-on-their-luck but good families, and who were looking for a new start in America. Their minds were pliable and they desperately sought hard training and discipline, preferring a way of life closer to what they had left in Japan than the difficult-to-understand American lifestyle. Ahiro chose only those who did not speak English, and the number of applicants who spoke only Japanese was more than most people thought. While English was routinely taught in urban Japanese schools, there were still the poorer rural areas where schooling was a second priority to farming and making a living; it was from these areas that most of Ahiro's students came.

Now Ahiro was the commander of his own small, personally trained strike force, recently down by three but with replacements already undergoing special education. As he himself had been raised to serve Yoriku, these men would be raised to serve him . . . and by serving him, they would exist, in turn, for Yoriku.

No order or spoken thought that came from Yoriku's mouth was a whim to Ahiro—it was a *necessity.* Charged now with guarding this apiary, the unhatched egg, and with seeing that the strange musician had anything and everything he needed to see this project to fruition and thus humiliate MedTech, Ahiro would not fail. It was not Damon Eddington's desires or Symphony of Hate that mattered, but the desires of Ahiro's savior. Every breath Ahiro drew, every sensation on his tongue, every color his eyes processed and sent to his brain, he owed to Yoriku. He would do anything and everything needed to see this assignment finished simply because it was what Yoriku wanted.

And to Ahiro, Yoriku was everything.

6

New Year's Day, 2124

In his dream, Damon was more than the musician, the composer, or the conductor. He was all *of those things, and more; he was the . . .* Creator. *A god, the Supreme Being, the Master of All Things Musical. He stood not at a podium but on a beautiful Greek pedestal made of majestic black marble and carved with regal faces and wings. His face was proud and passionate and his arms were poised over an orchestra of thousands; a hundred violins fanned as far as he could see to his left, every one an exquisite, fabled Stradivarius even though the last of the Italian master's instruments had disappeared in 2064. Cellos, violas, double basses, and English horns, all thundering out Mussorgsky's classic* Night on Bald Mountain *in its bold original version. Two dozen grand pianos and twice that many harps, and at the far left rear, a row of tubular bells and xylophones added exquisite accents to the magnificent ocean of sound cascading toward him, a waterfall of notes trimmed with melodious ringing and ringing and ringing—*

"What!"

Damon sat upright, rubbing the backs of his knuckles against his grainy eyes and eyebrows. God, he thought blearily, what a helluva dream! He could still hear the bells—

Ringing.

"Oh, Jesus," he said aloud in disgust. He wasn't still hearing his dream; it was the damned *phone.* His fingers scrambled for the VidPhone amid the junk on the bedside table, but when he hit the Receive button all he got was voice-over and the screen stayed black. Not for the first time, he wanted to pick the device up and hurl it against the wall; phone calls in the middle of the night were always bad, not that he had any family or friends to worry about, but being jarred from sleep by someone who didn't have the courtesy to show his face was fucking harassment. "What?" Damon demanded in as surly a voice as he could manage. "Who the hell is it?"

"Merry Christmas, Damon. A week or so belatedly."

"Keene—is that you?" Damon struggled to pull his sleep-stiffened body into a sitting position, fighting off the sheets twisted around his legs and waist. Christ, he thought, I must have been conducting in my sleep. "Jesus," he said again. "I was up working all last night, Keene. What time is—God, I've been in bed less than an hour. What the hell were you thinking to call this late?"

"Just thought I'd call and give you a little present, but—"

Damon sat up straighter, moving more toward wakefulness. Unwillingly, his fingers clutched at the bedsheet and closed in a fist. "Present? What present? Do you mean—"

"—if you don't want it . . ."

"Come on, Jarlath," he said. He had to stop himself from screaming; one wrong word and this bastard would enjoy hanging up on him. "No more games, please. You woke me up and scared the hell out of me besides. Let that be enough."

"Actually," the faceless voice of Keene continued as if he hadn't heard, *"I can't honestly call it a Christmas present, can I? It's more like an . . . Easter egg . . . waiting for its daddy."* The man laughed suddenly, and the cheap speaker in Damon's VidPhone turned it into a sort of unpleasant croaking, as if there were a swollen frog on the other end.

Now Damon's feet slid over the side of the futon to the cold floor and he started feeling gingerly for his worn slippers with his toes. "An egg? Really? Oh, my *God,* Keene! Where did you get it?"

On the other end of the line, Keene chuckled a little more quietly. *"Don't ask a question like that, Damon. I wouldn't answer anyway. Just be at Presley Hall inside of an hour to meet your fellow celebrants."*

"I'll be there, no problem." Having successfully found his slippers, Damon had the receiver jammed between his chin and his shoulder and was already yanking on his trousers. "Presley Hall, you said?"

"Right. And one more thing."

Damon frowned and paused, looking automatically at the VidPhone as a change came over Jarlath Keene's voice. Still nothing; he wished he could see the man's face on the screen, but Keene obviously had the video setting on the other end locked out. "Yeah, what's that?"

"Don't look for me to be anywhere near Presley Hall until your project is completed, my friend. I'm out of the loop on this one from now on. No matter what happens, it didn't come from me. Understand?"

Damon nodded solemnly, then remembered that Keene couldn't see him. "Yeah, right," he said hastily. "I understand your point completely. But what if—"

"Good-BYE, Damon."

Damon started to say something else but was rewarded by the dial tone of the VidPhone instead. *Damn!* What if he needed supplies? More assistants? Well, Keene *had* said something about "fellow celebrants" waiting at Presley Hall. He'd have to go there and see for himself, make sure these people knew who he was and the personal vision and motivation behind this project. God help everyone if Synsound had tossed a couple of their lower-level hack-'em-up bioscientists on this project. Out of the loop? Damon would scream so loud that Keene would hear the racket outside his freakin' bedroom window all the way on the posh East Side.

Even at six-thirty A.M. on New Year's Day there was human garbage on the streets. Damon walked the twelve blocks to Presley Hall in the cold dark, his thoughts bouncing between what waited at the concert building and idly wondering what this city had been like two hundred—no—three hundred years ago. Surely things must have been cleaner, safer, prettier then. His heavy, rubber-soled hiking boots were impervious to the unidentifiable trash that was strewn across the streets on the first day of the year 2124—paper, discarded food for the rats and the homeless, disease-riddled men and women, jelly junkies who might have been twenty years old or sixty. Heated sidewalks installed citywide more than a hundred years ago had eliminated the threat of hypothermia for the homeless and the addicts, and now both seemed to flourish as easily as the fist-sized cockroaches that scuttled around the sidewalks and reared in attack stances before they were kicked aside. When Damon got to Presley Hall and climbed the shallow steps to the private employee entrance, he passed a sexless, gray-garbed figure hunched over something shiny and brown that squirmed and clacked in his hands. Damon shuddered and quickened his step, turning his face aside as he went by but not moving fast enough to avoid hearing the nasty *crunch* of the insect's shell; he'd heard people talk about the vagrants preying on the giant roaches for food but had never seen it before tonight.

A quick press of his open palm against the Hand-

Print Scanner and he was inside Presley Hall. As the metal door slid closed behind him, Damon thought the place was deserted. Not a normal morning person, he had never been in the building at this time of the day, and it was an eerie feeling; although he was standing in a smaller side foyer, the hall still gave off the impression of vast emptiness, and the smallest noise—a tiny screech of the sole of his boot across the floor tiles, for instance—set off a chain of soft, unpleasant echoes. There was something terribly lonely about a building that was designed to hold tens of thousands of people being empty, a desolate, *looming* feeling—

"Mr. Eddington?"

Damon whirled in surprise. "What—!"

The white-haired man standing behind him looked almost as startled as Damon felt. "I'm so sorry," the man said hastily. "I didn't mean to sneak up on you. My name is Michael Brangwen, Bioengineer Level Three." He rushed on, his white mustache bobbing in a nervous smile as he thrust a pudgy hand almost into Damon's stomach, forcing the musician to accept the handshake. "We were told to meet you here, and I thought you'd be expecting us. This is Darcy Vance, Level One."

A long-faced young woman with streaked blond hair and steely blue eyes nodded at him but kept her hands in the pockets of her lab coat. Above the collar of the magenta-colored blouse she wore under her jacket, her face was as pale as an eggshell, her expression as serious as Brangwen's was enthusiastic. "Pleased to meet you," she said. Her voice was much prettier than she was; clear and even, it reminded Damon of a firmly played clarinet. "Didn't someone tell you we'd be waiting?"

Damon cleared his throat, trying to work air around the leftover swirls of surprise in his stomach. "I, uh, was told to meet people here, but not really where they would be."

Brangwen began walking—ambling, actually—across the main waiting area of the hall and Damon followed reflexively. He'd been in here a thousand times before but apparently Darcy hadn't. Despite his anticipation of what was to come, watching her was like having a fresh perspective on the old Presley Hall. She was clearly taken with the fake marble floor tiles and the marbleized columns that were easily six feet around and gave an illusion of support to the soaring domed ceiling by the main entrance. Almost everything in the entry sections was white—the floor, the pillars, the walls, even the ridged metal ceiling—to further the impression of clean stone and Romanesque space. Damon thought it was too bright and outright painful on the eyes, and he found the transition to coal-black inside the concert hall itself too abrupt. Nevertheless, he could understand why someone who had never seen it before would be impressed. It *was* quite an engineering masterpiece.

"It's such an honor to help you with this project, Mr. Eddington," Michael Brangwen said excitedly as they turned into the first of a series of twisting hallways that Damon had never known existed. Brangwen spent half his time walking backward so he could look at Damon while he spoke. "I *love* your work. My music collection is extensive, and I have your entire works, you know, even your first recording."

Brangwen glanced conspicuously at Darcy and she blinked, as if suddenly realizing it was her turn to talk. "I'm afraid you'll have to be lenient with me, Mr. Eddington." Her face, so pale beneath its tied-back mop of wavy hair, looked pained as a faint blush spread across her nose and cheekbones. A single, small curl fluttered against the worry creases in the high expanse of her forehead. "Like you, I'm very involved in my work. I don't watch movies or listen to music very much, so I'm not familiar with your achievements. I—I'm sorry." She brightened. "But I *am* delighted at the prospect of working with an alien, so you can be assured that I'll be giving my best efforts to your project. You'll never find anyone more dedicated."

Well, Damon thought resolutely, despite Vance's Level One rating, at least they were both bioengineers and not fledgling bioscientists, new hires that Human

Resources had decided should cut their teeth on a project the department considered unimportant. And Michael Brangwen was familiar with and appreciated Damon's music, even if Vance didn't. Considering Damon's track record with the critics and the public, being a hit with one out of the two assistants—fifty percent—wasn't bad. Besides, what really mattered was his music—the Symphony of Hate—not the past work history of these two. Enough of the courtesy crap. "Show me the egg," he said simply.

"Oh, yes—of course!" Brangwen's hands fluttered in the air as the group turned down a final hallway and stopped at what looked like a freight elevator. The older man gave the button a series of impatient pushes, as if he could make the elevator arrive faster by sheer will. "I guarantee you'll be impressed. This is unlike anything else that exists in our environment. Few people have ever seen an alien egg in the real world, much less handled one and lived to talk about it." The elevator doors slid open and the three of them stepped inside, with the senior bioengineer talking the entire time. When the elevator stopped, Damon followed the other two down more corridors, feeling numb from Brangwen's constant chatter, bewildered at the turns and twists; by the time they had stepped off a third elevator and descended a final flight of stairs, his entire sense of direction was blitzed. The thought of memorizing the route was daunting.

"Such a *fantastic* idea to use the sound of the alien in your Symphony of Hate, Mr. Eddington," Brangwen was saying. "It would have been *great* in your Fourth Symphony, too, the *Maestro de Santana*—"

They went past an orange door, then Darcy Vance stepped to the side and let Damon pass as Brangwen used a cardkey to open another door, this one made of sliding steel. Then they filed into the outer chamber of what looked like a huge apiary. Twelve feet to Damon's left rose an unbreakable glass wall crosshatched by steel beams; the room stretched another dozen feet to his right, where an extensive sound mixer console swept around the corner. Farther down from it were more consoles covered with dials and screens that Damon didn't understand—equipment for nurturing and hatching the egg and, Damon assumed, monitoring the alien once it was born.

"—you know, in the third movement when the explosions came?" Brangwen paused, apparently expecting an answer.

Damon barely heard the man. There, separated from the human world by only a few square inches of glass, rested the alien egg. It was hideously beautiful: an elongated gray oval of moist, lumpy flesh that held the key to his life's masterpiece . . . so close! Damon pressed his fingers against the outer glass of the cage and smiled, wishing that all these glass barriers would bend in and let him stroke the shell; he felt giddy, breathless—as though he were experiencing that once-in-a-lifetime feeling of his first public performance all over again. "When can we hatch it?"

"Oh, anytime." Brangwen's voice came from just over his left shoulder and Damon stood, reluctantly moving away from his view of the modest-looking glass box that housed the egg. "Everything is here and ready. Containment, medical monitoring equipment, the sound equipment you'll need on your end—everything."

"Wonderful!" It was all Damon could do to keep from rubbing his hands together. He scanned the room but didn't see what he was looking for and a tiny spot of worry began to prickle in his stomach. The only people present were himself and the two assistants. Damon swallowed with difficulty. "Then where's . . . the donor clone?" Vance and Brangwen exchanged meaningful glances and Damon's niggling feeling of apprehension burst into outright fear. Immediately his stomach began to burn in protest. "What's the matter?" he demanded. "Why are you two looking at me like that?"

When Brangwen still kept silent, Vance finally took the initiative and spoke. "We don't have one."

"What!"

The young woman spread her hands in a helpless gesture as Brangwen's expression changed into something resembling a distressed puppy's. He began to nod rapidly as she explained. "The fact is, the support systems that Synsound had built to maintain the egg and house the alien were astronomically expensive, not to mention the . . . ah . . . expedition costs in obtaining the egg to begin with. I mean, *look* at this place." She waved at the recording and monitoring equipment in the room and at the reinforced space spreading into darkness beyond the high glass wall. "Two months ago, this was nothing but unused basement storage. Surely you realize that none of this was here. The containment area, the quartz wall, all this was custom constructed for your project, the egg was obtained for you, and Michael and I were transferred to work with you. With all these expenses, adding the price of a clone was out of the question. We were told that a single clone costs more than all of this put together, and that the money just isn't there."

Damon felt like someone had whacked him in the chest with a hammer and was still happily beating away at him. "No *money*? After all this, they're saying that there's no more money? That's what they *always* say, don't you realize that? But what the hell is it supposed to *mean*?" His voice was escalating dangerously toward a shout.

"Mr. Eddington, I assure you, it's not up to us," Vance said hastily. "None of the construction decisions were shown to us for approval or comments. We're transferees, not new hires. Our salaries aren't even competitive with normal market rates. They're only giving us enough money to get by on because they . . . know we want to work with you on this."

Brangwen placed a sympathetic hand on Damon's shoulder. "She's right, Mr. Eddington. It's Mr. Keene and Mr. Yoriku who make the budgetary decisions—mostly Keene, I think. Like Darcy told you, he said that the setup was so expensive—the cage, the equipment, especially procuring the egg—that there wasn't any money left for a clone." His expression was grave.

"I mean, *think* about it. Clones are medically engineered life-forms with a market value of well over a million dollars apiece. Not only are they meticulously regulated by the Life Engineering Administration, there are at least a half-dozen nationally advertised organizations that constantly monitor the number of clones manufactured and the uses to which the life-forms are put. Plus they have informants *everywhere*—we'd never be able to get one legally. Then there are the religious groups that blame every bad thing that happens in society today on clones. All these groups are typical; they're always vocal, vying for media attention and ready to do anything to get it. All the horrible red tape notwithstanding, Synsound would never chance so much negative publicity—controversy is one thing, screwing around with the federal government something else again. Finding out that Synsound had taken an illegally procured clone and used it in a fatal experiment involving an alien . . ." Brangwen's voice trailed away. "God, I can't even *imagine* the implications."

For a moment Damon felt his knees try to buckle. Not far from where they stood was one of the rolling console chairs and he stretched out a hand and grabbed at it in time to keep his balance. "So what do we do?" he asked hoarsely. He pulled the chair around and sank onto it gratefully. "We have all this—an outfitted recording studio, a huge room with a cage, and probably more equipment and monitors than any of us have ever seen in one room—but we have an egg that we can't hatch. *What do we do*?" He searched Brangwen's face and the older man dropped his eyes, but when Damon looked to Darcy her gaze was even and clear.

"We'll have to use a live subject."

Damon gaped at her. "You mean *kill* someone?" When she folded her arms and said nothing, Damon covered his face with his hands and shuddered. He had a sudden inkling that the hands he lifted to his face felt exactly like a face-hugger would, and he let them drop rather abruptly back to his lap. All the fury and disappointment of a moment ago abruptly dissipated, leaving in its wake a deep, unaccustomed dread. "No, oh, God, no. I don't want *that.*"

Brangwen cleared his throat and touched him tentatively on the shoulder again. As he spoke his next words, he kept ducking his head lower and lower. "Well, it's not like murder, you know. You can't be blamed for killing someone who *wants* to die, remember? There are people who actually *want* to hatch alien eggs. Religious nuts—fanatics—who spend their lives trying to find a way to be a host."

Damon rubbed the back of his neck, trying desperately to concentrate on the situation. It had all been so simple: go to Keene and say what he wanted, and he would get it. That's how it had always been, yet now he was expected to beg. Too many people thought pleading for your needs was either an art form or a rare sort of verbal parrying. If he understood Brangwen correctly right now, the man was telling him that there were people who *wanted* to die, who would stand by and allow the creature waiting inside the egg—an eight-legged nightmare that he thought looked vaguely like a cross between a thick-bodied scorpion and a wasp as big as a man's head—to wrap around their face, then penetrate—

It was too awful to contemplate further.

He swallowed again, this time with difficulty. "And where do we find these . . . people?" Damon managed in a raspy voice. "These . . . fanatics?" Damon suddenly felt exhausted, already overwhelmed by this project of his own making and the unthinkable acts it seemed to be spawning. The concept that Synsound would destroy a human being rather than pay to sacrifice a clone was mind-boggling.

Darcy Vance stepped forward. Her arms were still folded across her chest and her expression was calm and cold, the perfect bioengineer and researcher-in-training. If she had any qualms about what they were doing, she certainly didn't show it; rather, now that Damon had hinted he might go along with it, she seemed to have all the answers and to be in a good mood besides. How courteous of me to cooperate, Damon thought sourly.

"I've already asked Mr. Keene about that part," she said crisply. "He said that if you agreed to the idea of using a live subject, all we had to do was ask Ahiro and it would be taken care of."

Damon raised his head. "Ahiro?"

"He works for Keene," Brangwen said. The older man looked nervous and exhilarated at the same time; his gaze kept darting back to the empty cage, as though visually testing it for strength. "And now that you've given the go-ahead, he'll work for us.

"Whenever we want him."

7

Darcy had finally gone home, as had Damon Eddington. At last Michael Brangwen had the apiary and sound lab all to himself, and he intended to make full use of it. He'd been waiting for this quiet time all day, and now he dug into the crumpled paper bag that had contained his supper—two microwavable mini-cans of pseudo-beef stew and a bag of trendy blue potato chips—and pulled out the last thing inside. As Michael held the syndisc up to the console's light and squinted at the fine print on the label, the technology that made it possible for something so small to hold such wonderful melodies stunned him, as it always did. His field was bioengineering—complicated, vast, *life.* For others to take inert materials like metal, plastics, and ceramic and turn it into music . . . *that,* to Michael, was sublime creation. Bioengineering? Bah; they worked with the materials that were already there, already *alive,* changing, replicating, healing. It was as though science had the supreme copy machine, complete with touchpads for quantity, size, color, and alterations. Geneticists had yet to discover the secret of bringing life to lifeless flesh, but Synsound . . . the company brought the breath of music to inanimate and inorganic materials every day.

So much to learn, to memorize, Michael reflected as he carried his new syndisc to the testing console. He could barely keep track of all the steps needed just to have a minimum sound demonstration—anything more was Damon's field. Knowing that Damon might have started setting up his recording preferences, Michael couldn't risk fiddling around with too much. He could have taken the syndisc home—he'd actually created a fine setup that wasn't too complex—but this seemed a more appropriate place for the music he was about to hear. The syndisc was used and quite rare, and Michael swore to his soul that the store clerk, a gum-chewing teenager with a half-buzzed haircut who couldn't find his own zipper much less a laser tag replacement for the missing sticker on the case, had really screwed up by shrugging and saying carelessly, "Five credits."

Michael turned the plasticized case over reverently and scanned the list of titles on the back. The syndisc was a re-recording of a 1989 CD titled "Chiller," performed by Erich Kunzel and the Cincinnati Pops Orchestra, and some of the individual titles were familiar—"March to the Scaffold" from *Symphonie fantastique*, "Pandemonium" from *The Damnation of Faust*, the Overture to *The Phantom of the Opera*—all fitting selections to prepare him for the work ahead with Damon Eddington. Others, like "Three Selections from *Psycho*" and "The Light from *Poltergeist*" eluded Michael, despite his intense interest in music and extensive collection of syndiscs. After a few moments of study, he slipped the syndisc from the case and placed it on the player. A quiet whirring sound and a press of the ENTER key was all it took to start the computerized sound commands.

The booklet accompanying the syndisc was missing, of course, and there was nothing to forewarn Michael about the forty-eight-second "Opening Sequence." Escalated high enough in volume to vibrate his teeth, the piece turned out to be a storm recreation containing peals of thunder and cracks of lightning realistic enough to make his heart hammer. Hands still shaking from the shock, Michael grinned and found the volume control, dialing it down to something more reasonable before a security guard or some other mope came running. *Wow!* he thought. Now *this* was music—strong, cell-shaking *sound.* Still smiling, he sat back on one of the chairs, folded his hands behind his head, and let himself be swept away.

The "Chiller" syndisc was over in slightly under an hour—long by today's standards, but nowhere near enough to satisfy Michael. Still, he pulled the syndisc out and put it carefully back in its case, then neatened up his work area and cast a last glance around the apiary. He had to go; if he didn't cardkey out pretty soon, someone in Human Resources would look at his time log at the end of the week and start screaming about unaccounted for overtime. Obviously he wouldn't put in a requisition for the time he'd just spent using the company's equipment to listen to his music, and frankly, Michael didn't care about getting paid for the overtime he put in on this project anyway. He was elated to have the job, thankful that his employment was going to last another few weeks or a month, or maybe more. And after that . . .

Michael pulled his coat out of the closet and shrugged it on, feeling suddenly very old. How much longer before he got that cheerful gold notice tucked into the envelope with his pay slip—*We're happy to announce your retirement!* He was already six months past the corporation retirement elective age enacted by Congress in year 2113, and the only reason he was still in Synsound's employment was because no one else had stepped forward and offered to work with the difficult Damon Eddington and the alien.

Sure, the offer hadn't been corporate-wide, but enough people had known of its availability that the company finally made it known to someone like Michael . . . who felt he didn't dare refuse. Face it, old man, he thought sourly. It's almost time to cut you out of the herd. You can barely keep up.

Michael sighed aloud and began making his way out of the building. Hearing his own plaintive sound made him alternately lonely and angry at himself—what good would it do to indulge in self-pity? People who did were perpetually angry, mean-spirited, and hated everything around them—Damon Eddington was a prime example. Speaking of Eddington, both he and Michael had seen the way Darcy ogled the hall's construction and size. Eddington might not appreciate her awe, but Michael could understand perfectly the way she felt—sometimes he was still amazed at it, too. He just hid it better, thinking it would look silly for someone his age to gape like a child at the building's architecture.

So many changes to keep up with in everyday life, much less in the field of bioengineering. Christ, sometimes the information seemed to fluctuate by the hour, like the hypermutant viruses it was rumored MedTech played with all the time. Everything moved too fast for Michael—viruses mutating, genetic engineering exploding into new realms, space exploration, and now alien experimentation—new information always popping up and needing to be memorized. The human race's voracious appetite for knowledge would never be satisfied; as a young man, he would have thought that was a good thing. Now he wasn't so sure.

So here Michael was, facing the end of his career with no particular specialty—bioengineers weren't really all that rare—or body of work to leave behind except an apartment filled with thousands of syndiscs and a hodgepodge of sound equipment strung together with old-fashioned electrical tape and blind luck—and don't forget the well-thumbed and expensive bioscience textbooks that were out-of-date almost as quickly as they saw print. No wife or girlfriend, no *family.* If he died today, not a single person would know or remember that he had possessed an insatiable appetite for all kinds of music—hellrock, classical, alternative, even the twangy country that was slowly dying out—everything. Again, he hated to let self-pity get to him, but *Jesus!* Sometimes he couldn't help it.

And tomorrow would bring another day of the Eddington project. Exciting, different . . . *terrifying.* The thought of nurturing and raising an alien hatchling scared the hell out of Michael, but what choice did he have? He couldn't refuse the assignment, or Synsound was sure to force him into retirement; the company—*Keene*—did not tolerate employees who bucked orders. A future with no job terrified him far more than the Eddington dilemma, which itself had implications reaching much further than the stolen egg and illegal hatchling. Retirement would mean a total upheaval of life as he lived it: he was already crammed into a small apartment, but he would have to move into one of those tiny retirement complexes on the far West Side, full of cockroaches and nosy, doddering neighbors who had nothing more to do than meddle in everyone else's business. What would they say when he blasted music from the Dead Visuals or Webster's Family Dummies at two in the morning?

On the other hand was the Symphony of Hate project. Michael himself had provided the supposed justification for the next step. But to sacrifice a person, religious fanatic or not, so that a creature that was little more than a wild, enormous insect could live . . . could their actions ever be absolved?

And there was Damon Eddington, of course, with whom Michael couldn't help but sympathize. Still young and inflamed, filled with self-pity or not, Michael saw Eddington as Synsound's victim, a man driven to the edge of sanity by uncontrollable creative impulses and Synsound's nasty policy of dangling its support always just out of reach. That was only the beginning, too, because in the younger man's music Michael heard everything missing from so many of the pieces recorded today—brilliance, passion, fury—all those wonders denied. No wonder Eddington was a dark and tormented soul.

But . . . what would be unleashed if Synsound continued to coddle its eccentric pet artist?

8

"Here you go, Chief Rice, the final results of the tests performed as a result of the Alien Research Lab theft."

Phil Rice looked up to see Tobi Roenick, the lab supervisor for MedTech's Coroner's Investigations Division, as she dropped a folder into the in-basket on the corner of his desk. The folder was red—a death investigation code—and pitifully thin. That pretty much said it all.

"Any results?" Rice asked, just to keep her in his small office for an extra minute. Tobi was a beautiful woman with caramel-colored skin, golden eyes flecked with brown, and a tightly cut cap of highlighted brown hair feathered around her face. Her movements were fluid and controlled, like a dancer's, the smile she gave him full and framed by red-glossed lips. For a moment all he wanted in the world was to ask her out to dinner and hear her say *yes*. But rumor had it that she was sharp-witted and could cut a guy down to size before the appetizer arrived if he said the wrong word; reluctantly, Phil decided to stifle his urge to issue the invitation for now. He liked living dangerously but he wasn't into masochism. Then again, she certainly was pretty . . .

In response to his question, Tobi picked the folder up again and held it sideways, then fanned its contents to emphasize the fact that there were probably only three or four pieces of paper in it.

"What do you think?"

Rice shrugged and leaned back against his chair. "There's always hope." He gave her what he thought was a winsome smile and their eyes locked for a moment.

"Nice try." She dropped the folder back on his desk and headed out. He was still reaching for it when she poked her head back around the door frame, a small smile playing across her mouth. "Hey, Rice."

He looked up in surprise. "Yeah?"

"You need to update those lines, you know. You sound like you've been watching reruns of *Dating Game 2100.*"

Rice opened his mouth to retort, but Tobi was already gone, and the fading sound of her heels in the hallway outside told him he'd have to raise his voice to be heard. No way; there was no telling who might be in the hall and listening. "Fine," he muttered. "If you don't like my lead-in, buy your own damned dinner."

He opened the test results curiously, but it only took a few seconds to confirm what Tobi had told him. A confirmation that the fingerprints had been lasered away, no genetic tracers, no implants, no retina records—nothing to tie any of them to any record in the United States. He hadn't expected anything, but what Tobi had considered a line was really the way Rice always felt, and the thing he considered his major and most annoying fault: his ridiculous, irrepressible optimism. This time, though, he'd bombed out. Sometimes he wondered if he'd ever learn his lesson.

Rice swiveled his chair around and looked out the window, smiling a bit when he remembered his job interview here six years earlier and how they'd touted an office with a window view as one of the major perks. At the cynical look on his face, the MedTech recruiter had back-pedaled hastily, saying, "Not that it makes any difference in the scheme of things, of course, but it does make the day-to-day chores a little more bearable. It's a stress reliever." Bearable, indeed; sometimes Rice thought he would have been better off without the chance to glance down and see Central Park and the Upper West Side. He wasn't fooled by the seasonal artificially engineered trees and grass or the brightly colored flowers that lined the walkways every spring when across the rest of the city the greenery could barely exist anymore. The foliage was an illusion, like printed jungle wrapping paper on a box that held a stew of teeming human bodies. The fact that he still saw hope for the people down there amazed even himself. At least the building was soundproofed and he didn't have to listen to the aircycles; he didn't think he could have stood that.

It was still early, not even three. He'd made the decision this morning to go ahead and use the alien as a bloodhound, way before Tobi had delivered the formal test results to his office. After all, if there'd been something in the results that would have given them a clue, she would have called him as soon as she received the information. A MedTech star performer all the way, Tobi would have never allowed the information to lag at the tail end of a chain of red tape; from the paper trail part of it, she wanted that egg back as much as Rice did. Having it out there—stolen right out from under MedTech's protective arms—was a fucking insult.

It was a damned good thing none of Rice's superiors were there to see the dark grin that spread across his broad face.

Finally, a challenge.

Rice had come from the NYPD a little over six

years ago, where he'd done a stint as an Undercover Operations Investigator. Before that, he'd been with the army's Special Operations Detachment, a twice-renewed tour of duty that kept him on Homeworld involved in the ongoing "cleanup" procedures. Ol' Blue the alien was a leftover from his final mission; tagged and captured by Rice himself, the former army man had been able to track the alien through computer records when the army sold the creature to MedTech's Research and Development Division. He needed to know where the life-form was at all times for his own peace of mind; after all, it was ol' Blue that had nearly killed him and ended his service with the army forever. Thanks to his final Homeworld battle with the alien, Rice could never go off-planet again. Hell, he couldn't even fly in an airplane; ol' Blue's offensive and nearly deadly swipe of claws had done soft tissue damage that made travel within a pressurized compartment permanently impossible.

Rice had thought working for the NYPD would be a suitable alternative to the excitement of the army's off-world war. He quickly learned that he didn't care for the constant emotional battering he felt when dealing with the victims and seeing people's lives destroyed by the sharks on the street, but for a while he'd been caught up in the chase, so to speak. Hunting criminals wasn't as physically challenging as whacking bugs on Homeworld, but it kept his mind in overdrive all the time; for a few years, Rice had actually been *happy*.

All that changed, however, when some enterprising young biochemist discovered that once fertilized by a drone, the liquid secreted by a queen alien as she laid her eggs could get a lab rat stoned. That same young man had then set about perfecting and distilling his product until it could be used by human beings, and after that, manufacture and distribution of this irreversibly addictive drug—named royal jelly, or simply jelly for short—were only a matter of diligent research. The biochemist's name was Christian

Bloomer, but his location was one of the best kept secrets the cops had ever encountered; when you were only twenty-four years old and one of the richest men in the world, it was easy to disappear into the masses.

To put it frankly, Rice got tired of jelly. It became the basis for everything in his work with the NYPD. Eventually the murders, thefts, fights, even the kidnappings almost always led to the drug and some addict or dealer trying to steal or score. He hated the stuff as much as the next cop but stopping it was like trying to stop the wind with a nylon net. Jelly was everywhere, and as fast as they did a sting operation in one place, two more sprang up to fill the gap. And stakeouts—God, how he hated *those.* Four years of drowning in that crap and he'd bailed and taken the job with MedTech.

At least here he occasionally got to work with the bugs again. The covert Alien Research Lab didn't need him often, but once in a while he'd get a call to come down to Sublevel Five and do containment or transport, or assist with some experiment or another. The harness they would use on ol' Blue tonight was Rice's invention, based on his work with the army and the small hive of aliens that MedTech put at his disposal downstairs. Rice had developed it and MedTech had footed the bill; now he and the mother company shared the patent, MedTech had an ace in the hole over a specific corner of the market, and Phillip Rice probably had a job for life.

Rice forced his attention away from the window and back to his desk, then reached over and switched on his computer. With more than an hour of daylight left and a rush hour coming at the end of that, he couldn't contemplate taking ol' Blue—his pet name for the older and bigger-than-average alien drone that had nearly killed him—out and onto the streets of Manhattan. Rice played with the on-line data regarding the city for half an hour or so, mapping out a number of possible routes out of Manhattan. Finally, he sat back in disgust. Why bother? Ol' Blue would take them where he wanted to go—which should be where he smelled the pheromones of his own hive. If the stolen egg was still in the city, the Homeworld creature would find it.

Rice ran his tongue over his teeth thoughtfully and stared at the glowing computer screen. While he might not know where ol' Blue would take them tonight, he'd damn well better know where they could or couldn't take the alien. A few clicks of the mouse and he switched programs and tapped into the one the major newspapers used to make up their layouts on what was happening with events around the city. A number of things showed up, including a Greenpeace rally at Times Square that didn't start until eight tonight—they'd be freezing their environmental butts off by eight-thirty—and a concert at Presley Hall that started at seven and ended at ten. That made both Times Square and Presley Hall off-limits until the crowds cleared out, and the people from the two events—especially the concert—would cause a surge into the restaurants and cheap shops in the area. If Rice's team and the alien headed west, then south, they'd have to pass the Port Authority, which might not be a good idea—way too many chances to run into jelly users there. Screw it. Rice was game for something to relieve the boredom; he and his team would go out late—after midnight—and march right up Fifth Avenue. Then ol' Blue could tell them which way was next.

"It's midnight in Manhattan, boys." Rice grinned at his two best security men. "You ready for this?" The bushes around them made crackling sounds, like plastic bags being crumpled, and Rice tensed. After a few seconds though, the GuardTech Robots stalking them on the other side of the still leafless vegetation slipped away. This time his smile was one of relief.

"Stop smilin' at me, you asshole," Eddie McGarrity snarled. He tightened his hold on the rear guidepole that angled over his head and was connected somewhere out of sight at the back of the complex metal harness wrapped around the Homeworld life-form. "I had a date tonight and it sure wasn't with *you.*"

"Luckiest day *that* woman ever had," Ricky Morez hooted. He inclined his head briefly toward the alien, unnaturally quiet within his titanium mesh jacket and alloy muzzle. The only sound they could hear was its breathing, a sort of low hiss that constantly echoed around the creature. "Did you tell her you play with bugs, big boy?"

"Hey, I'm still in the 'making a good impression' phase," McGarrity protested with a toothy grin. "I'm not looking to scare her off."

Rice snorted. "Don't worry, that'll happen naturally." He tugged on the guidepole at ol' Blue's left shoulder and the alien obliged with one long-strided step in that direction, then another. "Look sharp, guys. This sucker may seem like he's under wraps, but he's always going to be bigger and stronger than us."

"And anything else on the street," McGarrity shot back. "At least we don't have to worry about getting buzzed by one of the aircycle gangs at this time of night."

"Fifth Avenue is a No Fly Zone," Rice reminded him.

"Like it makes any difference."

"Where're we going?" Morez asked as he tightened his grip on the right guidepole, prodding the alien back into a straight-ahead direction. Maneuvering the creature using the harness and guidepoles was vaguely like steering an oversize canoe from the far rear—provided the canoe was equipped with a motor that ran in unpredictable directions.

"It looks like we're headed—"

Ol' Blue suddenly tossed his elongated head like a horse and made an abrupt right turn that nearly dragged Rice off his feet; Morez dodged out of the way and fought to keep his hold.

"Whichever way he wants!"

* * *

It took damned near two hours just to get past Rockefeller Plaza, and ol' Blue kept trying to go west. Rice and his men kept up a steady resistance, hoping to keep the alien on Fifth Avenue until they were at least past Bryant Park, and preferably Herald Square—not that it really mattered. For all Rice knew, ol' Blue could be leading them right into the heart of Penn Station. Sometimes Rice wondered about the way his own mind worked; had he really believed he and his team would be leading the Homeworld creature through an empty city just because they'd chosen the early hours of the morning? Not likely.

People were everywhere. Though most wisely kept their distance, crossing the street or ducking in doorways when Rice and his group approached, there were a couple of dorks on nearly every corner who had to try to get a better look at the alien, an occasional late-night tourist with his happy disposable camera who wanted a picture. Rice would've thought they'd seen enough of the bugs on the thousands of videos from the Homeworld Wars and, of course, the films that Hollywood pumped out by the dozens, complete with SoundImmerse and holograms that made audiences bob and duck from their seats. But hey, what could beat the real thing?

"I think we're headed toward Presley Hall," Morez said. His young face was creased with worry. "That might not be such a good idea, boss. I heard they got a run of nightly concerts going on."

"Tonight's concert was over at ten," Rice told him. "Last of the strays should've cleared out by eleven-thirty, twelve at the latest. That's why we waited so long, despite McGarrity's belief that I planned this entire trip to intentionally screw up his date."

"Yeah," McGarrity grated, "you're doing real good so far. On *both* accounts."

Before Rice could retort, the alien jerked slightly. All three men clutched uneasily at the handles of their guidepoles, then ol' Blue fell back into that strange, half-bent gait that became more pronounced in the larger aliens. "So far," the youngest member of their team agreed. Morez glanced at Rice. "But what if he gets really ticked off, Chief?"

"It won't make any difference," Rice insisted. He wondered if he was trying to reassure his men or himself as the life-form twitched again and swung his head back and forth, as if searching out the pheromones from his hive.

"The harness keeps the hands next to his sides so he can't grab or scratch anything, and the muzzle won't let him open either mouth wide enough to bite." Another loping set of steps and the alien paused. "Come on, Blue," Rice urged. He tugged at the guidepole, trying to get the creature back in gear. "Sniff those pheromones, boy. They're from *your* hive. Find that egg, buddy."

A few more feet down the street, and the creature jerked again, harder, as a couple of stoned yuppie secretaries started staggering toward the team and its harnessed creature, intent on "petting" the alien. McGarrity had hardly finished bellowing at the women and the team was cruising past West Forty-sixth and Diamond and Jewelers Row when ol' Blue went, as Rice would think of it later, completely ballistic.

The MedTech trio might as well have been holding ol' Blue with a harness made of rubber bands for all the control they managed to maintain. McGarrity was the biggest man of the three, and he had the dubious honor of being the first to be yanked off-balance when the alien suddenly crouched so low to the sidewalk that the blue-black bones guarding his chest cavity brushed the concrete. When ol' Blue followed his squat by rearing into a stance that was nearly ruler-straight, McGarrity went soaring into the street, the handgrip of his guidepole bouncing wildly before falling uselessly to the ground.

"Hold on, Rick—!" Rice never got the chance to finish his shout. One moment he was clutching his guidepole with every ounce of muscle he had; the next he was flat on his back on the filthy walkway, staring at the sliver of smog-encrusted night sky barely visible beyond the faraway tops of the skyscrapers. He heard someone grunt and turned his head to see Morez in a heap fifteen feet away. Rice rolled to his right and saw ol' Blue racing up West Forty-sixth, the three alloy guidepoles flapping behind him like heavy feathers.

"Come on!" he yelled as he scrambled to his feet. "We've got to catch him!" A solid round of curses from both his men told Rice they weren't hurt, and by the time Rice had managed to increase his speed to a sprint, the other two were right with him. Under normal circumstances, they wouldn't have had a prayer of catching up with the alien, but ol' Blue's balance was off, skewed by the harness that wouldn't let him swing his sinewy arms. Every third step or so one of the guidepoles would slip beneath the sharp claws of his feet and make him stumble; once he went all the way down, twisting on the sidewalk for a precious three seconds before he was upright again. Still, the Homeworld creature's stride far outdistanced theirs, and when they finally skidded into the alley into which ol' Blue had disappeared, they were in time only to hear the alien's screams of rage and watch helplessly as he rushed two men at the alleyway's far end.

Rice put an arm out as McGarrity pulled a laser pistol and started to head into the alleyway. "Don't bother, Eddie!" He had to yell to be heard over the combined roars of ol' Blue and the shrieks of his victims. "It's already too late—look!" McGarrity and Morez followed Rice's pointing finger and both blanched. Thirty feet down the rubble-strewn passageway, the creature was still roaring and hissing as he busily rammed himself headfirst against what . . . *little* now remained of the two men who'd been his target. The brick walls of the buildings at the dead end were splattered with alien mucus, human blood, pieces of bone and bits of brain.

"Jesus," Morez hollered. "What the hell's his problem? He was fine a minute ago!"

"I hope he stops here, Chief." McGarrity's voice was loud but shaky. "If he doesn't, I think we're fucked."

As if on cue, ol' Blue suddenly backed away from

the carnage and crouched, rocking unsteadily on his jointed legs as his barbed tail flicked dangerously in the air behind him. Cocking his head, they saw him struggle to move his arms and when that failed, he managed two wobbly leaps forward, then leaned over and nudged tentatively at the scarlet mass of flesh, severed body parts, and bloody sludge. Dripping strands of tissue hung from the alloy muzzle, and a solid line of greenish slime leaked from between the alien's teeth, as if he could taste the meat just out of reach. Apparently satisfied with his handiwork, ol' Blue leaned back, then rose and stalked to a point midway between his two fatalities and the MedTech team. There he paused, tucked his head close to his chest as he settled into a crouch, and waited.

"Well, I guess that takes care of them," Morez said dryly as the men edged into the passageway. "Jeez, talk about a temper." When they got to the creature, McGarrity and Morez cautiously reached for their guidepoles, but the alien offered no resistance.

"Hang on to him," Rice ordered. "I want to check out these two. And be careful he doesn't start up again."

McGarrity snorted. "Not much to see down there."

"Hey, Chief—given his recent history, I don't think I'd take too long if I were you." Morez shifted nervously as ol' Blue's hard, dark skin trembled. "We probably ought to remember that we don't know *why* he did what he just did."

"Yes, we do," Rice called over his shoulder. He reached down and poked at something small on the ground but didn't pick it up. "Bull's-eye. An empty jelly vial—that's what must've set him off. I think our dead pals here were a dealer and a junkie." Rice hurried back and slipped his fist into the handgrip on the left pole. "Come on. Let's get out of this dead end." The three of them began to hurriedly maneuver ol' Blue back toward the front of the alley where it intersected Forty-sixth.

Morez looked at him questioningly. "A jelly deal did *that*?"

Rice nodded, straining with the effort of forcing ol' Blue to turn back toward Fifth Avenue. "Oh, yeah. We learned early on that the best way to kill off these things on Homeworld was to capture a dozen good-sized drones and turn them loose in a different hive. These things hunt by scent and hearing, but identify strictly on smell and are extremely territorial. Each hive has a unique scent, and when one of 'em gets a whiff of a colony that's not their own, they go berserk. That stuff in the alley was nothing." Rice shook his head as he kept a steady pressure on his guidepole. "You ought to see the attack technique when there's a couple dozen of them tearing at each other."

"Thanks, boss, but I think I'll pass," McGarrity said. "Hey—where're you going?" he asked in surprise as Rice pulled on his guidepole, hauling the alien in a semicircle that turned him back toward Central Park and MedTech. "I thought we were headed toward downtown."

"Another time," Rice said grimly. "I haven't given up the hunt, but right now we've got to get Blue back to MedTech before somebody videos us." He jerked his head back in the direction of Forty-sixth and the other two men saw people starting to gather at the mouth of the alley halfway down the block. "Nobody'll complain much about those two, but we can't let this happen again. Too many people on jelly—next time it might be someone who'll be missed." He scowled. "I'm going to have to work a little on the control aspect of this harness. Let's go, and try to act normal."

Morez gave Rice a look that said he was crazy for suggesting such a thing, but McGarrity laughed heartily. "Oh, yeah, Phil. Who's going to notice? I take my pet bug for a walk every night about this time, just like the rest of the dog owners. Say . . ." He grinned mischievously at his teammates. "Did either of you remember to bring the *pooper scooper*?"

Morez rolled his eyes and Rice groaned. "That's disgusting, McGarrity."

McGarrity opened his mouth to reply, but Morez cut him off. "Of course it is, Chief. And it's a perfect example of why this fool's here with us, instead of on a supposed date with some mythical lady."

"Mythical, my ass. I *told* you," McGarrity said with a sulky expression, "I had one all set up."

"I'll believe *that* when I see it," Rice said. "Come on, you bastard," he snapped at the alien as it tried to twist in the opposite direction. "Another time—stop trying to go backward."

"Look who's talking, loverboy." McGarrity fought with his guidepole and finally got ol' Blue going in the direction Rice wanted. For the time being, the return trip to MedTech looked okay.

"At least I've got prospects," Rice said smoothly.

"I think all this stuff about dates and prospects is nothing but dream talk from both of you," Morez said. "And I've got a hundred credits—on *each* of you—that says you can't each bring a date to my house for dinner."

"Say what!" Phil demanded in astonishment.

"Uh-oh," McGarrity muttered.

"I'm giving you two a chance to put your money where your big mouths are," Morez challenged. "My wife and I make a fine pot of spaghetti—"

"With real meat sauce?" McGarrity's eyes were suddenly shining. He looked ready to drool.

"For you, Irish, we'll splurge." Morez sent McGarrity a mock scowl. "But you *have* to bring a date. No date, no spaghetti. And no excuses."

Phil chuckled. "You're in trouble now, McGarrity. We'd better schedule this for five or six months from now."

McGarrity said nothing, but Morez's eyes narrowed intelligently when he glanced past the alien's dark rib cage and locked eyes with Rice. "Well, I don't know, Chief. Being familiar with the both of you, I really have to wonder which one of you is going to have to pull a magic trick here."

"And what's that supposed to mean?"

This time it was McGarrity who laughed. "Maybe he's suggesting *you'd* better learn the word *abracadabra*!"

9

Darcy Vance spent a lot of time in the lab staring at the egg. There wasn't much else to do at this stage of the project, not until Ahiro showed up with a subject to host the alien hatchling. She knew that Michael came in late at night and used the elaborate equipment setup to play the newest of his ever-expanding collection of syndiscs. It was too bad she didn't have a hobby like that to occupy her free time; she'd probably be a lot less miserable if she did.

The alien part of the Eddington project though . . . that had promise. Finally, something besides MedTech's frogs and bacteria, and endless experiments trying to find a more economical way to provide the inoculation serum that was given to newborns to protect them against HIV, ebola, measles, and the rest of the long list of diseases that had been wiped out at the end of the twenty-first century. Darcy had taken the job here at Synsound a year ago, lured by their offer to promote her to bioengineer and increase her salary by twenty percent. Unfortunately, her pay as an entry-level bioscientist at MedTech had been nothing to crow about, and the twenty percent didn't make a dent in her student loans and all the charged credits she'd run up during her years at school. She and her father had gone their separate ways when Darcy had first entered college, and now, without family to help bail her out, Darcy was stuck with the bills; the HUD/Education Dept. was authorized by law to take forty percent of her salary until the bills were paid. Not much was left over to devote to entertainment . . . or a hobby that required tangible materials. Things like rent and food tended to take priority.

The Synsound job was a major disappointment. While it meant more money in her paycheck and toward her bills, the work was dull, dull, *dull.* The Synsound recruiter had contacted her, not the other way around, and Darcy now believed the woman had been nothing more than a Synsound shark whose sole purpose was to steal away the competitor's employees. Darcy had been led to believe that she would be working with the genetics engineering department, designing new clones for the shows, finding ways to reengineer existing ones when the paying crowds had grown tired of them. No wonder she'd jumped the MedTech ship—who wouldn't have? Instead, Darcy had become a sort of android repairperson, and the tiny lab and tinier office to which they relegated her and her work was filled with spare parts, growing cultures of android flesh, and the oily smell of the lubricating fluid that was used in the mechanical compartments of android bodies. Rather than searching for a cheaper way to manufacture inoculation serum, now Darcy spent her days tracking down obsolete machinery parts and hunting for a way to make android skin more rubbery and resistant to tearing.

After a few months of this, Darcy had swallowed her pride and decided that earning a little less money wasn't so bad if in the long run it paid off with steady promotions and job security, but when she checked back with MedTech she discovered that in its eyes, she'd committed the ultimate sin. Synsound was, oddly, MedTech's largest thorn, something about the music company being responsible for having to construct the force field that had cost the company nearly a billion dollars. Had she been a Synsound employee *first*, MedTech would have happily stolen her away just as Synsound had done. As an employee who had "defected," however, Darcy found she wasn't wanted back.

A surreptitious job hunt among the smaller companies proved fruitless; no one would give her uninspired academic record and short work history more than a cursory review before saying, "We'll call you, Ms. Vance." She had shot herself in the foot by leaving MedTech, and now she was stuck; MedTech couldn't even be persuaded to give more of a job reference than the legally required confirmation that she had once worked there.

Suddenly Damon Eddington's dreams had shone into her drab world, breaking through the murky haze her workdays had become like a red laser beam. Darcy had always wanted to work with animals or alien life-forms, and most of her classes in college had been geared toward that field. Unfortunately, she was seriously lacking in the concentration and application department; a dreamer at heart, Darcy spent far too much time thinking about all the radically experimental things she could do if she were a high-level bioengineer instead of applying herself in the classes required to really get that degree. Things hadn't changed much in that respect; here she was again, watching the egg do nothing in the physical world but envisioning with perfect clarity the thing it would someday become. She knew Eddington was disappointed about her lack of a musical background, but she couldn't—and wouldn't have, had she had the funds—change that for him. She and her coworker had agreed from the outset that coddling Eddington was to be Michael's responsibility; Darcy had no patience for such emotional frivolity, and chronicling the existence of the alien that would be born was to be her duty.

An alien . . . Could something like that be controlled? Perhaps trained? Common sense reminded her that they weren't exactly dealing with a friendly puppy here. Compassion? Attachment? Ludicrous concepts all, yet they represented the exact things Darcy had wondered about for years, since the first news that the creatures had been discovered during the colonizing expedition to Homeworld. After all the years of dreaming, she finally had a chance to find out if the situations she'd concocted in her head, exaggerated theories really, held even the most remote grain of truth. How many people had been in the position that would soon be available to her? She would be here to watch it grow from a hatchling, from the moment of implantation to birth—

Well, that part bothered her. Darcy could play the dispassionate scientist on the outside, but inside she was horrified that they were going to use a human being to host the alien hatchling. To see Eddington's ambitions become a reality, someone was going to die . . . and with her hunger to be a part of this assignment so strong, was she any less a guilty party? Michael had stubbornly pointed out that the . . . "donor" would be someone who wanted to do it, an addict so dedicated to the sensations created by royal jelly that he would donate his body to the continued existence of the alien species. But those people were . . . *demented*, so overtaken and mentally enslaved by their addiction to jelly that they barely knew which way was up anymore, much less the worth of their own lives. Was it really scrupulous to take advantage of that?

On the other hand, they couldn't work or function in normal society any longer, and they would never heal. Did the justification for using someone to hatch the alien egg rest in the concept that the donor was a walking dead person anyway?

Darcy simply had no answer.

So many possibilities . . .

Ahiro walked the streets at about twenty minutes to midnight. Few areas in Manhattan were dark at night anymore; pockets here and there—most of the interior of Central Park, of course—and Third Avenue was no exception. His target was in Midtown, two doors in on the southwest corner of East Forty-ninth and Third Avenue, but Ahiro was too cautious, too distrustful to go straight there. Instead, he wound his way from Synsound's West Side corporate offices through the Theater District, then carefully doubled back into the maze of buildings that made up the Garment District and beyond, turning east into Murray Hill to finally get to his Midtown destination.

The Church of the Queen Mother.

No aircycles or big money mechanical escorts here—mostly derelicts and down-on-their-luck bums looking for a way to pass the time with a cheap, temporary diversion. The "temporary diversions" strolled the streets in the form of underdressed prostitutes and jelly dealers, all ready to duck out of sight at the first sign of a cop jalopy. Tonight was cold and damp, a hint of more stagnant rain about to fall on the city rather than January snow, but that didn't seem to bother the hookers; the women wore short, strapless dresses and dirty high heels with worn metal tips that shot sparks off the street grates, and the males on the take kept the jock T-shirts and denim jeans as tight and scanty as possible.

The building that housed the church was easily over two hundred years old. In a more prosperous time in the neighborhood a century and a half ago, it might have been an elegant restaurant or a quaint antique shop, but any evidence of its original purpose or the way it must have looked as new construction was long gone. Now warped and cracking boards were nailed over exposed layers of rotting insulation and mortar in a haphazard effort to keep the place from literally spilling its guts onto the sidewalk. Bent and rusty nails jutted everywhere from the mildewy walls that ultimately led to the entrance—a triple set of double doors that consisted of more boards crisscrossed and impossible to close, useless against the New York elements. Those, perhaps, had once been floor-to-ceiling show windows.

It was absurdly easy for Ahiro to slip into the place, and no one noticed him despite his clean, dry clothing or well-bathed skin. This was his first visit, and the inside was bigger and better lit than Ahiro expected, but it didn't matter. No one paid him any attention, and he supposed that was because jelly junkies came in all kinds—bums, clerks, bankers, executives—a lot of them still grasping strings that led tenuously back to the normal parts of their lives. Not for long, though; royal jelly tempted them all and, once it had them, never let go. Fools, all, for invariably believing themselves to be the stronger.

Rumors on the street claimed the building had once been a church rather than the restaurant or store that Ahiro suspected was closer to the truth, but if this building had ever housed a real place of worship, it bore no signs of it now. There were no pews or altars, and certainly nothing so conspicuous as confessional booths. The walls looked as if they might have once been paneled, but time, insects, and moisture had destroyed all but the faintest resemblance to the out-of-date decorating method. Other doorways branched off the main room—leading to unused closets, maybe to a basement no one dared explore, and all except one were blocked by the telltale chaotic pattern of nailed-in-place boards. The exception was a heavy, worn-looking door at the far rear that was firmly shut; Ahiro had to peer fixedly at it to confirm that the signs of deterioration and chipped paint were nothing more than a craftily applied makeup. Ahiro grinned to himself; no doubt a closer inspection would reveal that the door was not only locked, but hardened steel under its painstaking camouflage. Beyond that barrier was an entirely different world from the one the jelly addicts saw, a side of their quiet, misery-filled church that they would never believe existed. No doubt their preacher, a bald-headed man in his mid-thirties with a baby face and calculating eyes who was in reality a highly clandestine MedTech employee, enjoyed all the comforts he desired as he passed out minuscule, carefully distilled measures of jelly with equally rationed doses of experimental drugs and medicine. To hear him tell it, the preacher was the only person to ever kick the jelly habit; in the real world, this self-proclaimed messiah had never put the taste of jelly on his tongue and had learned his evangelist skills by training in a class filled with hundreds of false preachers-to-be just like him.

Keeping carefully in the back, Ahiro watched as the preacher doled out the vials of jelly, each time pronouncing *"In nomine Matri Regina"* in a monotone voice. Not for the first time, Ahiro wondered how the man could keep a straight face as he mouthed those ridiculous words. It was the scientist thing, no doubt, like Darcy Vance and Michael Brangwen. The man behind the flowing pseudo-holy robes no doubt viewed these pathetic wrecks that were once human beings as no more than test subjects, lab monkeys, dogs, and rats with human skin and burned-out souls. And dozens of them shuffled quietly forward with heads bowed, an endless line of disciples to a chemically induced vision they could no longer live without, eyes closed, mouths in their gaunt, dirty faces open to receive the rapture, and repeat after me—

"In nomine Matri Regina."

Idiots, every one. This place was a farce, a testing ground for MedTech's most controversial and covert drugs and medicines and one of thousands like it around the world. The antiqued miniature image of an alien queen that squatted on a pedestal next to the spot the preacher stood was manufactured specifically by a secret division of MedTech, and the company made them by the hundreds. All these destitute men and women—

Ahiro's mind cleared suddenly as his searching gaze fell on one man in line. He recognized the man instantly from the graphics file Keene had downloaded onto the data terminal that Ahiro linked into the Synsound mother system each morning—this was the man Keene wanted Ahiro to take back to Damon Eddington, the same person who would host the alien hatchling.

He just didn't know it yet.

Ahiro watched him take his turn with the preacher and receive his token taste of jelly. He downed it and drifted back outside with the others, gazes heavenward as they stared at things that only they could perceive. The buildings, the air, living creatures in unseen dimensions—in the normal world, who knew what really went on in the minds of the jelly addicts?

This particular man had curly, too-long gray hair that had receded far beyond the crown of his head. His eyes were so sunken that their shade was undeterminable; the shabby red coat draped loosely around his shoulders as protection against the weather only enhanced the pallid color of his vein-mapped skin. The faintest trace of what the man had once looked like showed in the still-thick, jet-black eyebrows and the melancholy set of his mouth as he turned when Ahiro tapped him lightly on the shoulder.

"One moment, brother," Ahiro said mildly. The Japanese man gave the junkie the calmest, most serene smile he could manage, reminding himself not to smirk because when it came right down to it, this man had only hours to live and should be treated with respect because of it. "You're a very lucky disciple tonight, my friend."

"I am?" There was a sense of childish wonder in the man's voice, of desperate, unfulfilled longing. His stare was unfocused and annoyingly dreamy, distressingly trusting.

"Oh, yes." Ahiro slipped a hand around one of the man's thin elbows and squeezed it reassuringly. "Tonight," he said with a confident smile as he turned the man in the direction of Presley Hall, "you will fulfill your destiny."

Someone had been found!

Damon tried to keep his end of the conversation going, tried to concentrate on Michael Brangwen's words—after all, the man *was* asking about his dreams and his music, his *life*—but Damon was having a difficult time keeping the thoughts and questions straight.

Someone had been found!

The words were like a silvery chant inside his head, repeated with medievally religious reverence. Any moment now, Ahiro, that mysterious jack-of-all-trades Brangwen and Vance had told him about, would appear with the human key that was necessary to breach the barrier that hindered further progress on Damon's biggest endeavor. He needed to get past his giddiness and pay attention, to concentrate; in fact, Vance was saying something to him now, asking the question that showed in the puzzled set of her long jaw and her frank blue eyes. Damon finally forced himself to pull his mind together and listen to her words.

"So, you want this alien for . . . ?"

Again? "For the music, Ms. Vance. *Its* music—the pure *sound* of it." Was his exasperation showing in his tone of voice? He hoped not. Ordinarily he wouldn't care; he was used to working alone, doing all of his own recordings and mixes, but this project was so far out of his normal realm that he didn't dare alienate the only two people who would be working with him on it. He knew nothing about the creature that would theoretically soon be at his disposal, *nothing.* How to care for it, control it, feed it . . . did they even eat? Damon had no idea, and he hated being this dependent on others, especially Synsound flunkies, willing or unwilling. This time, however, it was a necessary evil.

"You think alien screams sound like music?" Vance made no effort to conceal her doubt.

For a moment Damon was angry. Then the feeling flashed away, replaced by a rare appreciation for her honesty—now *there* was something seriously lacking in that bastard Jarlath Keene. He heard no derision in her voice, only bewilderment and genuine curiosity. She simply couldn't *appreciate* the potential here, and after all, Damon was the artist, not her. Wasn't it up to him to show her—and others—the beauty in his art? *He* was the one responsible for bringing his virtuosity to the rest of the uncomprehending world. A hard task, indeed.

"They sound like . . . hatred," he explained. "Fury. Don't you realize that the scream of an alien is representative of the only things left in the world today to which people, the public in general, can relate? They identify only with violence and anger, *hate.* Refined to its purest form, the sound of an alien scream is the only thing left in the heart of a human being."

"Oh, that's *wonderful,* Mr. Eddington!" Brangwen broke in, his face lighting up. Vance looked at them both skeptically, but didn't interrupt as the older bioengineer continued. "Can't you see how we're bringing the two fields together, Darcy? I think it's great—science serving the arts. Especially *your* art, Mr. Eddington. We've got a golden opportunity here to meld the two fields into something completely original, perhaps even create an entirely new genre."

Vance slipped her hands into the pockets of her lab coat and chewed her bottom lip for a moment before looking again to Damon. "But . . . you have no desire to study it in any other way, Mr. Eddington? No interest in what its thought processes are, or how it exists in our world despite its obvious differences?"

Damon waved his hand impatiently. Ah, here at last was the *truth*. Vance was preprogrammed; attempting to or believing he could change her thinking would be nothing but wasted effort on his part. In some fields, the differences were simply too great. "I'm a composer," he said shortly. "Not a scientist. The science end is yours." He raised his hands in front of his face and flexed the fingers, first one at a time, then simultaneously. In the movement of his own body he saw and felt the fury inside him even if they didn't, that never-ending rage that always boiled when he thought of Synsound and Keene, and all those simpleminded, malice-hungry masses who devoured the parent company's so-called music. "I deal in what is heard and felt by the soul, not in the biological processes of the physical world. Music is the only thing that matters to me. I want this egg to hatch, and this . . . *thing* . . . to be born shrieking in blood," Damon said fervently. "I want it to fight and kill and scream. And I want to record every sound." He curled his hands into fists, unintentionally punctuating his words.

Someone had been found!

Before Damon could continue, the door to the apiary behind the three of them slid open with a clang. The trio turned together and for the first time Damon saw the fabled person who must be Ahiro. A tall, lean Japanese man, he had slicked-back black hair and a jagged scar that ran diagonally across his right eyebrow all the way to his cheek. Deep-set black eyes stared steadily back at Damon, and Ahiro's movements, smooth and controlled, reminded Damon of a watchful cobra. Walking dutifully at Ahiro's side was, thank God, the cultist who would hatch the egg—

"Ken?"

Damon heard his own voice squeak out the man's name as though it were something else, a strange new sound synthesized from rubbing a tangle of wires together.

The face that swiveled toward him was a lifetime removed from the man Damon had known in college as Ken Fasta Petrillo—"Ken Faster" for short. Most of the man's once-lush auburn hair was gone, and what was left encircled his skull in overlong whitish strands that were matted with dirt. Royal jelly had done its work on Ken: while Damon knew that the man was the same age as himself, he looked decades older. The eyes, though . . . they were still the same. Blue and faraway, lost as he always was in the daydreams and rhapsodies of his own making.

Druggie or not, there was nothing wrong with Ken's memory or the connections his mind made. When he saw the composer, his mouth stretched into a long, dry-lipped smile that was painful to see. "Why . . . hello, Damon."

"You *know* this man?"

Damon glanced at Brangwen and saw the bioengineer's look of horror; he had no choice but to nod. As usual, Vance's expression was watchful, but indifferent. "He was . . . *is* the best guitarist I've ever heard." He glanced at Ahiro, but the Japanese man remained stone-faced. "I . . . want to talk to him," Damon said uncertainly. Ahiro nodded and tilted his head toward the table at the far end of the outer apiary area that the team sometimes used for breaks. Damon sucked in a breath and motioned at Ken. "Come over here, okay? We've . . . lost touch."

Ken obeyed without comment and settled onto a chair at one end of the table, seemingly much more comfortable than Damon. Damon wanted to stare at his onetime friend, but at the same time he found the eye contact unbearable. "Ken," he finally began, "do you . . . do you know why you were brought here?"

Ken smiled again, that same chapped stretching of his mouth. "Oh, sure, Damon. Your man explained everything on the way." He nodded, as to confirm the words.

Damon tried to swallow and found his mouth dry. "But what you've volunteered for—I mean, how did you get this way?" Too blunt perhaps, too prying; it was simply the way it came out. He had to know, though; how much easier it would have been had Ahiro brought back a total stranger!

Ken didn't seem at all offended at Damon's inquiries. Instead, he did his best to explain, his expression sincere. "I started with the jelly, Damon. You know how I always was when we were in school—I wanted to try everything, and I did. It didn't matter what: Ice, StarGazer, jelly. If it was out there, I wanted to do it at least once, and I didn't believe the stories about jelly being instantly addictive. Hell, the feds claimed the same thing about Ice and I'd pulled through it without a hitch, remember?

"At first the jelly wasn't that different, a new kind of high, but that was all. I did it a couple of times and was ready to move on. I don't think you ever knew I was using. At the time, I—*we* had stuff planned . . . a couple of gigs set up, advertising posters set out, remember that?"

Damon nodded reluctantly. "Yeah, I do."

Ken grinned with pleasure and leaned forward. "Well, there you go. Then all that stuff in my personal life changed and everything went in different directions, you know, at the end of college. At first I was freaked out about it, but then . . . Damon, I started hearing the *music*."

Damon frowned. "Music? What music?" A dozen yards behind Ken's chair, Damon saw Ahiro move into the waiting alien enclosure; he punched in a code on the keypad that was wired to the glass and steel box that cradled the alien egg inside the cage; with a barely audible *whoosh*, the airlock released and the box's hinged top eased open. Damon knew he should stop him before things went too far, but a part of him wouldn't allow his limbs to move. If Ken noticed Ahiro's movements or the sounds behind him, he ignored them all.

"Oh, Damon," Ken said wistfully, "you should've heard it. If you had, I don't think you would have gone out on your own. I'd take a hit of jelly and then I'd play the guitar, play like I'd *never* been able to play before." Ken's smile was shy and vaguely boyish, as though he were proud of himself and wanted to say so, but was afraid he'd be accused of bragging. "Some people said I played worse," he confided, "but I heard it as better and I knew that they just couldn't hear—their ears were crippled, blocked by the noisy mess of this city. Oh, no, my playing was definitely better, *much* better." The addict stared at his fingers for a moment, seemingly bemused. "So," he said finally, "instead of quitting, I took more of the stuff."

"And you got hooked," Damon said hoarsely. On the other side of the quartz wall, Ahiro had carefully lifted the egg from the glass box and was carrying it over to a different table, one with four infrared stimulators built into it. He set the egg precisely at the center point of the sensors, then rotated it so that the bottom part of each slit in the egg's top faced a sensor. In a moment things would have gone beyond recovery, but Damon couldn't move. His legs felt filled with lead and he could barely get his words to squeeze out.

"But that wasn't the *point*, Damon. Don't you see? After a while, I didn't need my guitar at all, so I sold it for cash to get more jelly. If I needed to play, all I had to do was move my fingers and I could hear it. The music, Damon. The *queen mother's* music . . . so beautiful. What did it matter that no one else heard it? *I* did, and it followed me everywhere, fulfilling me, nourishing me. That's what counted." Poor foolish Ken, with his hallucinations and mystical music that only he could hear. He sat, utterly clueless, as Ahiro carefully unlocked the clamp that sealed the egg's occupant from the rest of the world. Now Damon knew that the point of no return had finally been passed, but that it was okay. With the sensors going and the clamp released, the sacrifice *must* be made. And Ken was already dead.

Damon cleared his throat, knowing that he had to ask the one question that would determine the sincerity of the addict's faith. "Ken," he said hesitantly, "did you ever consider . . . that maybe the music wasn't really there? That it was in your mind, caused from taking jelly?"

Unexpectedly, Ken laughed. "So what? If it is, the queen mother put it there, and it keeps getting more exquisite, more captivating. It's become church music, Damon, like Bach but so much more sublime. A choir of thousands, right here." His former friend raised shaking hands and rubbed his forehead, smoothing the skin back as though the abundant hair of his early twenties hadn't been slowly destroyed by the chemical components of the massive quantities of jelly he'd consumed through the years. "Finally, he continued, "I realized that I had to worship at the source, in The Church of the Queen Mother. But even that isn't enough. To truly experience it, I have to give myself to it. *I must become one with it.*"

Damon's mouth felt like it was filled with sand. "So you're willing to really join with the egg? Let it . . . ?"

"Exactly."

The stimulation sensors on the egg table began to glow as they reached their peak. In another second the air in the entire apiary took on a visible *vibration* as delicate lines of scarlet light shot from the sensors and grazed the egg just below the bottom of each slash. Damon wanted to tell Ken to wake up—*You're going to be killed, you idiot!*—but he couldn't; this was what Ken *wanted* to do. "But, Ken . . . to die like that . . ." Those were the best words Damon could offer.

Ken's eyes fluttered briefly, as if the man were contemplating a quick nap, then he gazed vacantly at the ceiling. "Not death, Damon. You've never been there and you just don't understand. I'd live on, in my God. Live on and *be* the music."

Damon rubbed his beard, willing his fingers not to tremble. This was Ken's choice, after all. He'd asked all the right questions and gotten the wrong answers, and it wasn't Damon's responsibility or obligation to tell another man, friend or foe, what he could or should do with his life. As Ken had emphatically pointed out, he'd made his own choices, had used jelly despite knowing the risks. He was an addict by choice . . . a *cultist* by desire. "And you have no doubts?" Damon asked softly. "No regrets?"

Ken started to shake his head, then hesitated. One shoulder moved the tiniest bit, a barely perceived shrug. "I'm maybe . . . a little afraid," he admitted. "But that's to be expected, don't you think?"

"Certainly," Damon agreed. "I—"

"It is time."

Damon and Ken both jumped at Ahiro's flat, cold voice. When Ken looked up at the oriental man, Damon was struck by how young the addict suddenly looked, in spite of the gray-white hair drooping on the dirty shoulders of his jacket. He'd been wrong in thinking jelly had turned the guitarist into an old man; rather, it had given him a strange, childlike innocence. Ken glanced back at Damon. "J-just a little—"

"This way, please." As if suspecting that Ken was on the verge of changing his mind, Ahiro deftly pulled the cultist to his feet and led him away from where Damon still sat at the table, head bowed. I should stop this, Damon thought again, but he felt utterly powerless. It didn't matter that it was Damon's project; he was not in control of this part of it and had absolutely no right to tell Ken what to do or how to die. But Ken had said himself that he was afraid . . .

Damon looked up in time to see Ahiro guide Ken into the cage where the egg waited. Once inside, he steered the addict onto an elongated chair at the front of the sensor table on which the egg sat. The stimulation sensors were at full charge now, speeding up the egg's awareness of human flesh and suffusing it with heat, and the knobby gray flesh of the egg's surface had begun to ripple instantly in response. "No—wait," Damon heard Ken rasp as the petaled top of the egg suddenly split into four sections with a noise that sounded like crackling plastic. "I—" Both he and Damon gasped together as Ahiro yanked Ken backward without warning and flicked a lever on the back of the chair; in response, metal shoulder braces sprang from the sides of the chair and with a flick of his wrists, Ahiro had locked them—and Ken—solidly in place. With eerie speed, the Japanese man was across the cage and by the door, out of the face-hugger's immediate range.

There wasn't even time for Ken to gasp.

Predictably, the parasite went for the host directly in front of it. When Ken opened his mouth to scream, the embryo's three-foot tail whipped around Ken's neck and nearly cut off his air. At the same time, it wrapped its limbs around Ken's face and the fleshy implantation tube shot down the addict's throat and halted his cry before it could start. The chair fell over with a crash and the shoulder brackets retracted automatically; inside of four seconds, Ken Petrillo was comatose on the floor, his mucus-coated skull encircled by the infant offspring of a life-form barely overpowered by mankind. The career of a once brilliant guitarist was forever ended.

Heart hammering, Damon's gaze danced among the other people in the room.

Brangwen was a mess, clearly the worst among them. Damon hadn't expected such a reaction from the man who had pointed out that this was exactly what someone like Ken wanted. Perhaps seeing it actually take place so close to all of them had made Brangwen feel a little too physically involved in the act. Sweating profusely, the older man's eyes were bulging and his hands were clamped over his mouth as though he might be sick at any time. Damon didn't know why, but he was gratified to see that for a change Vance was frowning and seemed a little pale around the edges; finally, Damon thought caustically, we find something beyond the scientist inside of her. He didn't know why she bothered him, except that she was even more out of reach than the festering, rabid masses that clamored for the endless menu of hate and violent music. At least the music *touched* them; for her, it did nothing, it meant nothing, it changed nothing, like screaming and waving your arms at a person who was blind and deaf. And there was Ahiro, of course, and Damon could read him like a VidDisc. A man of backbone and concrete, a *machine*; he had no feelings for the man that Ken Fasta Petrillo had once been and never would be again. Of all the people in this room, Ahiro cared less than anyone about Damon's dreams other than to do Keene's bidding and draw his monthly pay slip. Bah—all of them were losers, unworthy of the supreme sacrifice that Ken Petrillo had made.

For a few minutes the four of them stood over Ken's motionless figure inside the cage, staring down at him. Finally, Vance spoke. "We should move the equipment out of the cage now. He may hurt himself on it later." Her voice had returned to its crisp and businesslike tone; whatever processes her brain had undertaken to accept the situation and put the unpleasantness behind her had been completed. She glanced at Brangwen and he nodded jerkily, perspiration still dribbling down his temples, then obediently positioned himself at the former guitarist's head. He bent and slipped his hands under Ken's armpits, then lifted the guitarist's torso clear of the floor with a grunt, his face showing a combination of revulsion and fear at being so close to the face-hugger. As Vance struggled to hoist Ken's limp legs, no one but Damon noticed the tiny blue vial that slipped from Ken's pocket and clinked to the floor. A quick glance placed Ahiro on the other side of the glass and already on his way out of the apiary, and as Brangwen and Vance lugged Ken away from the overturned chair and closer to the quartz window, Damon swept Ken's final vial of jelly from the floor and into his own pocket in a single fleeting motion. It felt unaccountably large, as though he were trying to hide something the size of a softball.

Stepping outside the cage, Damon watched through the glass as the two bioengineers carefully positioned Ken so they would see him immediately when he woke, then moved out the chair, the table, and the equipment that had been used to stimulate the egg. For the first time, Damon became aware of the moist, nearly tropical breeze from the opened cage door as it bled into the cooler air of the outer apiary; with it came the smells of mustiness and high-strength, industrial plastic. After a few minutes Brangwen and Vance backed out of the cage a final time and closed it securely behind them.

"How long will it be?" Damon asked moodily.

"It could be hours, it could be days," Vance answered absently as she peered at a computerized checklist, then made a couple of notations with an electronic pen. Something in her voice made him glance at her; there was no denying the eagerness shining in her eyes as she looked from her checklist to the unmoving man inside the cage and back again. So much for the moment of imagined empathy.

Brangwen was breathing hard from the exertion of helping Darcy move the hatching apparatus. "We'll have plenty of advance warning. Why don't you try to get some rest?"

"I can't leave," Damon began. "It's too far to travel back and forth. I might not get back here in time if something goes wrong, or it starts to hatch—"

"That's what the cots in the other room are for." Vance made a final note on the tablet, then dropped it next to one of the computer consoles. "Amazing," she said unexpectedly, "that he could be so dedicated to a strange creature, a different *life-form*, that he gave his life to father its child."

"That's technically incorrect," Brangwen said reproachfully as Damon looked at her in surprise. "There's no breeding proce—"

Vance shot him a reproachful look. "I'm not talking about scientific methodology here, Michael. That part of it is as predictable as the theory of gravity . . . and about as dull." Damon turned to watch the two bioengineers, fascinated enough by Vance's startling deviation from her normal demeanor to pull his attention away from Ken. "I'm talking about the *philosophical* end of it. We have used science as the means to justify a man's willingness to die so that an alien might be birthed from his remains."

"What's the difference between that and the saints of Catholicism in the first millennium?" Brangwen asked.

"That which is seen, and that which is not," Damon said, leaving his post at the glass to join the conversation. "They never saw their God, but Ken could see his."

"You think that's it? Somehow I doubt he ever saw a real alien," Vance commented.

"But he *heard* it," Damon reminded them. In his pocket his fingers rolled around the vial of royal jelly, warmed to the temperature of human flesh by his hand. "Constantly."

"He *thought* he did," Vance shot back just as quickly. "No one else heard anything. I think Michael's right in that respect—it comes down to belief. Faith—which comes in countless forms. New scientific experiments are conducted on the concept that something about the individual research will turn out differently, even if no one is sure what the result will be. And what's faith but a feeling inside you that doing something is *right*?"

Damon turned his back and headed toward the room and a waiting cot, smiling to himself. He was sure she hadn't meant to, but Darcy's words had vindicated every aspect of Damon's involvement on this project. His final word was barely audible.

"Exactly . . ."

12

Exhaustion didn't matter. The sleeping room that had been set up off the apiary was barely the size of a closet but far enough away from the apiary to dull the sounds of Brangwen and Vance's preparations to muffled bumps and murmurs that reminded Damon of being put to bed as a child while his parents watched the vidscreen in the living room. While his childhood hadn't been stimulating, it had been reasonably secure, and Damon had thought that the faraway murmurs would enable him to sleep, at least lull him enough to get him a nap. He had collapsed onto the army-style cot with relief and welcomed its cradle of metal bars and rigid canvas. The pillow beneath his head was of considerably better quality than the cot, the balancing factor that kept the bunk's occupant from giving up entirely. Soft pillow and softer noises be damned, Damon found he could only doze; any would-be rest was fragmented by past recollections and the shattered life of the man in the cage within the apiary, a man who'd once been one of his closest friends.

The hours dragged by, turning into two-hour shifts that were traded with Brangwen and Vance. Nothing Damon did while he waited—slept (sort of), ate, or stared at the insensate man, stopped the flow of forgotten memories, flash scenes of an earlier and somewhat happier Damon, himself as a young man whose face was not so thin and twisted by a mask of bitterness. Ken, too, a meatier-framed man with auburn curls that drove the women in the audiences wild, clear, sparkling eyes the color of the ocean at sun-splashed midday. They'd blasted through the final year of college together, Ken's oh-so-talented fingers easily keeping up with Damon's complicated compositions, coaxing spectacular rhythms and innuendos from every piece. There was the drug thing, of course—with Ken there always had been—but it was no big deal, a little experimentation by someone eager to test it all; Ken's earlier guess that Damon hadn't known about his experimentation with jelly was right on the money. A few gigs, some advertising, and suddenly there they were, the two of them, with a few more messages on the answering machine than they could handle. Private parties and weddings had turned into nightclubs that wanted them to play for two- and three-week Friday and Saturday stretches, Manhattan and New Jersey radio stations that hinted at interviews and a live song performance or two to go with it, and . . .

Synsound.

The message from Synsound had been specifically addressed to Damon, so he had returned the call without thinking anything of it. After all, he was the managing end of the duo, he set up the gigs, kept their schedule, wrote the music, balanced it all between the last four classes that would give him his bachelor's degree in musicology. Synsound's offer had at first shocked him, then insulted and angered him; after two weeks of thinking it over, Damon accepted it. It was Synsound that made him realize that Ken was too heavily into drugs, and Synsound wanted nothing to do with the part of the duo who had a taste for chemicals. Ken, Damon had thought, could be replaced. Three weeks to the day after he'd received the telephone message, Damon moved out of the rent-controlled apartment he shared with Ken in Spanish Harlem and into the loft that would be his home for the next decade and a half. He'd thought the new place was temporary and romantic and part of the "dues" he would have to pay as he made his way to the top. That apartment was the same, luxury-filled rat hole he still occupied.

Damon started and shook his head, trying to clear out the disturbing old memories. He rolled over and squinted hopefully at the LED display on the wall clock, but only an hour and a half had passed—it felt like years. Burying his face in the pillow, he tried to sleep again, succeeded only in another half doze that mixed remnants of reality and recollection into a barely decipherable collage that ran through his head with amazing speed and the worst possible clarity.

Ken Petrillo—*Ken Faster*—had not been at all replaceable. Not once during the ensuing years did Damon encounter anyone with a fraction of the amazing dexterity, the instinctive *feel* for a guitar that his old college roommate had possessed. Damon's exquisite compositions suffered immensely at the hands of lesser artists, until in desperation he began performing the pieces himself, working at them stubbornly month after month while he stayed in near poverty and his career dripped along like a faulty faucet. While his pieces would never fulfill their true potential—losing touch with Ken Petrillo had ensured that—if he worked hard enough at it, and long enough, they at least met Damon's rigid standards.

And sometime soon the man who could have filled in the missing piece needed to make Damon everything he'd ever wanted to be a million years ago, the same man who was now locked inside an unbreakable cage and impregnated with the seed of an alien monstrosity, would die.

Eyes open and staring at the black void of the ceiling, Damon finally gave up on sleep. Hate had a way of robbing a man of rest, and right now Damon couldn't decide if he hated Synsound or Ken Petrillo more. The same old fears were back, thoughts and terrors he'd overcome—or so he'd believed—years ago. Once again his career and his future rested on Ken, only this time its direction had veered drastically. Once he had been afraid that he would never be anything successful without the former guitarist, would never progress beyond his own cloak of hostility. But progress he had, to new and greater heights of loathing, and here again, he was dependent on Ken Petrillo. Sometimes, during quiet times when he had no choice but to contemplate his own existence, Damon could almost see his life spread out before him like pieces on an enormous game board. His mistakes—and God, there were so many!—were twisted, unrecognizable lumps amid the quieter beauty of an occasional success. Tonight he fancied he could see Ken trapped within his own square on that huge board, a broken and irreplaceable game token, too far gone to repair.

"Mr. Eddington? Wake up. It's time—Ken's coming around."

Damon sat up too quickly and got a head rush for his trouble, wondered fleetingly if the dizzy spell was at all reminiscent of a jelly high. What could be so special about the drug that men would go beyond the wreck of their physical lives and give themselves spiritually to a creature with no compassion or love, and which had acid for blood and killing teeth? Against the flesh of his thigh, the vial of jelly hidden in the pocket of his pants was strangely warm, soaked with the heat of his body.

What, indeed?

Damon swung his legs over the side of the bunk and steadied himself as Vance hurried back into the apiary. He could hear the equipment's humming and buzzing all the way in here, needles swishing across the surface of graph paper—old-fashioned methodology but dependable—and the whine of laser printers competing with the cricketlike workings of computer disk drives. Pulling his thoughts together, he stood and found enough coordination to go back into the apiary. Part of him dreaded what he was about to see; the other couldn't wait for the hatchling to rip its way into being and start the treadmill moving toward Damon's dark concert.

Vance had her ever-present computer clipboard clutched tightly in hand as she stood in front of one of the medical computers, comparing data on the clipboard to the output scrolling across one of the eighteen-inch monitors. Brangwen worked diligently at one of the keyboards, inputting and sorting selected bits of information almost as fast as they came out on a line printer that was hooked to another computer about three feet away. More data spewed out of two laser printers in a font far too small and full of medical symbols for the old dot matrix to handle; Damon stared at it uncomprehendingly for a moment, then gave up. He could read music, not scientific hieroglyphics.

All three of them jumped when Ken began to wail inside the cage.

"Sweet Jesus," Brangwen said in surprise. He flipped frantically through screens of information on his terminal, his chubby fingers punching hard on the keyboard. "He can't be hatching already—he just woke up."

"Then what's the matter with him?" Damon strode to the glass wall and pressed against it, but Ken didn't seem to notice him. "Is he in pain? Already? Can't you give him something—gas or a spray of anesthetic?" The crying didn't stop.

"He shouldn't be in any pain yet," Vance said with a scowl. "Victi—er, subjects generally claim to feel better than normal during the incubation period. Chemical analyses routinely indicate exceedingly high levels of endorphins and adrenaline during the growth period, and a total cessation of the body's immune system." She tapped her lower lip thoughtfully. "He was out for about fourteen hours, but that's well within the normal range. I really have no explanation for this behavior." She glanced sideways at Damon and seemed vaguely amused. "And no, Mr. Eddington, there's nothing we can give him that will decrease the, ah, *impact* of what he will experience when the alien hatches."

"Well, *something's* making him crazy," Eddington said softly. "Are you even sure he was impregnated? Maybe it didn't take."

Vance and Brangwen exchanged glances. "There's never been a known instance where a hatchling failed to implant an embryo inside the human host," Vance said flatly. "This is an extremely hardy and adaptable life-form. It doesn't even require its host to be in particularly good health."

"Oh" was all Damon could think of to say. He waved at Ken through the glass, but the guitarist continued to ignore him. On the other side of the wall, Ken Petrillo had finally stopped yelling; now he was stalking erratically around the cage. At the times when he was close to the glass, Damon was surprised to see that Ken looked healthier than he had when Ahiro had first brought him in. Finally, the guitarist stopped and tilted his head against the back wall, as though he were listening for something they couldn't hear. That was impossible, of course; there were enough microphones and recording devices in there with him to capture the sound his blood made when it flowed through the arteries in his body.

Without warning, he registered Damon's curious face and rushed to the glass where the composer stood. "Where's the music gone?" Ken screeched. *"Where's my music?"*

"What?" Damon said stupidly, flinching away from the palm Ken slapped against the window.

"Bring it back! Bring back the music—PLEASE!" Ken was howling now, bouncing off the walls in the cage as if he were wearing one of the rubber supersuits that were so popular among the kids nowadays. He staggered past the hatchling's discarded shell, then abruptly bent and picked it up, holding it at face level and staring into the tangled, drying flesh of its underside. "Where is it?" In the apiary, the three of them

heard his whisper as though he were standing in their midst rather than segregated safely in the confines of the cage. "It's not in my head anymore," he murmured piteously. "Or in my . . . heart. Is it in here?" He pressed the dead, brittle flesh of the embryo against his ear like a seashell, his face rapt; after a few moments Ken's face crumpled in disappointment and he flung it aside. Startling Damon again, the guitarist at last locked gazes with him through the glass. "You never said you were going to steal my music, Damon," he said sadly. His expression was condemning and made Damon want to hang his head in shame. "You never told me that. *Where's the music?*" Ken buried his face in his hands and sobbed as Damon started to say something, but he turned away before Damon could get the words out . . . a relief, because the musician had no idea what would comfort Ken Petrillo now.

Ken stayed away from the glass for the next two hours; sitting with his back against the far wall of the cage, he seemed content to stare into space and hum to himself, his own melancholy attempt to replace the songs in his head that were gone forever. Damon felt like a thief, the thought that he had robbed the guitarist of his wonderful music somehow far worse than the fact that Petrillo would soon die. Computer tablet in hand, Vance tried futilely to get Ken's attention, wanting desperately to ask him technical questions. At times the man was barely cognizant of his surroundings; at others, his eyes were sharp and quick, following the movements of the trio around the outer lab with a strangely calculating awareness.

At the start of the third hour that Ken had been awake, Vance's fingers began flying over the dials and keys on the consoles. "His vital signs are through the roof," she told Damon and Brangwen. "Look at the sensors. I've never seen anything like this."

"The birthing process has *got* to start soon," Brangwen said as his gaze flicked from monitor to monitor. "There's no way his body can survive much more of this. His heart rate is up to one-sixty bpm and his blood pressure has tripled. Much more of this and he'll end up with a cerebral hemorrhage."

"He could die before the alien is born?" Damon paused and looked up in alarm from where he was readying the settings at the recording console.

Vance shook her head. "I doubt it. I've read all the records associated with alien-implanted subjects and there's never been an instance where a hatchling died in the host's body or during the birth process—a still-birth, in human terms. At this point the embryo would survive anyway." Her face was grim. "I do have to warn you that your friend in there—"

"He's not my friend!" Damon said sharply. "He's just someone I used to know!"

"Fine." Vance's voice was flat. "Your *acquaintance* is going to run out of endorphins very shortly. He's going to experience a lot of pain, and as I told you earlier, there's nothing we can do to alleviate that."

"That's . . . most unfortunate." Damon turned back to the console and adjusted the recording levels again. "But he made his choice."

Vance looked at him impassively as Brangwen ducked his head, then all three of them jerked when something whacked into the interior glass of the cage. Vance and Brangwen leaped to the VidDisc that was suspended overhead and swung it down and forward, aiming the huge metal camera directly at the cage. Ken was up, finally, and staggering around the cage like a drunken man; his mouth was twisted in surprise and sweat coated his face and head. "Hurts!" he squawked. "Please—" His words became garbled as the front of his chest suddenly convulsed and swelled. Damon hit the Record button and gritted his teeth; was that a *cracking* sound coming from Ken's chest?

In the glass enclosure, Ken's cries choked off and he fell to his knees. He tried to crawl forward and retched, once, then twice; a third spasm sprayed black-red blood from between his lips into a puddle on the floor. One arm reached behind him as though searching for something, then his balance gave out and he slid all the way to the floor, eyes staring at the ceiling, mouth working soundlessly.

"Is he dead?" Damon demanded. "What about the alien? What—"

"Be patient!" Vance snapped. "I told you, it's coming!"

Indeed it was. There was a final convulsion and the hatchling ripped through Ken's chest and the flimsy, dirty clothes he wore. Lying on the floor, the bones of his rib cage splayed jaggedly from top to bottom, nothing remained of Ken Petrillo but a depleted husk—

And food for the infant alien.

The newly born creature's cries were shrill and loud, sharp enough to pierce through the exhaustion that tried to dull the senses of the three people who watched it with horrified, wide-eyed fascination. The bloodstains painting the shiny brown carapace and mouth seemed to add a curious *bubbling* sound to the life-form's birth melody, a ringing din that only increased as the creature twined the segments of its legless, elongated body around Ken's corpse and began to feed.

As Vance wrote frantically on her computer pad, Brangwen turned away with a shudder, his face gone the pale gray color of oatmeal. Of the three, only Damon was transfixed by the raw beauty of the alien's nativity music. He saw nothing but heard everything—everything he'd hoped for and more, a wail of hunger and want that equaled the unrealized dreams deep within his own shredded soul. "Beautiful," he breathed as his fingers danced over the slides and dials of the recording console. Tears of gratitude and appreciation gathered in his eyes and finally leaked down his face. All of it had been worth it—Ken's life, everything. "So very lovely, so *unique*. No one else will equal your song, no one else *can*!"

Hours passed without rest as Damon manned the recording console and watched the alien grow, never fully comprehending that the nourishment it ingested had once been a living man he had called a friend and partner. "Yes," he told it gleefully, "eat and grow big, and strong, my little prodigy." Damon's eyes were ringed with shadows of exhaustion but he dared not leave the console. Everything here was new, every sound priceless—he couldn't take the chance of missing the smallest one. The smile he sent toward the glass cage was dark with yearning and allegiance. "My little *Mozart,*" he said breathlessly. "So young and talented . . . so *hungry.*"

Across the room, Vance and Brangwen charted the alien's rapid growth as the full circuit of the LED clock's display chronicled the demise of all facets of the newborn phase of the life-form. Before being cast aside, the brown, cockroach-colored shell deepened to blue-black and cracked apart to allow the emergence of the first of the coming three stages. The creature that clawed its way to freedom was as dark as its last husk and armed with an undersized but fully evolved set of teeth. A mere eighteen hours later it had long, limber legs to go with its arms, a half set of the customary bony crests along the sleek, reverse arch of its spine, and the smooth sweep of its head had begun to lengthen and compress at equal intervals as it separated from its back.

Seventy-two hours—only three days—and Damon stared across the apiary at the fully grown Homeworld creature he'd wanted for so long. Seven feet tall without straightening, Damon could feel its rage, see the fury in every jerking movement the life-form made. They were so alike, creator and child, linked by spirit and Damon's experience, each condemned to a life of unwilling imprisonment and servitude. Damon knew what it was like to *be* an alien in this world, to be unappreciated and misunderstood, to be condemned for his very existence in a society that had no place for him. Separated from him by clear quartz was the physical manifestation of everything Damon had weathered, all the suffocating frustration and overwhelming wrath, the embodiment of his life.

Mozart.

It was a perfect name for a perfect being, a thing of

deadly magnificence with a voice like combined black gold, Scriabin's *Poem of Ecstasy* and *Poem of Fire* made flesh to stand before Damon and the world.

Finally, as the creature's feasting ended with the last of Ken's remains, Damon left his post at the recording station and stood by the glass wall, palms resting lovingly against the cool quartz surface. "This is what you gave yourself for, Ken," he whispered. "Isn't he beautiful? And it was worth it, wasn't it? Oh, God, yes." Watching Mozart pace restlessly around his cage, Damon felt the last scraps of guilt fall away. This was not a life or a friendship sacrificed to fulfill the greed of an audience or the mere hunger of a musician, oh, no. It was something so much more, so *immense* in the way it had given everything that Ken had wanted. The culmination of Ken's life stood in Mozart, breathing and hissing, the source of Ken's music and his god. As had been the guitarist's paramount aspiration, Ken had become a part of the life-form, the *god* . . . had helped it come to *be* in a way no one else could ever claim. For his part of it, at the end Damon had done all right by his late comrade Ken Petrillo.

For a moment Mozart registered Damon's presence and paused, cocking his massive, eyeless head as though trying to discern exactly what a human being was. A silent ten seconds and the alien turned and slunk away.

The only thing that had bothered Damon earlier, and still abraded at his peace of mind, was Ken's final, coherent question.

"Where's the music?"

13

"Mr. Eddington?" Darcy touched the dark-headed musician gently on the shoulder, trying not to startle him. "He's fully grown now."

When Damon turned his gaze from where he'd been sitting at the recording console, his eyes were blank and rimmed with red. She heard the bones in his neck crack with movement as he reached up and removed his headphones. "Huh—what?"

"The alien has achieved its maximum growth potential," she explained patiently. 'It won't do anything now unless we arrange it. Why don't you go home and get some rest?"

For a moment Darcy thought he was going to refuse. She wondered how could he stay here like this, night after night, living on the fat-loaded fast food substitutes that they had delivered. Personally, she longed for a freshly cooked meal, something actually put hot on her plate directly from the stove. She'd had way too much of cold and greasy over the last five days. Finally though, Damon stood. "All . . . all right." His concentration seemed to be off-kilter, then he brightened. "And I'll get the master soundiscs, too. For my composing." The musician rubbed a hand over his face and looked surprised at the uneven growth of stubble there, usually so carefully clean-shaven around the double points of his sculpted goatee.

"You'll feel better after you manage some real sleep," Darcy said as she offered him his coat.

"Yes, yes," Damon agreed absently. He took the coat and squinted at it as if he didn't know what it was, then blinked and draped it over his shoulder. The corner of his mouth turned up as if he'd finally realized how far gone he seemed. "I guess I'm pretty well burned out."

"We'll see you in the morning," Darcy said, intentionally turning toward the door that led out of the apiary. Damon followed her lead unconsciously, but stopped and looked back when the door slid open. "Take good care of him," he instructed her and Michael solemnly. "Of Mozart."

Darcy and Michael both nodded, and after another second of hesitation, Damon stumbled out the door and was gone.

Neither of the bioengineers said anything for quite a while as they moved around the apiary, finalizing the computer data and organizing the mass of paperwork that had been generated by this phase of the project. "So," Darcy said eventually. After all those hours of alien screeches and Damon's chatter, the unaccustomed silence was getting to her. "Do you think he's crazy?"

Michael shifted his attention from the last of the data he was inputting into one of the computers. "Crazy?" He took a moment to eject a disk from one of the floppy drives, labeled it, then slipped it carefully into a storage case. "No," he said at last. "I don't think so. He's dedicated to his music, that's all. That dedication requires methods that are somewhat out of the ordinary, but . . ." Michael shrugged and gave her a small smile. "He's . . . *intense.* I believe that's what the school generation calls it these days."

Darcy slid her hands into her pockets, then drifted to the glass and watched the creature inside for a few seconds before replying. "But it seems like such a waste," she said distantly, "using the alien like this. We have a spectacular opportunity to study its behavior, yet all we've done is lock it away and fill its cage with a bunch of microphones. I've always wondered if these things are capable of . . . attachment."

"Attachment?" Michael stood and stretched, then walked over and stood beside her to peer at the alien. Inside its cage, Mozart shifted into a jittery crouch, as if the unseen presence of the two humans posed a threat.

"Yes." Darcy bit her lip absently, then rubbed her temples. "Attachment in a nearly one-on-one situation like this, born from simple familiarity. This isn't a med lab filled with chimps and rats and a couple dozen scientists working under genetic managers and research assistants. The three of us—and maybe Ahiro once in a while—are the only people this alien will know. Perhaps there's a chance it would begin to recognize us, to accept us."

Michael ran his fingers over his chin and frowned. "And then what?" he asked pointedly. "Do we try and train it? Even if the study was successful in the form of actual results, what would humankind do with the information? We're dealing with a life-form that has a brain with functions we aren't even close to understanding. Your interest in this is high, so I probably don't need to tell you that the military has poured millions into attempts at cloning sterile replicas for warfare purposes. So far, they've gotten zilch; the aliens' biological makeup is so convoluted we can't duplicate it yet. Plus I'm sure there's a whole underlying branch of the government that we've never heard about that exists just to keep tabs on other countries around the world and make sure that if we can't replicate them, they can't either."

"I know all that," Darcy said. "I'm quite up-to-date

on my alien research, thank you." Still, her words weren't biting and she inclined her head toward the creature in the cage. "Don't you find it at all interesting that the woman who originally discovered these things claimed she and her crew were responding to a beacon sent by a derelict ship? We've always assumed these things are instinctive beings with no thought but to kill and procreate, but what if such a ship had actually existed? The government still maintains that her story was a myth and that she died of natural causes on a prison planet where she was incarcerated for military negligence. But what if it's the government that's lying, Michael? Others claim she wasn't sent to the prison planet at all, but was a refugee from yet *another* disastrous encounter with the aliens on her escape craft. If her claims were true, it could mean they possess at least enough intelligence to use space travel as a means of transportation."

Michael shook his head. "I don't buy that at all. You don't have to know how to pilot a vehicle to jump in it when it starts to move. Anyway, that spaceship thing is speculation only. Her story was never proven."

"It was never *disproved* either. Instead—so they say—she was thrown in prison on charges that most people still find extremely questionable. Surely I'm not the only scientist to look at these aliens and notice that in captivity they seem to be significantly underdeveloped. Some of the eggs laid in the pseudo-nests now have three petals rather than four, as though they're regressing genetically. Why is this happening? If it was once possible for them to build a ship and travel through space, why can't we communicate with them on some level?"

"There's no proof they can build anything," Michael insisted again. "And even if they could, why would we *want* to communicate with them? You're not looking at these creatures objectively. These aren't civilized beings, Darcy. If what's-her-name—"

"Ripley."

"Okay. Darcy, don't you see all the holes in your theory? You claim that Ripley says she responded to a beacon from an alien ship, but I distinctly remember that she never specified it was an *alien* ship, just a derelict. You've rearranged the facts to support your case, but they're inconsistent. No one ever said that the aliens used the beacon to draw her ship down to the planet surface—if there was such a beacon, it was probably a help signal sent by the space jockeys from the derelict." He looked at her and shook his head. "You're acting like there's probably a whole *planet* of these things somewhere besides the place we've always believed they originated." Michael waved a hand toward the cage. "Jesus, Darcy. These Homeworld creatures are the scariest, most dangerous things the inhabitants of Earth have discovered to date. Do you actually think we'll ever be able to control them? No wonder the government wants to squash any notion that a whole world of the things exists somewhere else."

Darcy's expression twisted into a sneer. "Because it's frightening, we should ignore the possibility that it's true? Now *there's* an intelligent way to deal with something." She glanced toward the cage. "And control them? God, no, Michael." Darcy's mood abruptly changed and she chuckled as the alien suddenly reared to its full height and swung its head, as if it had heard her voice through the soundproof quartz window. Then the creature flipped lazily on its back and stared upward, no doubt inspecting the roof of the cage in its own unknown way for a nonexistent path to freedom.

Darcy's laugh made her coworker raise his eyebrows. "What's so funny?"

"No human being has ever survived a face-to-face weaponless encounter with an alien without being cocooned as a future host. The ones who *have* later turned out to be already impregnated with the embryo of a drone or queen. Control them? Face it, Michael." Darcy's tone was cynical, her eyes wide but faraway as she gazed at some imaginary situation beyond the one that existed on the other side of the quartz wall. "A person could spend years working with one of these things, and I sincerely believe there would be recognition between the alien and the researcher. A bond between scientist and subject . . . perhaps. That's what I'd like to find out. But they'll *never* be truly trainable or controllable. No matter how much time is invested, I think the most you could ever hope for would be for it to pause a moment before it kills you."

14

Damon set the vial of jelly on his nightstand reverently, then sat on the edge of the bed and stared at it for a while. When he'd been a child, he had done the same with the infrequent gifts his parents had given him. It was such a rare thing for his parents to buy him anything beyond the obligatory item or two at Christmas and a card on his birthday that the unwrapped boxes sat there for days before he would open them. He didn't shake them or inspect them, or try to peek beneath the wrapping paper, preferring to build up the anticipation to a point where it became nearly unbearable. Looking back, he realized that he'd driven his parents to distraction over this—*"What the hell is the matter with you, Damon? Just open it, for God's sake!"*—and more than likely had inadvertently narrowed his chances of receiving more. But once it was opened and no matter how good it had been, the surprise was *gone* forever—never again would a magical moment be waiting for him inside this particular box, and it might be a year or more before the next one. Instinctively he believed that moments that came so infrequently should be savored, extended. *Treasured.*

Freshly showered, his beard trimmed and with some real food in his belly, if it hadn't been for the bone-deep exhaustion creeping through him, Damon thought he might feel almost normal for the first time since Jarlath Keene had called him in the middle of the night. A full eight hours sleep would round everything off and clear his head for his work with Mozart tomorrow. Sighing, he pulled his gaze away from the vial and crawled beneath the blanket, tucking it snugly under his chin. The loft was cold tonight and he could hear the drafts soughing through the cracks around the window frames and pipes, but under the covers his body heat built quickly; it wasn't long before he stopped shivering and felt quite comfortable.

Damon's eyes opened of their own volition and he found himself looking at the vial of jelly again, Ken's final gift to him. There were too many large windows around the flat for it to ever be dark in here; changing neon lights from the electronic billboards erected on the roofs of the buildings across the street spilled in his place like a cold, muted rainbow, a living snake of color that cycled unceasingly around him. Despite his bleariness, Damon's mind found the pattern right away: the colors made a full circuit every six seconds, bathing the jelly vial in luminous yellow and combining with its natural blue color to make the fragile glass tube glow like a wide spot of green laser light. The first time Damon saw it happen, it was beautiful enough to take his breath away, and it wasn't long before he started anticipating the sequence. When he finally fell asleep, the jelly's glow was the last thing he saw, implanted into the optic sensors of his retinas and carried brightly into his dreams.

But rest was an elusive concept. Damon's sleep was broken apart like a child's jigsaw puzzle with pieces that refused to fit; every time his consciousness pulled him out of darkness enough to know who and where he was, Damon would invariably find the vial of jelly in his sight, radiant with the lights of the neon-coated night beyond his windows. Hour after hour, until he became convinced that it was jelly he was missing; *that* was the thing that would mysteriously pull it all together for him, fill in the deep and hideous hole that had always been present in his life. Turning away from the sight and sweating despite the cold air against his face, shivering under the heat of the thin blanket, twisting and fighting against the rough weight of his own pajamas until he sat up in frustration and lowered his head to his cupped hands.

From the world on the other side of the fragile panes of window glass, Damon could hear the ceaseless growl of Manhattan traffic—people, out at all hours, aircycles, buses, even the faraway roar of the hypertrains in the tunnels, the new vehicles so loud that the newspaper vendors routinely sold earplugs. Beyond that . . . nothing.

"Where's the music?"

Ken Fasta Petrillo was gone now, dead, but his words lingered in Damon's mind. What could be in that vial that would make a man with unequaled guitar skills abandon his genius in favor of elusive notes that no one else could hear?

The queen mother's music . . . so beautiful.

. . . Fulfilling me, nourishing me.

It keeps getting more exquisite, more captivating . . . so much more sublime.

I can do this, Damon thought. I'm much stronger than Ken ever was, much more in control of myself and my destiny. If Ken could try and then kick Ice and StarGazer—and he did—I can do the same with jelly. I am a true artist; my love and dedication to my work is worth the risk, worth the pain of recovery, worth *everything.*

Perhaps it was the lack of sleep that made him vulnerable and trivialized his fears and the well-known warnings, let him brush aside the human evidence that wandered the streets every day. Most likely it was soul-deep desire that enabled him to reason away his fears as he picked up the jelly vial to inspect it—

—then uncapped it, rolled the delicate vial in his palms, and drank.

He had expected it to be tasteless; instead the inside of his mouth was bathed in the flavor of scorched cotton candy and, strangely, rich red wine . . .

Awake, Damon dreamed.

No longer did he watch Mozart from the protected side of the apiary. He *was* Mozart—

In the womb. His first inkling of sentience was the demand to be *free*, to be out of this hot and confining space, to still the unceasing thudding of its foster-creature's heart and feed on it—

Birth. Ripping clear of the birth enclosure with wet, red fury, so much energy and hunger, turning it all against the corpse of the being that had hosted him—

Growing. Voracious appetite barely appeased by cold, dead flesh as his body swelled and split his first bloody brown carapace, stretched again and formed legs and arms, magnificent in the sinewy power and brutal strength as they reached far above his sharp-toothed head. A final evolution and he was complete, massive, unstoppable—

And FREE! Charging the flimsy transparent walls that held him, feeling them crack under his blows like so much ancient crystal. The world beyond was like a table prepared for him, and he feasted mercilessly on those fools who had made him beg for the smallest of necessities, his parents, the nightclub owners when he was a youth, Keene and his fat witch of a secretary. Then he moved on and up, to Yoriku, whose company had patronized and laughed at him, ridiculed him under the guise of a helpful sponsor; he reveled in the feeling of the man's head splitting between his massive jaws, tasted human blood as it jetted between the razored teeth of his double mouths. Not yet finished, he took his rage to the city and its children, vented his unchecked hate as he worked to slaughter thousands amid the cruel, lazy public, all those people too stupid to know what pure sound was, too idiotic to appreciate the beauty of true music. But through it all—

Silence.

Total, maddening. In his rage and his joy, as he reveled in the carnage he created, every time he opened his splendid mouth with its row upon row of sharp and lovely spears, not a scream came out.

Not a hiss, or a cry. Not a single beautiful shriek.

Or a note of music.

Damon gave his own howl when he came back to himself as the frigid blue light of dawn trickled through the windows of the loft. The perspiration streaming down his forehead felt like ice water, the soaked strands of his hair like sharp icicles against his chilled skin. It would have been so *good*, if only—

If only. The next best thing, he thought acidly as he wadded up the blanket and threw it across the room along with the emptied jelly vial, to *someday.*

Wasn't that always the way?

Vance and Brangwen were already in the apiary, puttering around their equipment and sensors like the dutiful little Synsound laborers they were. Damon ignored them, dismissed the startled looks on their freshly scrubbed faces as he marched to the glass of Mozart's cage and raised his fists over his head. "I want to hear it!" he roared. "I want to hear the music! Sing for me, damn you—*come on!*" Damon's voice rose to a scream and he pounded on the window.

The fire-tempered quartz didn't so much as vibrate under the composer's onslaught. Mozart hunkered down momentarily and swung his dark, elongated head from side to side a few times, but the only sound the three humans heard through the speakers was a soft, low hiss. After a few moments the alien turned the spiny expanse of his back to the window and retreated as far as he could go into the shadows at the far end of the enclosure.

Damon whirled, making both bioengineers flinch and step back. The skin beneath his dark eyes looked as though it had been painted with a wash of deep violet; his hair was wild and falling into his eyes. He slapped it away. "Get something for him," he demanded. "Something he can fight—something he can *kill.*"

Vance frowned. "Like what?"

"I don't *care,*" Damon snarled. "Whatever you can get your hands on. Just make sure it's alive when he gets to it.

"I want to hear him scream with joy when he rips it apart!"

15

"Well, here they are," Brangwen said unnecessarily as he set the two cages on the floor next to the feeding door. He was puffing from exertion and completely stressed out by those fools down at the animal shelter. What difference did it make to them *what* he did with the animals, he wondered irritably, when it meant two less animal mouths for the city to feed?

Both Darcy and Mr. Eddington came forward curiously while Michael shrugged off the green jacket he'd worn to the shelter. He wasn't a total idiot; they'd never have given him the cat and the dog had they seen his lab coat. As it was, he'd lied through his teeth on the adoption forms. Yes, there's someone home to walk and feed them; no, I won't have the cat declawed.

"What did you get?" Damon asked eagerly.

Michael thought the man was looking worse with each passing hour. Gone was the unique, deep-thinking gaze that had impressed Michael so much; in its place on Eddington's face was a mask of gaunt desperation. "A cat and a dog," Michael said testily. "That's what we all agreed on."

"I *know* that," Eddington said sharply. "What *kind*?"

Darcy bent and undid the catches on the smaller carrier, then flipped open the lid. Wide yellow eyes surrounded by a ruff of thick orange fur stared mistrustfully up at her, and the feline meowed harshly as she lifted it from the box. Darcy ignored the noise and scratched the cat's head. "Tabby," she said simply. "In other words, your basic alley cat."

The look Damon directed at the cat was clearly disappointed. "What about the dog?"

Michael shrugged. "Who knows? A street mutt, maybe a little larger than most. Enough scars to see he's been around awhile and probably knows how to fight. Take a look." He flipped the latch on the dog's case and opened the door, then reached inside and found the leash still attached to the dog's collar. After a few seconds of steady tugging, the dog came out. Not particularly friendly, it kept its ears flat against its skull as it eyed the room and its occupants with suspicion; it didn't bother to acknowledge the cat in Darcy's arms. The dog's tail stayed tucked protectively between its legs.

"Crap," Damon said in disgust. "The thing probably doesn't weigh forty pounds."

"Forty-two," Michael said pointedly. "And he's the biggest one they had. When I told them I was interested in something bigger, they told me anything larger than forty-five pounds is euthanized if it's not picked up by the owner within two days. They're so seldom adopted that they don't even bother offering them to the public." Michael watched as Eddington extended his hand toward the dog experimentally and the dog gave a low growl and backed up a couple of steps until it hit the end of the leash. "At least he's not fawning over us," he offered.

"He might as well be," Eddington grunted. "He's too small to do much else."

"There's always the newspaper," Darcy suggested. "We could check out the ads, see if we could come up with something better."

Michael looked doubtful. "I think those are almost always puppies. Most people who get rid of full-grown dogs are picky about where they go. You know, the 'free to good home' syndrome."

"Well, this is what we've got, so let's just try them and see what happens," Eddington cut in. "Maybe they'll do the trick." He turned his back and headed for his recording console and Michael shot a glance at Darcy. Her shrug and curt nod said it all.

I doubt it.

"Okay, I'm ready." For the first time since he'd barged into the apiary this morning ranting like a madman, Eddington looked almost like his old self again—alert, eager, his eyes sharp and focused as his gaze tracked Mozart in his cage. "You can put them in anytime."

"Here we go," Michael said. He inclined his head and Darcy gave a final, companionable rub on the cat's head. The thing had been purring for the last ten minutes, and although Darcy's face was as cool and expressionless as it always was, Michael was certain she felt like a traitor to the animal.

But work came first, and she leaned over and pushed the tabby into the smaller, one-way feeding channel that led to Mozart's cage. "So long, furball."

Without letting himself think about it, Michael did the same with the dog, avoiding a bite when he shoved on the dog's rump only because the interlocking entry valves automatically closed and prevented the dog from coming back at him. "He's in."

"There you go, Mozart," Darcy said softly as she knelt close to the window and peered into the alien's cage. "A couple of visitors for you."

Michael saw Damon tense at his console, then jab the Record button as Mozart caught sight of the animals and stalked toward them. The older man's breath caught in his throat, and he had a fleeting moment of empathy for the composer. What *would* the alien sound like when he screamed? Would it be as beautiful as Damon believed? A sound trickled through the speakers, but it was devastatingly disappointing: nothing more than one of Mozart's dark hisses, a sound that reminded Michael, and no doubt Damon and Darcy, of a noise he'd heard only from filmdiscs . . . the drawn-out sizzling of red-hot iron dipped in water. The cat squalled suddenly, followed immediately by an admirably savage snarl from the dog that made Michael's eyes widen; whatever the canine had learned from life on the streets, it had become quite adept at making itself *sound* larger than it was.

But for Mozart . . . hardly a challenge. A blur of bluish-black motion and it was done, as difficult to Mozart as stepping on an ant was to a man, like the hand of God descending and wiping out someone or something's existence with barely a warning. Four seconds of silence, and Damon's shoulders slumped as he pressed the End Record button. "It's not enough," he said dejectedly. "These animals were . . . they were nothing. *Nothing.* Can you hear him now? He's *laughing* at us, for God's sake. Cats, dogs—to him these are only contemptible amusements." His hands came up and he rubbed jerkily at his face, then looked at his palms oddly. Michael wondered briefly if Eddington was hallucinating. "We need to get something bigger. Sheep, cows, *bulls*, for God's sake. If we don't give him something he finds competitive, this is all he'll ever give us. Hissing—nothing more."

Neither bioengineer said anything, but Darcy's eyes were narrow as she glanced Michael's way. It wasn't difficult for Michael to remember their unspoken exchange earlier today.

I doubt it.

* * *

The cow turned out to be about as worthless as the sheep did, and privately Michael thought the apiary was starting to smell like a barnyard as well as occasionally sound like one. He had been vaguely worried that people on the streets would notice the crates on the loading docks outside and wonder why a concert hall would be unloading animals, but no one ever did; once inside and emptied, the containers stunk of animal sweat and manure, and the group was stuck with them for days until workmen were found who were security-cleared to come into the apiary to haul them away. Michael had seen Darcy, whose demeanor was usually so cool and unaffected, sniffing the arm of her jacket with a repulsed look on her face as she realized that the smell of the animals was seeping into all their clothes. The alien had made short work of the cow, which had done nothing but freeze in place and low mournfully as Mozart disemboweled it. The sheep had been quicker and had at least given Mozart something to chase, but its end was swift and produced only a few pathetic, panicked bleats on Damon's recording.

The three of them endured each other's monotonous company for four endless days before the crate from India finally arrived. The creature inside it packed a lot more force and raw strength than anything they'd pitted against the Homeworld life-form so far. As revolted as he was by the continued killings and by the sight of Mozart's messy but methodical feasting afterward, the expectant atmosphere was contagious and Michael couldn't help being excited about the struggle to come—though not nearly as electrified as Eddington was. When the crate finally arrived, Eddington had become so much of a basket case that he could barely communicate with Michael and Darcy; his words tumbled over each other and he left sentences dangling and directions incomplete. It was a good thing the two bioengineers had worked enough with Eddington to know the details of each attempted recording session.

"Get ready to let him loose," Eddington said. His voice was shrill. "One, two, three—*now*!" He slammed a hand onto the Record button and watched, eyes bulging, gaze fixed on the view into the cage, ears attuned to every pinpoint of sound the earphones would feed into his head.

The workmen had carefully prepositioned the crate at the entrance to Mozart's cage and made the hookups, and now Darcy hit the lever that simultaneously lifted the front of the shipping container and slid open the largest of the entries into the alien's enclosure. Inside, Mozart advanced almost carelessly, lulled by the docile animals pitted against him before now, expecting another easy kill and subsequent meal.

Stupid but ill-tempered, the wild gaur bull shook its head and snorted, then lowered its head and lumbered all the way into the cage. When its red-rimmed eyes fixed on the alien, it bellowed. The noise was loud and long, and the animal sounded like a massive horn reverberating inside the chamber; the sound rose and fell, punctuated with the huffing of its solid breathing as it leaped sideways, hoofs scraping across the textured plastic of the floor in a move surprisingly quick for an animal of its size and bulk. Still unsuspecting, Mozart went into a half crouch and began to advance as the gaur bull tensed and its massive head dropped as far as it could on its shoulders. Another bellow hammered through the speakers, stronger, this one clearly a warning. Mozart moved closer, unaffected by the animal's noise, still apparently assuming this was another of the placid creatures he'd faced over the past week. It was a significant misjudgment, and the alien was unprepared for the bull's heavy-bodied charge and the long, curving horn that pierced his left side, sliding neatly under the row of armored ribs as the steer's weight drove him backward. Acid blood sprayed the bull's face and it went crazy with pain, lurching and almost going down on forelegs that suddenly seemed far too small to support its weight. Its bawls filled the speakers, escalating to a frenzy as Mozart's screams of pain and fury joined in and the alien began swiping at the bull with razor-edged claws, splitting the animal's thick hide in a dozen places.

Outside the cage, Michael glanced quickly at Darcy, then at Eddington. The musician was rapt with attention, his fingers sailing over the dials and levers on the recording console. "Listen to him sing," Eddington managed. He raised one hand, spread the fingers, then folded them into a fist. "It's *wonderful* . . . like catching lightning in your hands!"

A roar of agony poured through the speakers. Michael spun back to the cage's window and saw that Mozart had his long, sharp fingers wrapped around his opponent's horns. Suddenly the alien twisted his lower body so that his tail was at right angles to the rest of him and flipped the segmented length of flesh like a whip against the bull's muscled flank. As the Synsound team watched through the window, transfixed, the gaur bellowed louder and tried to pull away, only to find Mozart's tail wrapped securely around its brawny shoulders.

In a final, thunderous bout of speaker fuzz, Mozart ripped the bull's head completely off its torso.

For a few seconds there was silence. The alien flung its trophy aside and backed away, as if waiting to see if the bull would somehow rise to challenge him again. Darcy and Michael stared at the blood spray on the walls inside the cage, looking through a spatter of red that oddly enough resembled . . . freckles.

Then Eddington sighed and punched a button on the console; the red light overhead that announced "Recording" immediately flicked off. "Tremendous," Eddington announced. "But too damned short." He made a fist again and held it close to his chest, as though he were trying to calm his pounding heart. His grin was dark and full of potential as he contemplated the things to come. "Now we know what he needs, though, what will make him truly sing. He needs something like himself that can *hurt* him, something that will make him the *victim* rather than the hunter."

* * *

Thus far, Darcy had been the person elected to approach Ahiro on an as-needed basis, and she didn't hesitate now. She had no idea how or what Ahiro was going to do to make Eddington happy, but that was his problem. One need only do the math to figure it out: she and Michael could merely work with what they had. If Ahiro did not supply the raw material, they could not be held responsible for a lack of results.

Darcy was becoming more suspicious about Eddington by the hour, but when she voiced her concerns to Michael, he brushed them off. "Don't worry about it," Michael said. "You're probably right; more than likely, he *is* addicted to something or other. So what? You know the statistics. Eighty percent of the artist and musician population are users. They take everything from jelly to marijuana, though the green stuff's nearly impossible to get now. Most of them will die before they see age forty."

"I don't want to work with a junkie," Darcy said stiffly. "I don't think they can be trusted. They're not stable."

"No offense, but when did Damon Eddington ever seem stable to you? Nothing about this project is normal." Michael shrugged. "Morals have their place, Darcy, but Synsound isn't a big champion of the majority. Save it for dinner with the folks—"

"I don't keep in touch with my family."

"That's not the point," her coworker said. There was a sharpness to his voice that suggested she was trying even his easygoing temperament. "This is not Sunday church. If you didn't know that when you took the job here, you must've been living in an ecology pod. Hell, most of the revenues in this corporation probably come from addicts who float through each day carrying discplayers. The headphones are probably implanted right into their damned brains. Besides, how can you complain about working with a user after the four of us all had a hand in the death of that Petrillo guy?"

Darcy finally stopped bringing up the subject, although her suspicions about Eddington were confirmed early one evening when she followed him into Gramercy and watched him slip into an alley off Irving Place just beyond the park. Peering around the corner of the building at the mouth of the alley, she saw him deep in conversation with a motley-looking guy who had a skullcap of hot pink hair, dark glasses, and a ring of oversize pearlescent beads imbedded in the flabby skin around his neck. It didn't take a Ph.D. to figure it out, and when Damon offered the man a stack of bills and accepted two glass vials in return, things were pretty much settled.

Like it or not, there could be no more denying that Eddington was a jelly addict. It didn't show . . . *much* . . . anywhere in his work, though. Whatever the stuff had done to him when he'd first started using, Damon had finally adapted pretty well. He never zoned out at the mixer console or lost control of his thought processes in the sense that he couldn't make decisions or operate the equipment. After nearly opening her mouth on two separate occasions, Darcy finally decided that silence was the best policy here; musicians were temperamental creatures, prone to solitude and a free creative license. Eddington wouldn't take kindly to her trying to bring down an iron fist, and Michael was right: who was she to tell him what to do, anyway? Besides, everyone knew once you tasted royal jelly, you were in it until the end. Like it or not. Ultimately she didn't care what he smoked or took or injected; he could do what he liked to his own body. She just didn't feel he could be trusted and was loath to turn her back on him.

Back at the apiary, Eddington began to put in as many hours watching Mozart as Darcy did, and she couldn't help but marvel at the way he stood at the window and murmured, palms and fingertips pressed hard against the glass as if he could touch Mozart through it, sometimes talking to the alien, more often addressing no one but himself. "I can feel you," Eddington whispered, "your rage, your hunger. But why can't I *hear* your music? Sing for me, so that I can sing for you. Give me more, Mozart, *more.*" His monotonous words were like a litany, and she was getting pretty tired of hearing them; the sooner Ahiro got back, the better.

Darcy had almost given up and gone home when Ahiro and two of his companions finally arrived with another animal crate. Ahiro led the way, steering the crate while the others pushed it along on a wheeled platform. On his way to the bathroom at the rear of the apiary's outer chamber, Damon froze at the sight of the covered container, the expression on his face a mixture of anticipation and misgiving. In his usual fashion, Ahiro did not smile or elaborate. "We have a beast for it to fight," he said simply. He and his men didn't wait to be told to slide the container into the loading position at the feeder door.

"What—what is it?" Damon's eyes were wide and beginning to fill with wild hope.

"It is extremely fast," Ahiro said. "With fangs and claws and the ability to defend itself." Without another word he grasped the heavy green canvas draped over the crate and pulled it away.

Darcy gasped and her hand went to her throat as a feral growl rumbled out of the exposed cage; cautiously she moved forward with the others for a better view. Inside the rough cage was a sleek and beautiful black panther with glittering golden eyes; at the sight of the people, the animal's mouth twisted into a snarl filled with sharp white teeth.

"You must have gotten this from the Bronx Zoo!" Darcy exclaimed. "How on earth did you get it out?"

"We do what is necessary to please Mr. Eddington and to continue the project," Ahiro said. He didn't bother to elaborate as his men used poles to reposition the front of the crate until it was pressed against the sealed entrance to Mozart's cage. When the end piece was pulled free, he jerked his head toward his two companions and they bowed slightly and slipped out of the apiary.

"I hope you weren't seen," Michael said in a worried voice.

"Who *cares* where it came from?" Damon said excitedly. He was giggling like a schoolchild, pacing at the rear of the panther's cage, his movements making the cat emit a steady warning growl. "Finally we've got something that will give Mozart a *real* fight. This will be wonderful, I know it!" He chuckled, then practically vaulted to his recording console, laughing outright as the panther hissed and swiped a paw between the bars of its cage at the movement. It took less than a half minute for him to rub his hands together gleefully and announce, "I'm ready."

Everyone in the room seemed to stop breathing as Ahiro tossed the canvas back over the cage so the animal inside wouldn't claw at him, then leaned forward and pulled the switch that opened the final barrier between it and Mozart's enclosure. Staying carefully expressionless, Darcy saw Damon smile maniacally as he hit the Record control and his fingers poised expertly over dozens of controls on the recording console. Ahiro's eyes were narrow and watchful, his merciless gaze riveted on the door to Mozart's cage as it slid open. Only Michael was frowning, his face pale around his wide eyes, as if he already knew the fate of the exquisite black cat. But . . . didn't they all?

When the door began to open, the caged animal dropped instinctively into a crouch and pulled its lips back to show those fabulous pointed teeth. There was nothing reticent or timorous about this cat, and the instant the gap was large enough, the panther sprang. A savage snarl filled the speakers as Mozart backstepped in surprise, then twisted away reflexively as he sensed the animal hurtling toward him in midair. When the panther struck the alien, it landed on his back and sank the claws of all four paws deep into Mozart's outer husk.

The enraged scream Mozart gave as the panther's teeth slashed at the back of its plated head sounded like a combination of overloaded boiler steam and maddened elephant.

The alien whirled crazily as it tried to throw the cat off, tail thrashing in the air until its barbed end scraped the panther's flank and parted skin and fur.

The cat's yowls joined Mozart's shrieks of pain and it released its hold and leaped sideways before Mozart could grab at it; without hesitating it charged again, this time slashing through the alien's tough carapace and ripping at the dark, knobby flesh of the life-form's midsection with gleaming incisors nearly two inches long.

Outside the cage, Darcy gasped and stepped up to the glass. "The panther's going to kill him!" She had to shout to be heard over the pounding noise coming through the speaker setup, and Eddington had no inclination to lower the volume. Rather, he seemed to be riding the waves of sound, swaying on the vibrations hammering through the apiary.

Ahiro answered from somewhere behind her, but she didn't want to take her gaze from the battle taking place inside the alien's enclosure to see exactly where he stood. "Not a chance." She sensed his amusement and decided he was patronizing her; his disdain made her want to slap him. Setting her jaw, she started to turn to scowl at him. "But what if it *does*?" she demanded. "Then we—"

"Look," Ahiro commanded.

She spun and cringed openly, feeling sudden sympathy for the cat as she registered the sight. Ahiro was right, of course; the panther had the spirit but never, in reality, a genuine chance. Separated by the wall of unbreakable glass, Mozart was a mere four feet away and Darcy had a detailed view of the front grip that Mozart had managed to gain on his adversary. Scratching and biting viciously to the end, the cat was flipped on its back and eviscerated while it was still struggling within the spiked hold of the alien. Its final scream of torment mixed with a sound from Mozart that was very much like a call of triumph.

* * *

"This is beautiful, exquisite!" He was talking out loud, but it didn't matter; none of the others could hear him over the screeching of the panther and the shrieks of Mozart. "Listen to it—fierce, orgasmic, *consuming.*" There is so much I can blend it with, he thought deliriously, Henze, Corigliano, Shostakovich, Honegger, Hovhaness, Nancarrow, all those twentieth-century apostles of rage and soul-grinding sorrow. How easy it would be to close his eyes and listen forever to Mozart as he envisioned the magnificent compositions to come—

The music stopped.

"No!" Damon leaped to his feet so quickly that his chair fell backward and landed with a crash on the floor that made the rest of the room's occupants jump. "Where did the music go—it must continue!" His hands twisted into claws and he wanted to dig them into his own face in disappointment. "Damn it—that was too *easy!"* His fingers closed into a fist as his eyes squeezed shut and his head tilted back. Tears of rage burned small, wet trails down his cheeks and his chest heaved. "It wasn't enough . . . I need *more.*"

"Mr. Eddington," Ahiro said quietly, "perhaps I can provide you with another animal, something larger?"

Damon sank to his knees in front of Mozart's cage; inside, the alien was already beginning the process of stripping the panther's flesh, feeding a voracious appetite that seemed never to be satisfied. "Another animal?" Damon whispered. "What animal? Look at him, Ahiro. A few minutes ago he was injured, cut in a dozen places by the panther. Now he looks fine and eats the same animal that wounded him." Damon let his head fall forward in defeat, resting his overheated forehead against the cold glass. Perhaps this was what Synsound and Keene had aimed for all along—to humiliate him, force him to surrender to the company's idea of "music" and use his fine composition skills for their profit. If so, he'd never felt so close to giving in. "It's no use—I'll never succeed in this project. Hell, Ahiro, no animal is vicious enough to keep Mozart busy long enough to give me what I want—what I *need.*"

As Vance and Brangwen quietly began the routine of assembling and analyzing the data recorded on their equipment during this last battle, he and Ahiro watched Mozart for a long time. Finally, Ahiro took a pair of tight black gloves from his pockets and tugged them on, then spoke in a voice that was soft and distant, and vaguely ominous.

"I believe there *is* one such animal, Mr. Eddington," he said. "Give me time . . . to capture it."

16

When Keene looked up from the contract he was reviewing, Ahiro was standing in front of his desk.

He didn't know how the ninja had gotten past Marceena and into his office, and he didn't feel comfortable asking. Something about the Japanese man frightened him, a ruthlessness that Ahiro kept carefully concealed in his day-to-day dealings in Synsound's business world but that shadowed through nonetheless. Keene doubted if Ahiro had simply walked past Marceena's desk, and it was a certainty she would never have let him in without at least hitting the intercom buzzer to warn him that someone was on the way; most likely, she'd never seen him enter the waiting room or slip past her.

"What do you want?" Keene's voice was sharper than intended, enough so to make him instantly regret the tone, but if the younger man noticed, he didn't show that either. Not for the first time, Keene noted the scar running across Ahiro's right eye; perhaps that was what made him look so sinister. He wondered briefly if the ninja had inflicted the wound on himself to purposely change his appearance. He didn't think it was such a farfetched possibility.

"Mr. Eddington requires an animal more suited to fighting with his alien," Ahiro said.

One thing Keene admired in the man—in *any* man, actually—was the ability to get right to the point. He capped his pen, placed it carefully on the desktop, and sat back. "We've already provided him with a bull and a . . . panther, wasn't it?" Ahiro nodded, and Keene drummed his fingers on the edge of the desk, trying to think. "What could we possibly come up with now? A lion would outweigh the panther, or maybe a polar bear. I'm told polar bears are the only animal natural to the earth that regard human beings as prey. Getting one, though . . . that could be a problem. If we go that far, we might as well try an Alaskan brown bear. Now there would be an adversary."

"I have a suggestion."

"Fine. Let's hear it." Now what, Keene wondered. Another trip to the Bronx Zoo? He'd squash that idea right now; the panther's disappearance had made the zoo triple their security force, especially since the fools were convinced that the cat was still on the loose within the zoo grounds. His idea about a bear was probably the best; if getting a polar or an Alaskan brown bear proved too difficult, grizzlies were easier to obtain. They wouldn't have to go as far north to do it.

But when Ahiro spelled out his plan, Keene had to admit it was something he'd never considered.

Five minutes later he sent Ahiro on his way and instructed Marceena to get Yoriku on the VidPhone. They hadn't spoken about Eddington and his project since the plans had been made for the initial abduction of the egg, but Keene hadn't been lax in his reporting duties; he had kept his superior up-to-date with twice-weekly memos transmitted with the originals of the mountainous reports from the two bioengineers working on the project. Keene didn't know what Yoriku planned to do with all that information, but he had no doubt the man had some future strategy already mapped out. Yoriku wasn't the only one trying to fine-tune this situation; the idea of choosing Ken Petrillo as their cultist had been conceived and implemented solely by Keene. Every time Keene thought of the jelly vial, in particular, he felt it indicated the caliber of the people with whom he had to deal. It was foolish enough that the composer so readily accepted the "coincidental" appearance of his long-lost partner, but how could Damon Eddington honestly believe that Ahiro wouldn't see and report Eddington's snatching up of the jelly vial that had fallen out of Petrillo's pocket? Ahiro saw *everything* and carried it all back to Keene—after, no doubt, he told it all to Yoriku.

As for himself, Keene had a serious problem with accepting that the cultist had still possessed an unopened vial. For heaven's sake, the man was a *junkie;* while going too long without a fix might drive a jelly addict insane, one of the most chemically interesting things about royal jelly was that its victims could take all they wanted—no one had ever died of an overdose. Since when in the history of drug-induced mankind did an addict ever exercise self-control? It was utterly ridiculous to think Ken would carry the stuff around and wait to drink it. Despite Ahiro's claim that Ken had pocketed his ration, what Ken had received at The Church of the Queen Mother before the Japanese man had caught his attention should have gone down his throat before he'd left the building.

So many questions . . . and now this latest, newest phase of the operation, as proposed by Ahiro. Far more risky, it would require advance approval from Yoriku—someone on whom Keene could fall back, if necessary. There was a definite risk factor here, and if heads ended up rolling because the bunch of them were caught, Keene wasn't about to go down alone.

When the light on the VidPhone flashed that the

connection had come through, Keene swiftly brought up a handheld recorder—one of those horrible little electronic devices that Damon Eddington detested so much—and slid it in place to the left of the speaker on the VidPhone, where it couldn't be seen by the caller. A flick of his finger before he opened the line and the cassette started turning. "Keene here," he said in as bland a voice as possible.

"What do you want?" Yoriku's face filled the screen, distorted by the usual static on the communication lines.

"It's about Damon Eddington, sir," Keene said. Something about Yoriku seemed . . . different. There was a downward twist to his mouth that Keene didn't like, a hint of something nasty in his eyes. Was it directed at him? Or had it always been there? Keene was beginning to wish he hadn't called, despite the need to cover his back. He could've given approval to Ahiro's suggestion on his own, depending on how brave he was feeling. Too late now, though.

"So?"

Keene blinked. He didn't recall Yoriku ever slipping from his ultra-polite Japanese businessman demeanor, even when he was dispensing the most unpleasant news—like sending a vice president to play travel coordinator. "So, uh—" He fought the unaccustomed stutter and won, started over in as smooth a voice as possible. "Damon Eddington needs to obtain a more suitable animal to fight the alien and make his recordings. Ahiro was just here and he suggested—"

"You're wasting my time," Yoriku grated. *"I've already talked to Ahiro about this."*

Keene literally *saw* the man reach forward and hit the Disconnect button on the VidPhone. A millisecond later he found himself staring with his mouth open at a blank screen; nothing looked back at him but his own stupid, dull green reflection.

"Shit," he said crassly as he reached over and stopped the useless recorder. His ears filled with the buzzing of the dial tone and he punched the Disconnect button on his end, then sat there with his finger on it, his mind still trying to work around his surprise at Yoriku's uncharacteristic bad manners. Beyond that were other issues—like his superior's claim that the matter had already been discussed with Ahiro, and thus presumably approved by Yoriku. That *had* been what he meant . . . hadn't it? If so, Ahiro must be clearing everything Keene told him to do with Yoriku before proceeding; therefore Keene's question was a repeat, something Yoriku despised as a prime waste of time—which in turn would rationalize his rudeness on the VidPhone. But if they were miscommunicating, Keene stood to take the full blame for the hunting expedition in which the brutally efficient Ahiro was probably already immersed.

Keene stood and fingered his tie uncomfortably. Here was an element of risk he hadn't figured into the stupid Symphony of Hate equation. He should still be safe, though; nothing that he could think of tied him to Eddington beyond that one telephone call about the egg—and he'd made that from a pay telephone in Spanish Harlem while his chauffeur had stood ready with an Electrostun pistol. In fact, Keene hadn't spoken with Eddington since that night, nor had the musician been in his office since last year. It rankled the hell out of Keene that Ahiro didn't respect him enough to act on his orders without having them preapproved by that bastard Yoriku, but at least Keene felt that he was reasonably isolated from the project and its potential ramifications. Had Yoriku found out about something, perhaps Keene's failed MedTech interview? Maybe . . . but probably not. Still, if someone over there had talked, it would go a long way toward explaining why Yoriku had acted so bent out of shape on the VidPhone. On the other hand, Yoriku might be extremely unhappy with Eddington right now. With Synsound's pet "arteest" on the road to addictive damnation, Yoriku would have to start cultivating another alternative musician for that small but profitable—and growing—quiet niche in Synsound's customers that Damon Eddington didn't realize indeed existed for his work.

Keene grinned to himself. That was a blow Yoriku wasn't going to get over anytime soon. Rumor had it—and gossip certainly procreated well in the heart of Synsound—that Yoriku *liked* Eddington's music so much that he had it piped into his penthouses and private offices. The thought made Keene shiver; how could anyone listen to that stuff if they didn't have to? Damon Eddington's early classical renaissance pieces had been pleasant, if not vaguely dull, but in Keene's opinion the later compositions had deteriorated into something that sounded like banshees being tortured. Any fool who would willingly listen to that crap deserved to be laughed at.

Keene laughed all right, every time his monthly pay slip was delivered and one twelfth of his six-figure salary settled nicely into his healthy global market fund. How contemptible that he would pocket so much of Synsound's money when less than two years ago he had longed to breathe the sterilized air of MedTech, Synsound's fiercest corporate rival. Now he hated both companies: Synsound for trapping him in a position undermined by the instability of Yoriku's continuously changing whims and refusal to share even a tidbit of his power; MedTech for handing him a humiliating rejection after six months of intense interviewing for a vice presidency slot in their marketing and development department.

"We're very sorry, Mr. Keene. We know the interviewing has been extensive and time-consuming. In the long run, however, the process empowers us all by giving us concrete details on which to base the conclusion, as unfortunately we did in your case, that a candidate such as yourself would not be suitable for the executive position that is currently available."

The royal *we*, the royal *us*. Presumably Keene was included in neither since his opinion that he would be a valuable asset to MedTech was summarily ignored. Twenty-three months since he had walked out of that building for the last time, and the degradation and rage still felt as fresh as it had when the words had first slammed into his brain.

So Keene sat in his mediocre-masquerading-as-plush office in the Synsound Building, and he laughed at MedTech as well, chuckled long and hard every time he thought of how he had made those self-serving and conceited sons a bitches look like basic horses' asses by engineering and seeing to completion a corporate theft the likes of which the company had never dreamed would take place. Too bad he hadn't been there to enjoy the expression on their uppity, blueblood faces the morning they showed up for work and realized their most secret project had been violated, their alien watchdogs were dead—not to mention the human security guards—and one of their precious alien eggs had disappeared.

And the game wasn't over yet. Revenge was like that; a pawn here, a rook there, sometimes bending the rules to keep the tournament never-ending. But always . . .

One piece at a time.

17

Michael was reluctant to admit it, but Darcy was right about Damon Eddington. Sure, he had tried to defend the composer and trivialize Darcy's idea that he was on jelly, but Michael hadn't really believed that a man with such a fine mind would let himself be dragged down the road to chemical insanity. Now, however, the evidence could not be denied. The musician *was* taking something, and it probably *was* jelly; while Michael dearly wanted to attribute the ups and downs of the musician's disposition to how well his Symphony of Hate was coming along, the drastic changes in personality were too apparent to be explained away by that. Now Eddington barely talked to the bioengineers, and Michael was sorely and constantly disappointed about that. At first Eddington had been fairly open with him, maybe a little flattered that his music was known to Michael; Darcy hadn't made any points by not being familiar with Eddington's work, but it hadn't been a prerequisite for the position either. He wished that Eddington would involve him more in the process of his composition, ask for his thoughts, let him listen to a segment or two and offer encouragement. But Michael didn't have the nerve to ask for any of that—after all, he was a man of science who, while he liked to listen to music and had plenty of ideas, possessed no real-world knowledge of how to combine the notes, how the instruments worked, or of what might sound good mixed with something else. In the reality of Eddington's Symphony of Hate, Michael Brangwen was nothing.

Jelly junkie or not—and Michael was somewhat mollified by the impression that the younger man had deteriorated only a little—watching Eddington work on a day-to-day basis was a fascinating thing, a privilege for the uneducated. Totally dedicated, Eddington worked as though the music were a physical thing into which he could submerge, drowning himself with whatever exquisite vibrations were being fed into his eardrums through the headphones. At other times it seemed as though the sounds that played in his headphones could be shaped by those fine, long-fingered musician's hands, sculpted into something that all could see as well as hear. Eddington worked his way methodically through all six tapes of the alien's sounds, using everything—even the one that contained only the noise from Mozart's short-lived episode with the cat and the dog and the hot hiss of the alien as they were destroyed. For some reason, those sounds stuck in Michael's head above all the others; in those, he believed Eddington had been correct; it was easy to imagine he heard Mozart's total disdain for all of them. Eddington was fitting every sound Mozart had ever made into the structure of his masterpiece, and Michael shuddered when he thought of hearing Mozart's insulting, steamlike tone at the base of some obscure piece of fine classical music.

While Damon stayed at his recording console, Darcy tended to Mozart. From his perspective, Michael was content to handle the paperwork and import the data that was constantly being jotted down on Darcy's computer pad. The young woman was a working machine, and reports were generated by the dozens. The laser printers ran almost constantly, their quiet hum sometimes undercut with the sharper metallic ring of the dot matrixes as they replicated simple bio readouts for distribution amid the myriad Synsound channels.

Darcy's devotion to Mozart captivated Michael nearly as much as Damon's commitment to his music; obviously she had been serious about the theories of attachment they had talked about while waiting for the embryo to grow inside Ken Petrillo. They were back to offering the creature normal food now, and she insisted on feeding the alien herself, shoving everything from thawed cloned turkeys to heavy slabs of nutrient-injected meat substitute through the slanted feeding tube. Her nimble fingers pumped out dozens of analysis reports every day outlining what she perceived to be Mozart's reactions to her presence as her soft voice droned through the speaker that she kept in the ON mode every time she was near the cage and she continued to direct smiles at his eyeless face. It frightened Michael inexplicably to see the Homeworld lifeform uncoil itself and move to the glass every time Darcy walked within two feet of the cage, regardless of whether it was time to be fed or whether the speaker was on or off. Everything they knew about these creatures suggested they couldn't see, at least in the way that mankind understood sight and optical recognition to work. The aliens did not think; they ate, they reproduced, and they killed, pure animalistic instinct in alien form. Why then, if the alien had no sight or sense of familiarity, did Mozart *always* know when Darcy was close?

Brangwen checked the wall calendar for the second time in less than ten minutes. It had been nearly three full days since Ahiro had promised Eddington a new animal for Mozart to fight. What would he bring back? A bit of a computer hack, Darcy had told him about an unsigned memo she'd come across in the data files that hinted the next creature might be a polar bear or something like it. The idea of a polar bear worried Michael; an immense creature, a polar could top twelve hundred pounds or more and would be nearly three times Mozart's mass. It might die in the process, but what if it managed to crush Mozart? A grizzly might be worse; it was well known that a wounded grizzly was one of the most dangerous animals on earth. It was doubtful that Mozart would be able to kill it with one blow, and an injured grizzly bear could very well go mad and rip the alien to pieces despite exposure to the creature's acid blood. And weren't Alaskan brown bears even bigger? Beyond some kind of bear, Michael just couldn't imagine what Ahiro had in mind, and that, perhaps, was the most terrifying thing of all.

He almost felt relieved when he heard the apiary's entry door slide open. Eddington was out of his chair in a flash and striding eagerly toward Ahiro, then he paused and took a step back. Curious, Michael and Darcy moved to his side and saw the reason for Eddington's hesitation. Ahiro had been sent to bring back a beast that would provide a battle for Mozart, but instead of a single covered cage like the one in which he'd brought the panther, five wooden crates, solid but not that large, were lined up along the outer hallway wall. Waiting silently next to each was one of Ahiro's men, ready to push them inside.

"What's in them?" Eddington asked excitedly. "Can we look inside?"

Rather than answer, Ahiro lifted one end of the nearest crate. It came free easily, obviously not held in place by nails or catches. In an unhurried move, he pulled the side piece free and set it against the wall.

Inside, unconscious and nearly naked, was a man.

"This is the first of five," Ahiro said without preamble. "They have all been sedated and fitted with shunts through which the required tranquilizer dosage is automatically being fed. The drug will keep them asleep until they are needed."

Eddington's face went white below the widow's

peak on his high forehead, throwing the ebony of his hair and the darkness of his eyes into startling relief. "You've got to be joking!" he exclaimed. "You've seen what Mozart is capable of—how can you expect a man to survive a battle with a thing that can kill bulls and panthers within minutes?"

Ahiro reached into the space between the two front crates and pulled something out. "With this," he said flatly.

Michael felt like he was going to choke. He recognized the weapon in Ahiro's hands from the NewsVids; the National Guard used Electrostun rifles regularly on looters in disaster areas, and it was a favorite for riot control. Before he could protest, Darcy beat him to the punch, though obviously for different reasons.

"Absolutely not," she said heatedly.

"It will not produce enough electricity to kill or permanently injure the alien," Ahiro assured her as he set the rifle down. "But it will cause it great pain and make it very angry. And it will even the odds . . . somewhat."

Michael finally found his voice. "Wait a damned minute here! Never mind the alien—these are people we're talking about throwing into that enclosure. Where did these men come from? You—you kidnapped them, didn't you?" The older man felt dizzy from shock.

Eddington cleared his throat nervously. "Well, look at this one. He's a mess—obviously they . . . uh, came from the worst bars and drug clubs in the city. They certainly aren't model citizens."

"Obviously *nothing*. We can't just go around abducting people," Michael insisted as a vein began throbbing nastily in his temple. He looked around the lab area desperately, wishing Darcy would back him up. As usual though, his needs and stark reality were at odds; she stood off to the side, her face professionally neutral now that she'd been reassured that the Electrostun rifles weren't set to kill. What were the men in these crates to her but larger lab animals, made available simply for scientific use? Her empathy was only for her project and Mozart. "We're still talking about human beings."

"You were not so sensitive about Ken Petrillo's well-being," Ahiro said pointedly. "Now you have become the shining wellspring of humanity?"

"Petrillo was a *cultist*," Michael said stubbornly. "He *wanted* to die, remember? Hell, you found him in The Church of the Queen Mother. You told him ahead of time what we wanted, and he came here of his own free will. No one dragged him."

Ahiro's black eyes didn't waver. "And these men are drunkards and addicts and criminals." One hand sliced through the air in the direction of the crates in a dismissive motion and he folded his arms stoically. "Left on their own, most of them will be dead within the year anyway. They will expire unnoticed, and their demise will have no objective and serve no one. The city and mankind will be that much better off. At least here, their ends can serve as research."

"Perhaps." Darcy's gaze flicked thoughtfully between the Electrostun rifle and Mozart. "But do we really *need* them? We have the technology that will make the alien scream in and of itself. Why must we sacrifice human life, too?"

Damon hesitated, but Ahiro laughed. "A creature that screams for no reason does so without passion, Ms. Vance, like a petulant child throwing an impulsive temper tantrum or a primate that beats its chest in the jungle simply to hear the sound that announces its territory. Motivation is the driving force behind any true experience. Is that not so, Mr. Eddington?"

Michael opened his mouth again, but Ahiro's sharp wave of a hand and next statement effectively stifled his protests. "But the decision, after all, is Mr. Eddington's. If he feels that to make use of this resource is unwise, improper, or . . . useless, then we will return these . . . *animals* to the precise locations where they were found."

Michael's neck joints felt like they were trying to turn through hardening concrete as he looked to Eddington. Surely, he thought, the musician would not go this far, even for his art. Surely—

But the look in Damon Eddington's sienna-colored eyes clearly proclaimed his decision.

"This all has to be changed," Eddington announced after the first crate had been resealed and all of the boxes carefully brought inside and stored against the wall of the apiary farthest from Mozart's cage. "I want Mozart's cage made bigger, more complex. Right now it's nothing but a big carton—he runs around in it like a rat in a shoe box. It needs to have places where someone can dig in and defend himself decently. No one will fight for long if there's no place they think they can escape the alien." He opened his arms as if he were going to hug Mozart's enclosure. "I need these fights stretched out to a more appropriate length of time. I don't have to see the battles, and I don't care if I can. As long as I can hear what's going on, down to the remotest detail, I'll have what I need." Sensing the crowd gathered outside his cage, Mozart shifted restlessly, then stood, his long tail unfurling behind him like a huge, overly fast anaconda. Eddington frowned. "But how are we going to do it? Somehow I doubt Mozart will sit back and let us redecorate his house."

"We can use nerve gas," Darcy said.

"I never heard of such a thing."

Darcy looked thoughtful. "It's something new, just developed by the army."

Eddington raised one eyebrow. "The army? How did we get it?"

Darcy gazed at him, her eyes unreadable. "Probably the same way we obtained the egg, Mr. Eddington. I wouldn't know the details, and they don't pay me to ask questions about anything that takes place outside of this laboratory." When the musician said nothing, she glanced back toward the cage. "In an area that tightly sealed it will be easy to incapacitate him," she continued. "Once he's totally under, I'll suit up and go in to custom fit a ventilation mask over his mouth that will keep the gas supply going only to him. He'll stay out until about two hours after he inhales the last of the stuff."

Michael scowled at her but she ignored him; he'd known nothing about the nerve gas either—Darcy was much more heavily into alien research than he—and until now he'd had some hope of making the project so unlikely to succeed that the prisoners would be released back into whatever hell Ahiro had pulled them from. Now that Eddington knew there was a way that the alien could be disabled, Michael's last hope of abandoning this cruelest of phases had disappeared.

And forge ahead he—*they*—did. Shortly after Ahiro had arrived with the man-crates, another unsigned data memo had come down from the executive floor, this time directing them all to stay within the apiary continuously until the completion of the project. That any one of the people involved with this project might have lives outside of Synsound was not a corporate consideration, and now even Ahiro and his men were with them almost twenty-four hours a day. Michael found more than a thing or two strange about the setup, and the fact that Ahiro and his team could work with raw steel and operate welders represented barely a fraction of his discomfort. The rest of it centered on the so-called "budget" that governed the Eddington Symphony of Hate undertaking. It was odd bookkeeping indeed that included exotic animals and equipment, massive amounts of steel, and unlimited overtime for bioengineers and service workers—or whatever Ahiro and his team were called—but not a single simple clone. At first Keene's assertion that a million-dollar clone was too expensive in light of the apiary's construction costs and the expenses of obtaining the egg had been a reasonable one, but that was pre-imported Indian guar and reconstruction, and certainly before the abduction of five men. Did their budget include jail bond for all of them if something went awry? Michael doubted it; it was far more likely they would all . . . *disappear* if the project and its horrible actions were exposed. Or worse, there would be some kind of paper trail that completely exonerated Synsound and its executives—and probably Ahiro—from any wrongdoing; he, Darcy, and Eddington would be the corporate sacrifices, the puny scapegoats for all the wrongdoing.

But ultimately Michael went along with it, because he must. Sometimes he felt like Mozart, trapped in the belly of the Synsound beast, being slowly digested by the hungry corporate machine. While Mozart slept soundly in one corner, the silent Japanese men worked with admirable speed and efficiency, putting up steel walls and welding slick metal tubes as they followed a blueprint that Michael and Darcy carefully laid out using a DesignCad program on the one freestanding computer in the apiary. The subbasement was extensive beyond the original walls of the alien's cage, and in Michael's opinion the steel walls that they requisitioned were manufactured and delivered with outlandish speed, then installed with a skill that seemed out of place in men also trained to perform such tasks as hijacking alien eggs and kidnapping men. Perhaps some of the men's swiftness in the renovation had to do with the alien slumbering not-so-peacefully at one end of the room; like a dog chasing a rabbit in its sleep, the creature periodically twitched and hissed and made the workers jerk with nervous fright.

At last the new cage was completed. The men withdrew and Darcy removed the mouthpiece she'd fitted over Mozart's face; forty-five minutes later—a significant miscalculation regarding the sedative's projected time frame that made Darcy scribble furiously on her computer pad—Mozart stirred. When he was fully awake, he hunkered down and swung his head to and fro, testing the smells and sensations of his new home.

"Some studies claim the aliens use an echolocation system that resembles that of Megachiroptera," Darcy said thoughtfully as the four of them watched the lifeform maneuver into one of the larger tunnels.

"What's that?" Ahiro asked. It was the first time he seemed curious about anything.

"Bats." Darcy flipped a switch near the feeding entrance and sound, painstakingly recognizable, began coming through the speakers—Mozart, hissing and slipping along the smooth, round walls of the corridors that now branched in several directions from the main compartment of his enclosure.

Michael stared into the cage, waiting for Mozart to reappear at the mouth of a corridor that appeared to lead to an escape, but in reality circled around and ended up back at the center chamber. "Wouldn't that require projected noise?" he asked.

"It would explain why they hiss constantly," Darcy pointed out. "The same noise, all the time, even when they rest. While the human ear can't normally hear the alien's at-rest sound unless leaning practically into the alien's mouth, our microphones easily pick it up. Surely you've noticed how exaggerated Mozart's hissing becomes during a conflict."

"I've noticed him doing a number of things," Michael said dryly.

"Yeah, well," Eddington cut in impatiently, "he screams, too. And *that's* what counts."

"Anyway, it's just another theory," Darcy said softly, more to herself than anyone else.

Eddington pressed against the glass, trying to peer farther into the cage. "These tunnels," he said for the tenth time, "you say he can't get into all of them?"

Michael answered him . . . again. "Positive. As you specified, we set them up so that there are several places inside where someone can squeeze into and be out of Mozart's reach. At seven and a half feet tall, it's physically impossible for the alien to get into them. None of those areas are permanent solutions, of course, because they're all dead ends. Eventually thirst, hunger, or the belief that they'll find an escape route will bring them out. False hope," he finished bitingly. "It seems rather cruel to me."

The others ignored his comment. "I was worried about disorientation, but Mozart looks like he feels quite comfortable with the changes," Darcy said, her gaze sharp as she watched the alien explore. "No hesitation whatsoever."

"Then we should be ready, right?" Eddington was so excited he sounded like he was in danger of losing his voice.

Eddington turned to look at Ahiro, but he had already gone to the first crate and was wheeling it toward them on a small dolly. Reluctantly, Michael put his back into helping Ahiro lift the drugged man and place him inside the newly reconstructed feeding cage to Mozart's enclosure. Sitting inside a garishly painted red square on the floor and slouched against the door before the glass box lowered, the captive looked absurdly like one of a dance club's human decorations gone too far over the edge, now nothing but a drunken, nearly naked male performer on display inside a small glass elevator. When they were certain he was balanced against the back of the area, Ahiro reached down and tore the shunt from the back of the man's bare shoulder. In a better life, their prisoner had been a redhead with a thick, enviable mustache and a thousand freckles spread over his skin; now it was hard to distinguish the blood blisters raised by the shunt's removal from the freckles and the dirt ground into his flesh. If nothing else, he had not yet joined the ranks of the malnourished; while the man was clearly sliding toward the inside edge of slender, his frame was still sturdy enough to be considered fairly healthy.

"The pain of removing the shunt will make him start to wake up," Ahiro said matter-of-factly. He dropped the bloody piece of plastic to the floor, then absently kicked it aside and pulled the lever that would lower the glass cage over the groggy man. "It is a powerful but short-lived tranquilizer, and he will be fairly cognizant within five minutes."

As Ahiro had predicted, the redheaded man's eyes began to flicker almost immediately, and it wasn't long before he was trying to pull himself upright. When the captive looked like he could concentrate, Ahiro relayed his instructions, his tone even and, in Michael's opinion, obscenely serene. "The weapon at your side is an Electrostun rifle," Ahiro told him calmly. "It is effective only within three feet of the creature you will encounter when the door behind you opens." The prisoner's eyes widened and Michael saw that they were a bizarre shade of reddish-brown that almost matched his hair. Once this had been a handsome young man.

As his predicament began to sink in, the man gasped and began slamming his hands against the front of his small prison. "No—please!" he cried. Twisting futilely within the small glass enclosure, the Electrostun rifle seemed to be the last thing he wanted to find. "Let met out—I won't tell anyone, I swear to God!"

"The harder you fight," Eddington interrupted, "the longer you'll stay alive. It's your choice."

Disgusting, Michael thought belligerently as he crossed his arms, how easily Eddington falls into his new role as *Executioner in the Name of Music.* Look at him, relaxed . . . *safe* on this side of the world while someone on the other side faces death. The fool—he doesn't have any idea what that really means. And Darcy—he didn't know whether to shake her or slap her—but he thought the chances were good that neither would bring her back to her senses. In the scientific realm, she was as much into this endeavor as Damon Eddington was on the musical end. At this point, if there was anything in the world that she wouldn't consider doing so that it would enable her to continue working with the alien, Michael couldn't imagine what it was.

Eddington pressed a button and a whine of hydraulics warned them that the feeder door was about to open. While Eddington hurriedly strode to his recording console, no one else on the outside of the cage moved. Inside, the redheaded man dropped into a crouch and whirled, eyes bulging as the door began to pull open. Barely two feet away, Mozart already waited on the other side, head cocked like a trained guard dog listening for someone to come into the house.

Eddington's voice came clearly through the overhead recording speakers, deep and pleasant as it was reproduced on the higher quality equipment. "If you remain in the small cage," he said clearly, "the alien will kill you instantly. Leave, and you may survive."

Liar, Michael thought sourly. The poor schmuck in there had no chance, and he would die fighting solely on the belief that freedom lay just down one of the tunnels. Already the redhead was clutching the Electrostun rifle and—

Finger on the trigger, the prisoner plunged out of the cage and faced the alien. Mozart reared on his hind legs and hissed, reminding Michael of a fully grown praying mantis he'd once seen in the aircycle garage here in the building. The bioengineer had wanted dearly to catch it—they were so rare and to find a live one in the midst of Manhattan!—but he'd had nothing with which to trap it. His attempt to pick it up with his fingers had resulted in a miniature version of the thing that now faced off with a human being on the other side of the glass wall.

"Come on, come on, come *on*," Damon urged breathlessly from the mixer console. Surely the man would fight—anything else was unthinkable. To let the alien just kill him outright—

With a bellow of desperation, their prisoner fired his weapon and lightning leaped from the muzzle of the rifle. One hundred fifty thousand DC volts turned the interior of the custom-built cage—and Mozart—a bright, sizzling white, the color of the outside world during the most charged moments of a vicious electrical storm.

Mozart rocked back on his feet and screamed as they had never heard him before. For a moment Damon literally lost his air; the sound boiled through them all like the soundtracks of the old NewsVids from the Homeworld War, raw footage shown on public stations to satisfy the public's never ceasing demand for bloodshed. In the alien's cry Damon heard the pain wails and curses of all the men wounded by fiery lead and cold steel, and the shrieking agony of a thousand women damned to be childless by mankind's careless wartime use of chemical warfare upon its own brethren. It was timeless and indescribable, the frenzied souls of millions screaming at God from the heated depths of a hell they'd never believed existed.

As the redheaded man vainly fought for his life, Damon heard Mozart's shriek again, and again, and again. Like a hard-headed dog that refused to learn its lesson, the alien would pause for a ten- or twenty-second interval, sway in place like an enraged baboon, then try to attack anew. His prey was weak and slow, his movements dulled by drugs or booze or whatever his addiction of choice had been; there was no strategy to the Electrostun hits he gave the creature, no attempt to herd it in one direction or another. Shocked, exhausted within minutes, and nowhere near either of the tunnels where if he would not find escape, he might at least rest, the doomed man managed a final two-second blast before Mozart leaped on him and tore him apart.

The alien's final scream was everything Damon had ever wanted: agony and fury, the instinctive roar of a beast's victory and revenge over a detested foe. It was dark and evil and fresh, and it pounded through him and everyone else in the room, giving of itself to them all, offering everything Damon had sought and everything he'd needed . . .

But never *enough* . . .

By the time they opened the third crate, the group had learned the value of keeping the men in the feeder cage for an hour or two to clear their heads of the last effects of the supposedly "short-lived" sedative.

The second man to go in was a drunkard rather than an addict. Everything about him seemed to shake or twitch, starting from his slack facial muscles to his continuously trembling hands and the jiggling gut that encircled his midsection like an overfilled balloon. Despite his yearning to get on with it, Damon heeded the advice of the two bioengineers and let the man sit inside the feeder cage for quite some time; besides, it was apparent from the way he kept staggering against the sides of the glass cage that the sedative had hit him harder than it had the first man, probably because of the alcohol residue in his system. If the chunky man hadn't been sleeping it off in his crate for nearly a week in between his capture and the completion of

Mozart's enclosure, Damon would have sworn the guy was still stone drunk.

Nevertheless, at the last instant the survival instincts kicked in and the captive gave it his best shot—feeble, short-lived, but enough of an effort and a lucky aim to make Mozart shriek with anger when the charge from the Electrostun rifle hit him full in the face. The sound was like white fire, sending heat racing along Damon's nerve endings as he closed his eyes and let the sweet euphoria take him . . . until the man with the potbelly and thinning white hair met his final fate in the claws of the alien.

Captive number three, while free of any aftereffects from the medication, was a coward and would have been an utter disappointment had not his screams had a pitch completely different from his comrades. Tall and thin, with dirty brown hair that curled onto his neck and muddy brown eyes that seemed unable to focus, he died the quickest of them all. His lisping breaths and shrill voice spiraled through the microphones to meld with Mozart's music until, with unaccustomed humor, Damon thought the man and the alien were yodeling together. Their victim refused to leave the cage, and the only reason the outer glass walls weren't smeared with blood and body matter was Mozart's disinclination to squeeze into it; instead, one long, ropy arm ending in a taloned hand shot through the door and dragged the cowering man out.

It was difficult, but they decided to wait a full twenty-four hours between each kill, wanting to keep the alien's appetite just this side of hungry. Damon fretted but the bioengineers insisted, worried that too much food in a short period of time would make Mozart lax and leave him open to permanent damage from the Electrostun. When Darcy pointed out that they knew nothing about the prisoners or their pasts, and that any one of them could be a former military man and know the creature's weak spots in battle, Damon acquiesced. With so far to go on the project, he didn't want the alien severely injured or worse; starting over was something he instinctively knew

Synsound would not do if Mozart were killed. Damon spent the time between the mini-combats as productively as possible, constantly plugged into his headphones and working the controls at the recording console as he mixed Mozart's frenzied harmonies with the mood-shattering pieces he'd selected.

Because the last one had been such a disappointment, to Damon the overnight interval felt more like a week. When Ahiro opened the crate, however, it was obvious the wait was going to pay off; the man inside was clearly the best of any of them so far. If his actions were on track with his appearance, he was going to be the prime candidate to substantiate Darcy's reminder that any one of these so-called street hoods might have been professionally trained. Of average height, this man was nonetheless superbly muscled. Square-jawed beneath a thick, shaggily cut head of blond hair, his face and hands were streaked with dirt. Enough time had passed to let the swelling go down, but it was obvious by the deep purple bruises beneath his eyes and across the misshapen bridge of his nose that he'd given his kidnappers one hell of a fight. Blood from the busted nose had dripped down the light beard that had grown during his sleep and onto his chest, drying in spots on the only thing he was still wearing—

"Boxer shorts?" Brangwen bent and peered at a wrinkled label sewn on the waistband of the colorful boxers, then frowned at Ahiro. His eyes were heavy with suspicion. "Tell me, what kind of a junkie wears designer silk underwear?"

Ahiro shrugged as he slid his hands under the unconscious man's arms. "One who steals from others," he said. "Then uses what does not belong to him."

Brangwen made no move to pick up his end. "I don't like this," he said. His voice was starting to shake. "I—I'm not so sure this one is like the others—"

Ahiro glanced at Damon and made no move to release the captive. "Mr. Eddington?"

Damon hesitated, but only for a second. Of course

the man was an addict, or a drunkard, or a criminal like the three who had gone before him. It was just earlier in his chosen "career," that's all—thus it wasn't as obvious. For all they knew, the young man could be a mobster or a dealer; perhaps he was one of the thousands of loan sharks who fronted money to people down on their luck and then brutalized them with impossible payback rates that compounded daily. "Don't be absurd, Michael," Damon said briskly. "Here—" He pulled off his headphones and dropped them on one of the console's shelves. "If you have a problem with putting him in, I'll help Ahiro do it."

Ten seconds of pulling and careful positioning, and Ahiro and Damon had the blondhaired man in place within the painted square on the floor. Without waiting for further argument—and working with Brangwen all this time had taught him that the older man could drag a disagreement on for days—Damon reached over and pulled the lever that lowered the three-sided glass cage after Ahiro ripped the tranquilizer shunt free. With a whine of hydraulics the compartment settled onto the floor and locked into place within its grooves. Damon rubbed his hands together, then cracked his knuckles as he stared down at the immobile form inside. "Now all we have to do is wait for him to fully wake up."

"I still say—"

Damon did his best to ignore Brangwen when he tried to follow Damon back to the recording console, effectively cutting off the bioengineer's words by slipping the headphones back on and conspicuously sliding the volume lever up; his wager that the older man hadn't a clue about when the console was on or off was true, and now all he heard in the headphones was Mozart hissing in anticipation within his territory, responding to the whine of the hydraulics. When Brangwen gave up trying to get his attention after a few minutes, Damon switched to his syndisc recording of Hovhaness with relief. Running mini-experimental mixes of Mozart's music and selected cuts from those of the old masters was so routine now that he could easily keep an eye on Brangwen, Vance, and Ahiro without destroying his concentration while the prisoner slept off the last dregs of the sedative.

"He's ready."

"Wha—!" Ahiro's voice startled Damon out of the light doze into which he'd fallen. Despite the delays between battles, Damon had, as usual, found time to catch only a nap or two, and those were right here, head down on the console. There were so many recordings to make, so many glorious noises to mix—he couldn't risk missing any more than was absolutely necessary . . . especially now, when he was so close to getting down the perfect mesh of alien sound and human voices backgrounded by a tapestry of finely seasoned classical drama. When he scanned the clock display, Damon realized almost an hour and a half had passed; the syndisc recording in his earphones had long run its course and he was back to the sounds that filled Mozart's cage: the breathy hiss of alien respiration, the occasional chalk-on-blackboard squeal of his nails across a stained floor pitted with the cracked remains of those who had come to . . . *visit.* "How long has he been up?" Damon asked in a cracked voice. He'd had a portable desk divider brought in to separate him from the constant distraction of Mozart's corral as well as the continual motion of the others; now he saw that Ahiro had moved it back against the wall, giving him a clear view of Mozart behind his sturdy glass wall and the captive, so far oblivious to Mozart's existence.

Ahiro glanced at the man in the glass cage. The prisoner was trying to stand up but he was too tall to fully manage it; his efforts made him look like a man doing a really asinine impression of an ape. Instead of pounding insanely on the glass as the others had done, he was inspecting the corners inch by inch, like a tropical fish exploring the boundaries of its watery prison. "Fifty minutes, maybe a little longer. I made Brangwen and Vance leave the main room so he wouldn't freak out so quickly."

Damon nodded; it was a good plan, and one they

should have employed earlier. The longer their test subjects beat on the walls of their cage, the wearier they were apt to be when they had to face Mozart. One of them had bloodied the knuckles of his hands just trying to break through. "Tell them they can come back in," Damon instructed. "He looks awake enough to me. Besides, physically he's the best yet." Ahiro nodded.

In under five minutes, the apiary lab was again running normally—Damon was readying his console, Brangwen was monitoring his data output, charts, and computers, and Vance was jotting notes on her computer pad, frantically trying to keep pace with what she perceived to be ongoing monumental events. At that notion, Damon couldn't help smiling; Darcy Vance seemed to think anything and everything that had to do with Mozart was some kind of commemorative event. Their latest specimen was still surprising them; instead of screaming uselessly at the glass—they always kept the speakers turned off until it was time to give instructions about the Electrostun rifle—he seemed to be trying to carry on a conversation with whoever came close enough to the glass for him to think they could hear. Like the others, he had no idea that no one could hear him and the angle of the cage and door prevented him from seeing the waiting alien.

Finally, they were ready. Damon had taken extra time on this one, and while he liked to think that every instance in which he'd recorded Mozart had been his best effort, every session taught him something he hadn't known before—some new way to combine an alien scream with the sound of a shrieking violin, a just-so clash of cymbals. From his position in front of the recording console, he nodded at Ahiro and the others and flipped the switches to ON. As Damon joined them, the remainder of the group gathered around the cage and stared at its occupant; the man inside had given up his efforts at communicating for the time being and now looked back at them expectantly. After the excitement of the first time, Damon had let Ahiro take the burden of explaining to the subjects just what was demanded of them, but this time Damon decided to do it. He expected a better-than-average battle from this one; perhaps watching the fight would infuse something extra into the mixes he created later on from the sounds.

As Ahiro toggled on the speaker to the cage, Damon began relaying the matter-of-fact instructions to the man inside. "Your attention, please. You see that there is a metal door behind you. In a few moments, we are going to open it and within reach on the other side is a weapon called an Electrostun rifle. It is charged but not lethal."

"Wait—please!"

Through the low-quality speaker on the feeder cage, the captive's voice sounded hollow and small, warbly, as though he were shouting to them from an underwater well. Damon ignored him; he'd hardened himself some time ago against the pleas coming from the prisoners and this man was no different from the others. Better fed perhaps, but beyond that . . . "When the door is open, you will find that there is an alien on the other side. Unless you defend yourself, the alien will destroy you immediately. To stay alive, you must exit the cage in which you are now and enter the area beyond it, pick up the weapon, and use it as necessary to get to a series of tunnels on the other side of the enclosure. The alien will be between you and the tunnels."

"Wait," the man said again. Damon looked up in surprise; by now most of the men had resorted to hysteria, but this guy wasn't giving in. *"You don't know who I am. If it's money you want, I work for MedTech. They'll pay any ransom—"*

"In the tunnels are areas that are too small for the alien to climb into," Damon said, interrupting him again with a confidence he suddenly didn't feel. "In those subtunnels you will be able to rest and plan your strategy. Estimated time to reach those tunnels is about five minutes, and if you do so without sustaining a mortal wound, we will incapacitate the alien, remove you from the cage, and release you." It was a lie, of course, and one that continued to infuriate Brangwen, but without motivation—the belief that survival was at least possible—the danger existed that the subject might not bother to fight until instinct forced him to do so. By then, Mozart would be all over him.

"Listen to me, please! Don't do this—I'm far more valuable to you alive. I'm the chief oper—"

"You know, he *does* looks familiar. I think I've seen him before," Vance said suddenly, her words unintentionally drowning out the rest of the man's sentence.

Brangwen's voice was almost at panic level. Perspiration was beginning to slide down the sides of his chunky face. "I *told* you he doesn't seem like an addict!"

Then Ahiro did something he'd never done before, and it was a damned good thing everything was set on automatic at the recording console. Without waiting for the go-ahead from Damon, he stretched past the musician and flicked the switch that opened the door separating the feeder cage from Mozart's enclosure. The man inside whirled, and whatever he had planned to say to further convince them to free him was lost forever as the hydraulics pulled the steel door aside. As they knew he would be, Mozart was already waiting on the other side, the faintly greenish saliva dripping from cruel, white teeth.

"Oh, *Jesus*," Brangwen whispered. His hand went to his mouth. "We've really done it this time."

"Mr. Eddington," Vance began to stammer, "I-I don't think—"

As Damon looked over at Vance in surprise, Ahiro's chilly voice overrode her words. "At this point, all your doubts are irrelevant."

Unwittingly emphasizing Ahiro's words, the man inside the cage shouted in fear and leaped into Mozart's domain. He feinted to the right and the alien moved with him, like a gangly grasshopper trying to walk on its hind legs. Sliding to a stop, the captive dodged backward, his lighter weight and better-balanced frame carrying the move smoothly as Mozart's longer limbs tangled and flailed for stability. Barely a double heartbeat had passed and the captive had the Electrostun in hand and was bolting for the tunnels.

Mozart hissed in frustration, mouth yawning. Angling across the reconstructed area, the alien's longer stride easily placed him between his prey and the round hatchway that led—or so the prisoner thought—to freedom and eventual release. Running, the bulbous head reaching—

The blond-haired man spun and gave Mozart a full blast from the stun rifle from less than a foot away.

Mozart had never been zapped that close. The charge hit him square in the center of the area just above his teeth and Damon could have sworn he saw the creature's head *glow* from it. The scream of agony that came out of Mozart's mouth made Damon gasp for breath as his fingers slid against the feeder cage's outer glass. "Listen to that!" he whimpered. "So passionate—so exquisite!" As the rest of the team crowded close to the window in an effort to see the fate of the man inside, Damon wobbled back to the recording console to check the equipment, the alien's scream still reverberating in his head. By the time he crossed the short distance, Mozart had already screamed twice more and Damon felt like he was teetering on overload from the sheer splendor of the Homeworld beast's howls.

"I think he's going to make it!" Brangwen shouted excitedly.

"No, he won't."

Damon shuddered and readjusted the speaker balance, then glanced back at the others. Vance was alternating between watching the mini-war within the cage and scowling at Ahiro. "What do you mean, 'no, he won't'?" she demanded. "How can you know that?"

"Because I used the remote control to reset the parameters on the Electrostun rifle," the Japanese man said matter-of-factly.

"What!" Damon exclaimed. "Damn it—*why?* Now the battle will end too soon!" His hands flew over the console as he jerkily tried to keep track of the man being hunted by Mozart.

Brangwen was as furious as Damon had ever seen him. "Then we'll have to gas them both," he shouted. "This time you've gone too far!" His face was red and his hands were balled into fists as he turned to race back to the medical control console. Inside the enclosure, Mozart gave another shriek, this time not as loud.

To everyone's amazement, Ahiro stepped bodily between Brangwen and the control panel. "Dr. Brangwen, if you try to turn on the gas, I will be forced to do whatever is necessary in order to prevent that."

"W-what!"

"I have my orders."

"He's in the tunnel!" Vance shouted. Her hands were pressed against the glass, her nose almost on its surface as she tried to see. "Now Mozart's going after him!"

"Damn you, *what* orders?" demanded Brangwen. His face was almost purple. "On whose authority? Step aside."

"I'm sorry," Ahiro said. His face was expressionless. "I cannot do that." Brangwen made a move to go around and Ahiro's hand landed on his shoulder. He did something with his fingers, the slightest of movements, and Brangwen cried out in pain. "If necessary, I will kill you."

Now both Damon and Vance gaped at him. Damon found his voice first. "Ahiro, what the hell are you talking about?"

The ninja released Brangwen and the older man backed away, rubbing his shoulder fearfully. "I have my orders," Ahiro repeated. "The man in the alien's cage has fired . . ." He tilted his head, mentally calculating. "Four times, I believe. He has one more shot, then his weapon will no longer work."

"But why?" Vance asked. "Michael was right, wasn't he? This man isn't an addict or a criminal. He's someone—"

A fifth scream from Mozart blasted from the speakers, the echoing quality clearly from deep within the small maze of tunnels that ringed his cage. Damon closed his eyes momentarily and lifted his chin, straining to catch every nuance.

"The poor sap's defenseless now," Brangwen said bitterly. "I hope you're happy, you . . . *assassin.* Who was he, huh? Some rival that screwed up one of our executive's golf games?"

Ahiro was unperturbed. "It is not my place to ask questions, Mr. Brangwen. I simply do what I am told."

"Yeah? Well, go to *hell*," Brangwen said with unusual hostility. "Why don't you do that?"

"Shut up, Brangwen," Damon said absently. "I don't want to miss this and you're breaking up my concentration."

"God *forbid*," Brangwen muttered as he stomped over to stand by Vance.

"He might still make it," she suggested. "If he gets to our—"

But a succession of high, tormented screams killed their final hope.

Although he didn't know it, the final man put in with Mozart had a distinct advantage over his four predecessors. Ahiro had willingly followed Damon's orders that the original Elecrtrostun be reprogrammed to function again, so not only was the final prisoner armed with a new Electrostun rifle but should he get that far, another waited in the tunnels. Unfortunately, his competence at the survival game was only a notch above the subject who'd chosen to meet death by staying inside the glass cage; clutching the stun rifle, he fired at Mozart twice, nicking him once and missing him entirely the second time. A fatal mistake, but Damon was extremely pleased with the way the quick, blaring scream from Mozart as he was hit mixed with the staccato wails of the dying man.

And Damon was, finally, finished with his grand composition.

Except.

He had no material for a finale.

In the days that followed the death of the last man, Brangwen avoided unnecessary conversation with Damon and ignored Ahiro altogether. The idea that the elderly man thought he was making an impression on either with his behavior made Damon laugh to himself; did he really think it mattered to Ahiro or him what Brangwen did? Ahiro had his own agenda and Damon didn't care to know it; Damon's own goal, his Symphony of Hate, was so close to completion that he could almost wave his arms and see the finest of Synsound's recording equipment adding the ferocious alien screams to the imaginary rows of orchestra instruments and musicians that would—or *should*—perform the rest of the composition. That was the only part of the dream that made Damon sad; how very unlikely it was that he—or any of them—would ever see a live performance by an orchestra. The few that still existed were populated mostly by androids: mindless, dull, not a shred of creative DNA in their cells. The mere idea made Damon shudder.

The finale. What to do for it? As usual, it was late and except for Vance and him, the apiary was deserted. Vance was there, of course, as she was every night; haunting the glassed-in walls of the enclosure, crouching and smiling at the alien, whispering to him in a breathy voice punctuated by gestures that Damon supposed she perceived as being nonthreatening. Personally, all Damon saw was a salivating monster who'd sooner rip Vance apart as continue to listen to her.

Yet . . . what if he was wrong about Mozart's inclinations, and Vance turned out to be even moderately correct in her hypothesis? Anyone with half a brain could see that somehow the alien always recognized her. While no one and nothing had been said about what would become of this project after Damon was through with his composition, already he was finding himself wanting to make more. The Symphony of Hate had been intended as his last work, but the sounds were so superb, so superior to anything contained in his prior mixes, that Damon couldn't help speculating that Synsound might let him keep the alien for future use. Of course, a lot would depend upon how well his Symphony of Hate masterwork sold in the stores and the clubs, but he would deal with that bridge when the time came. The dreams were there, but right now he still had this finale business to contend with.

What was missing? Damon pondered the question long and hard, and it was watching Vance's never-ending efforts to communicate with the alien that made Damon finally pinpoint the elusive, missing component. Thus far, nearly every sound that Mozart had uttered had been connected to pain and unenlightened rage—the creature had no idea what either notion meant, but did both out of undiluted instinct. The missing element was so common, so *rudimentary*, that it'd been staring Damon in the face the entire time. What Damon needed was a sense of compassion, of *intimacy*, neither of which the alien could feel.

Or could he?

There she is, Damon thought as he stared at Darcy Vance. Wrapped up in her foolish, ostensibly useless research with Mozart, Vance was oblivious to Damon as he flushed a vial of jelly from the pocket of his pants, uncapped it, and drank. Royal jelly, the essence of the beast itself, and it would tell him what it needed, show him what to do. It always did.

His tolerance level for the jelly was climbing, and now Damon seldom lost touch with consciousness or reality during his bouts of dreaming while he was awake—daydreaming his parents and teachers used to call it. Not for the first time, Damon wondered how many odd memories were buried in his subconscious, bits and traces of forgotten words and songs that he hadn't written down and which could have been worked into this grand theme. As he fought to keep a grip on his surroundings, a scrap of memory floated into his head like a crumbling leaf, the faintest strains of a barely remembered rendition of Wagner's "Liebestod" from *Tristan and Isolde.*

Love, and death. Love was a concept unknown to Mozart, as alien to him as most of his biological makeup still was to humans. Did he feel attachment for anything? Any*one?* Most bioscientists and bioengineers scoffed at the theory, but some, like Darcy Vance, still speculated. And wasn't it true that with one person, Mozart was closer to affection—or what passed for that emotion in the mind of a Homeworld creature—than with anyone else?

The thing that was missing, Damon realized, watching through slitted eyes as Darcy Vance moved around the apiary, was true *loss*, the pain of something treasured now gone forever. So far his composition was a melody of ignorant rage and instinctive bestiality, but to make the public he so despised truly *hear* it, he would have to do something to bring to Mozart the kind of anguish the creature had never expected existed.

Damon blinked and suddenly saw himself as Vance might: eyes dark with fanaticism, tracking her every movement around the lab, watching her as she watched the alien, and it in turn watched her, a ménage à trois of hunger and obsession.

Liebestod, Damon thought again. *Love-death.*

19

"Good morning."

Surprised, Phil Rice looked up to see Tobi Roenick standing just outside the door to his office. He smoothed his hair without thinking, then mentally cursed at himself for doing it. What was it about her that made him feel like a high school boy? "Come on in," he said hastily. "Have a seat."

She cocked one eyebrow but accepted the invitation, dropping gracefully onto the upholstered chair at the side of his desk. Behind her the door drifted closed, effectively cutting off the sounds and traffic from the hallway. The white MedTech lab uniform that Tobi wore did little to camouflage her spectacular figure, and when she crossed her legs at the knee, Rice caught a shimmer of silver given off by the material of her stockings. He had to force his gaze to stay on the red folder in her hands. "I found something on the data system," she announced. "A match that I thought would catch your interest. It has to do with the missing egg."

Now it was Rice's turn to lift an eyebrow. "Oh, really?"

Tobi placed the folder on the corner of Rice's desk and opened it; while it wasn't exactly thick, Rice could see a definite increase in the number of papers inside. "Do you remember that theft from the Bronx Zoo not so long ago?" she asked.

"Yes," Rice answered immediately. "One of the big cats—a panther, wasn't it?—disappeared without a trace. They're still looking for it."

"Well, wherever it is," Tobi said, "I'll bet it's with our egg."

Rice leaned forward, his eyes gleaming. "What did you find?"

Tobi tapped a line of data with a long, carefully manicured fingernail. "A fabric match," she said with a satisfied smile. "NYPD's evidence department apparently just got around to uploading the information. Seems they found a swatch of material hanging from the fence around the cat enclosure. They had no clue what to do with it, of course, but the information went into the network. Same material, weave and content—which, by the way, is a highly specialized Japanese product *not* commercially available in this country." She gave him a suddenly girlish grin, pleased with herself. "I caught it on a follow-up sweep. I don't give up very easily."

"So our ninjas struck again," Rice said softly, drumming his fingers on the edge of his desk. "But what on earth would they want a jungle cat for?"

"Sounds to me like they've got some kind of collection going," Tobi commented.

"Maybe. In any case, that's really great work," Rice said. "You find anything else?"

Tobi shook her head. "Afraid not, Chief—"

"Phil."

She looked at him keenly, then let a small smile play across her lips. "Okay, *Phil.* I didn't find anything else. But I run follow-up reports on a daily basis." Tobi shut the folder with a muted snap and stood with that same vague shimmer of silver around her legs. "After all, having an unhatched egg unaccounted for in the city is a pretty serious health hazard."

Rice ignored the tinge of sarcasm in her voice. Why, he wondered, did Tobi feel it was necessary to always go on the offensive? "Will you keep me advised of the results?" He shoved his hands into his pockets, afraid that what he was about to do would make them visibly shake. He was still singed from her crack about how his lines had sounded like something from an old dating game show. If she didn't like innuendo, fine; he could go for the straight-on approach. But it was now or never; what better place to give in to a wild impulse than in his office with the door closed, where no one could see him get knocked down to size?

"Of course." She turned to go.

"Would you like to go out to dinner sometime?" he blurted.

If she was startled, Tobi didn't show it for more than an instant. "I think that might be fun," she said. Without missing a beat, she brought her wrist up and glanced at her watch, then looked back at him. Not for the first time, Rice was struck by the impression that every move she made was as graceful as a ballerina's. "Right now I have to get back to work. Call me and we'll pick a day."

After she was gone, Rice sank onto his chair and tried to decide if he'd just snagged the biggest prize this side of Central Park or was just plain out of his mind.

"Tonight."

Rice said the word so softly that Eddie McGarrity almost didn't hear him. "What'd you say, Chief?"

The two men were in the room in the far rear of Sublevel Three that Rice had claimed as his and ol' Blue's back when he first took the job, an area he jokingly called "Detention." Standing at the far back wall, Rice smiled widely and looked ol' Blue up and down.

Unable to move, the alien was fastened securely within his harness, itself hitched snugly to six alloy anchors in the floor braces. "I said, *tonight.* It's time we take him out again to hunt."

McGarrity rubbed his chin thoughtfully. A rugged guy in his mid-thirties, without his MedTech security uniform and helmet McGarrity's blue eyes and blond crew cut made him look more like a teenaged line-backer than a seasoned defense veteran. "I don't know, Phil. It's been weeks since the egg was lifted—will the scent still be there? That's a helluva long time."

"Oh, it'll be there all right." Rice went back to the chair by his worktable and sat, then stretched until he could hear the joints popping in his neck and back. Too much tension, caused by some seriously unfinished business; tonight he was going to rectify that. "Even if the damned thing somehow got hatched—hell, *especially* if it hatched. That baby's got to be around Manhattan somewhere. I've had sniffer dogs at all the checkpoints off the island—bridges, tunnels, ferries—*every*where, and the animals would've picked up the scent if someone tried to smuggle the egg or a hatchling through. So far the patrols have gotten zip, which means it's still in Manhattan. Somewhere on this overcrowded piece of rock is the smell of ol' Blue's hive, and no air filter I've heard of can eradicate *every* molecule of the pheromones from these creatures. One whiff, a *trace* of his own hive, and Blue'll be off like a rabbit headed for a family reunion."

"And what if he smells something he doesn't appreciate, like last time?" The third member of Rice's elite team had come into the alien's detention space in time to catch the gist of the conversation. "Are you up to a repeat of the last trip's action?" Despite his question, Ricky Morez followed McGarrity's example and began suiting up for the coming excursion, carefully checking his gear and ammunition.

Rice chuckled. "Not this time, boys. You think all I've been doing is waiting for ol' Blue to catch up on his beauty sleep?" He got up and went over to the alien's side, then plucked a small metal control box from where it hung on the mesh that pinned the alien's arms against his ribs. "Check this out," he said as he held it out.

Both his men leaned forward to peer at the object. Sized to fit comfortably in the palm of a hand, the gray box Rice held had a single, thumb-sized red control button; from the bottom of the square piece of metal, a generous length of thin steel tubing wound its way up to ol' Blue's bottom jaw, where it ended in a surgical implant several inches behind the alien's final incisor.

"What does it do?" asked McGarrity. "Shock therapy?"

This time Rice laughed outright. "Get real. It'd take a helluva lot more juice than we could get out of a lightweight box like this to slow up this creature. Huh-uh, this baby's filled with Surgealyn."

"I've heard about that stuff," Morez said as he fed the straps of his holster through his belt loops and buckled it in place. "Heavy-duty shit. Who made up the box?"

"My latest project," Rice said smugly. His thumb skimmed teasingly along the surface of the brightly colored plastic button and he gave ol' Blue an appraising scan. "A slight touch and our little baby gets sleepy. Another one, and . . . *wham.* The miracle of air-powered intravenous injection."

"I thought Surgealyn was an anesthetic for humans." McGarrity slipped his helmet on and fastened the chin strap. Gone was the boyish blond haircut; now only his eyes showed in his chiseled face, blue and hard beneath the shining white headgear with a blazing red *MT* across the left front. "Has it been tested?"

"It was originally developed for humans, but Medical Engineering did some custom redesigning specifically for our purposes. At my request they came up with a chemical modification to keep it from breaking down in an acid-based bloodstream, a supercondensor to triple the dosage strength, and an accelerator to jump-start the process, all in a handy box the size of a vidscreen remote control. When we're ready to go, I'll attach it to my guidepole just above the handgrip." Rice glanced up at the alien's eyeless head. "You might have a different biological makeup, but we could still knock your ass out cold, couldn't we, Blue? Let's hope we don't have to go that route." He hung the box carefully back on the mesh and ol' Blue quivered, as if he could sense the drug and what it might do. Rice grinned. "Don't get nervous, old boy. We plan on keeping your ugly self awake . . . at least until we find the bastards who stole our egg."

"I'm ready," Morez announced. "By the way, did you see the inter-office memo about Sumner?"

"Yeah, I read it."

"Who's Sumner?" McGarrity asked. "Someone I should know?"

Rice snickered as Morez rolled his eyes. "Only the guy who signs your pay slips, you ignorant jackass. He's missing—no one's seen him for two weeks."

McGarrity shrugged. "Maybe he decided to take a vacation. A couple of weeks is nothing. I knew this one guy who—"

"Sure," Morez scoffed, "and since when does someone go on their vacation and leave their metallic amber Lexus Air Coupe at a stoplight in front of the World Trade Center with the engine running and blood on the steering wheel?"

"Ah. Well, maybe he didn't go on vacation." McGarrity looked over at Rice. "Is this something we're going to be involved in, Chief? Hell, I never paid attention to the fact that the guy existed here at MedTech. If we're going to tackle a missing person on him, I'm going to need more information, a scanned photo, the data files—"

The black man shook his head. "That's a situation for the cops, and from what I understand, the city's brought the feds into the investigation. I guess it's too much for the metro guys to figure out. Hell, we've got all kinds here, including our share of jelly addicts and dealers—especially those. I'm out of the murder business, and to be honest, most of the missing people or homicide victims in Manhattan are never found anyway. If the perp can get the body into the water, the pollution'll liquefy most of it inside of twenty-four hours. Half of the shit in the rivers is probably melted human remains."

"We'd just be stepping on the cops' toes anyway," Morez pointed out. "Trust me—you don't even want to try *talking* to feds on a case. They've never heard of the word *teamwork.*"

"God knows that's the truth." Following the example of his men, Rice was fully suited, and now he shrugged into the straps of an oversize white backpack and hefted it until it was comfortably in place against his back. "Right now our job is recovery of stolen property. Okay, men. Let's go *hunting.*"

20

"So," Brangwen said around his last mouthful of food, "now that you have it all, what's next?"

Damon toyed with his own food for a few seconds before answering, pushing the remnants of whatever it was—something chow mein—idly around on its plastic plate. This was the first meal the bioengineer had shared with Damon since the fourth man, the one who'd claimed to work at MedTech, had been killed by Mozart somewhere in the tunnels. Tonight Brangwen was dressed to go out; his normal white lab coat had been swapped for a white sports jacket over a mauve shirt above tan slacks. The bioengineer had been especially careful about food spills, and cinched smartly around his neck was a white leather tie that Damon thought looked absurd. "The easy part," the composer finally answered. "Plugging the alien cries into the framework I've already developed, melding the two in the right places."

As usual, Vance had rushed through the evening's meal and was now back at her self-appointed post in front of Mozart's cage. It had become almost normal to see the alien on the other side of the glass wall; no matter where Vance chose to sit along its length, Mozart invariably found her and settled on the other side. Damon looked over at her, then picked absently at a few crumbs on the tabletop. "But . . . I don't 'have it all,' as you put it." In a way, he wished he did, wished the project was over and the Symphony of Hate completed. He was getting tired of the apiary, with its quietly filtered air and constant hum of small ventilation ducts, miles of steel-protected wiring and hydraulic-driven equipment. Every time he tried to catch a nap, he saw blinking console lights and heard the drone of laser and dot matrix printers in his head, like some stupid commercial ditty stuck in his brain.

Brangwen's eyes widened and he brushed off the table fastidiously, then leaned forward. "You don't? You mean—"

Damon spread his hands. "I mean I need something *more.* One more piece." Brangwen looked utterly puzzled. Jesus, Damon thought in disgust, it was useless, like handing a violin to an airhammer operator. How could he make this man understand, who listened to anything as long as someone stopped long enough to slap a brightly colored label on it that said it was music? "I'd go in there and face Mozart myself if I thought I would get the sound I'm looking for," Damon said grimly.

"My *God,* Mr. Eddington. What more can it do?" Brangwen stared first at him, then looked over at the creature squatting restlessly by the window across from Vance. "How much louder can it scream?"

If nothing else that the other man had said to him in past conversations illustrated his ignorance of Damon's dreams, this final question did. When he answered, Damon had to speak through clenched teeth. "It's not the *volume,* Brangwen. Can't you understand that, man? Christ, we can turn it up as loud we want. It's the *quality* that's significant, that makes the music understood by those who hear it." Without realizing it, Damon's hand slipped inside the pocket of his pants and around his stash of three vials of jelly; as always, the substance picked up body heat and magnified it, gave back more than it received. He prided himself on his ability to keep the vials in his pocket without downing all of them at once. *That* was the kind of rigid self-control that set him above and apart from spineless addicts like Ken Petrillo who would've swallowed the contents of all three within a few minutes. "For God's sake, don't you get it?" He couldn't keep the frustrated tone out of his voice. "What matters is the thought behind the scream and what *caused* the scream, what *made* the music. Those are the things that are conveyed to the listener through the sound. Pain—physical emotional, or . . ." His fingers tightened longingly around one of the hot vials of jelly and for an instant Damon had a flash memory of the scene that had played in his head when he'd downed his first dose. "Or spiritual," he finished.

"Well," Brangwen said brightly, "I don't think you're going to find what you're looking for tonight." He stood, then leaned over the table again. Despite the night-on-the-town outfit, Brangwen's face suddenly looked tired. "Look, Mr. Eddington, everybody says that if an artist or a musician goes too far into their work, they lose touch with the rest of the world and it affects their progress. I've heard that writers read outside of their genre to keep their viewpoints from getting stale and to bring more creativity into their stuff. Why not get your mind off Mozart and the Symphony of Hate for a few hours? I've got passes to the Helltones' concert upstairs. It's so far removed from your stuff that it'll clean out your head and make you look at this project like it was brand-new. What do you say—care to join me?"

For a second Damon's mouth dropped open. "No *thanks*, Brangwen. I *hate* that trash. I'd sooner have my eardrums punctured than listen to it, and I promise there's nothing in that show that will in any way improve my creativity *or* influence my music." Damon shot him a sideways glance. "But thanks for your concern."

Brangwen gave him a sheepish smile, as if realizing he might have gone too far. "I hate it, too," he said confidentially. "But I think it's important to be familiar with all aspects of contemporary music. If you limit yourself to certain kinds, how will you know what else is out there? And what will you compare it to?" He shrugged. "If you never listen to their music, how will you know what you missed? For that matter, how will you know you *hate* it? At least this way you know what the critics are hearing, too."

"You're assuming that crap is music," Damon said sarcastically. He knew Brangwen was probably lying—no one listened to music they truly *hated*—and his mouth twisted. "Forgive me if I don't think it qualifies."

"Yeah, well." Brangwen shrugged again, then looked across the apiary to where Vance knelt in front of Mozart's cage. "Darcy, how about you?" he called. "Care to take a breather from the job and join an old man for an evening? I'll even spring for a drink afterward."

Damon tensed; for a long moment Vance seemed to consider her coworker's offer, then she shook her head. "No thanks, Michael. I'm going to stay here and observe Mozart."

Brangwen's pudgy face sagged in disappointment, then he recovered and fussily smoothed his tie. "Okay, if that's what you want. You guys have a peaceful evening." He chuckled. "I'm sure *I* won't—my ears'll be vibrating for a week. See you later." With a final cheerful wave, he ducked out of the apiary.

Damon stared after Brangwen for a long time, wondering if the older man knew just how insulted Damon had been to be invited to the Helltones' concert. For a second it seemed he had, then the bioengineer had brushed it off, but Damon couldn't. Of all the groups around right now, he found that particular band of mutated androids particularly distasteful. Damon scowled to himself and shook his head. Brangwen and the rest of the insidiously empty-headed people like him who paid good money for those tickets deserved to lose their hearing—they certainly wasted it—and with the concert speakers blasting out that garbage, they just might. What would be going into their ears tonight wasn't real music anyway.

He turned his attention back to Darcy Vance and watched her without speaking, feeling his pulse jump nervously. Preoccupied with Mozart, she appeared to have forgotten Damon was still in the apiary with her—as usual—and he watched, enthralled, as she slowly held up one hand to the glass directly in front of Mozart and rotated it. Inside his cage, the alien tilted his head thoughtfully as if he were aware of her experiment, his sharp white grimace never wavering. Was it processing her movements? Memorizing them? How? Perhaps the bioengineers and bioscientists and yes, even the warfare units of the armed forces had been wrong in their declaration that the aliens couldn't see. This creature's cage was soundproof unless they turned on the two-way speaker, and safety necessitated that the air supply from the rest of the building be completely neutralized before it entered the enclosure. No smells got out—thank God—and no smells got in except through the feeder cage doorway. How, then, did Mozart know—always—the exact location on the glass surface at which he could reach out his claw-tipped fingers to mirror Vance's? It was eerie how every time she brought her fingertips to the glass, never quite touching the surface, the alien's were always on the other side.

Keeping carefully silent, Damon drew one of the vials of jelly from his pocket and broke the seal, downing the contents in one gulp. The physical reaction was nearly instantaneous: every one of his senses shifted into overdrive at the same time as his mind spun ahead to that maddening *if only* speculation. *If only I could make the alien scream for the loss of something it values.* Of all the sounds that existed in the known universe, *that* was the *if only* that Damon needed to finally complete his Symphony of Hate, to *fulfill* him and his dark musical child.

The second phase of the jelly's reaction made him relax, instilled him with confidence and a feeling of serenity when he should be anything but. On the other side of the apiary, Vance had rearranged her position to settle Indian style in front of the glass just to the right of the feeder cage; Mozart crouched on the other side, somehow, as always, sensing her presence. A glance at the speaker showed Damon that the red light was glowing; Vance had hit the Toggle button so that Mozart could hear the small world that existed just beyond his glass barrier. Her whispery voice floated across to Damon, the jelly expanding his hearing ability until every word was as clear as if she were speaking to him from a foot away. Soft, slightly lisping, the sound of her voice—

"I'm sorry, Mozart. I haven't been feeding you lately, have I? I haven't had *to."*

—unaccountably erotic. There it was again, as Damon watched with wide eyes . . . that human hand to alien hand against the glass, a mankind to alien life-form bond that no one could explain. What was Mozart feeling, right now, as his deadly fingers stroked the quartz glass? Did the huge, carapace-covered creature feel desire? Or were his movements nothing more than an often-repeated "scratch test" of the glass as he continued his search for a weak spot in the walls of his prison?

As the glow of the jelly in his system reached its peak, Damon stood and walked soundlessly to the small group of instruments next to the recording console, his steps slow and precise, measured for efficiency in every way. There weren't many instruments down here—a few guitars, a double bass, a small keyboard—but they were all cabled to the amplifier on Damon's sound console. The keyboard, he decided after a quick study of the array, would serve his needs as well as anything else. Keeping his mind purposely focused on what his actions would ultimately achieve rather than the steps necessary for him to get there,

Damon quietly disconnected the instrument and drew it free of the tangled web of electronic cables and plugs. As he silently carried it across the apiary and stopped behind Vance, his pulse stuttered crazily when Mozart shifted without warning, as though he could see Damon coming up behind his mentor but could do nothing about it. Did the creature have a sixth sense? Did he *know* what Damon was about to do? But the alien only rocked back on his haunches and was again still.

Almost panting, Damon squeezed the plastic warily a final time before he raised it over his head. Countless sacrifices had been made throughout the ages in the name of the arts, and just because this was the twenty-second century didn't mean that all the offerings were over. In a way, Darcy Vance was like Ken Petrillo. The former brilliant guitarist had given himself completely to bring life to one of the creatures that helped to create his life drug and bring unheard melodies into his mind; Vance would soon have the ultimate opportunity to test her own theories and find out if Mozart did, indeed, feel an attachment for her. The keyboard's case was hard, but not, Damon hoped, hard enough to kill.

He didn't want her dead.

21

Occasional free passes to some of the concerts at Presley Hall were one of the few things left that Brangwen liked about his job. At first he'd been thrilled—well, mostly—to be involved with Damon Eddington's Symphony of Hate project, and if he didn't exactly agree with the motivation behind the composition, well . . . that wasn't his decision to make. He could live with the Ken Petrillo part because *that* decision really had been Petrillo's—the cultist hadn't been kidnapped or forced into submission. He hadn't been *murdered.* But the five others . . . their deaths were heavy on Michael's conscience. He hadn't really been truthful when he'd told Eddington that he, too, hated the music of the Helltones, but it was better to be diplomatic than intentionally annoy people, and he really did believe it was vital to keep your mind open. Eddington had looked insulted and Michael had almost apologized, then had changed his mind. After all the things that

Eddington had been a party to over the past weeks, Michael shouldn't have to apologize to the composer for anything. Besides, Michael had jumped at the chance for passes to the concert when he'd seen the notice in the local employees' newsletter. The three of them were still under corporate orders not to leave the building until the Symphony of Hate was completed, and the concert was a prime opportunity to get away from the project without stepping on his employer's toes. He'd never really expected Eddington or Vance to accept his invitation, and the truth was, he was tired of Eddington and his alien screams, of Ahiro and his dark, ominous eyes. Even Darcy, with her obsessive observation of Mozart, was starting to get on his nerves. They'd gotten so deep into this assignment that Michael was hearing Mozart's hissing and screaming in his sleep and waking up in cold sweats with the shrieks of the creature's victims echoing in his brain. Tonight, if only for a couple of hours, Michael could let the Helltones drive it all away.

A veteran employee, Michael had ceased to be impressed with Presley Hall's construction the second year after it was built, over a decade ago. He'd spent too many hours in its back rooms, basement laboratories, and employee lounges where the staff bitched all the time about how hard it was to keep the cheap white tiles clean and get up the stains of God-knows-what left by the maniacs who had attended the previous night's concert. He didn't know why he'd decided to eat his dinner with Eddington tonight; frankly, musician and murderer didn't follow the same path in his logic and Michael had been unable to think of Eddington as anything but a cold-blooded accessory to murder since that MedTech executive had been thrown to the alien. The disappearance had been in all the papers but Eddington was too wrapped up in his composition to care and Darcy was too involved in her part of the project to keep in touch with the outside world anymore unless it related to alien research. Michael wasn't stupid and it didn't take a doctorate in physics to know that Ahiro was Keene's—or someone's—corporate hit man; no doubt he'd known everything from the start, including the exact identity of the man he and his team had dragged from a car in front of the World Trade Center late one night. In a way Michael still felt a reluctant sort of pity for Eddington; he'd once told Darcy he didn't think the man was crazy, but after all this, he'd reconsidered that opinion. How far could you—*should* you—go to immerse yourself in a dream? And how much should a man be allowed to do to see it to reality?

Michael frowned as he fed his pass into the ticket reader at the front door. He shouldn't be thinking about the Eddington project tonight; he didn't *want* to. Tonight was supposed to be a break from work, a much needed sweeping out of the brain cells by something that had nothing to do with the Symphony of Hate or Eddington or his infernal alien. As part of trying to push it out of his thoughts on his way up to his second balcony seat assignment—not bad for an employee pass—Michael stopped and bought a soft drink and a bag of candy to munch on during the show.

By the time he climbed into his seat, the Helltones were already onstage and starting to hammer out their first song. The view from the balcony was pretty good—in fact, Michael preferred it to a ground-floor seat—and there was a fifteen-foot vidscreen to the right of the group on the stage to give the audience close-up shots of Synsound's latest hit group. The vidscreen itself was a pretty fancy job that had been customized to match the sculpted flesh of the lead singer, and the first thing that filled the screen was a top-to-bottom shot of the singer that made Michael shudder. So much for getting away from Eddington and his damned alien; Michael had never thought about it before, but the face of the Helltones' top android star was a synthesized amalgamation of human and Homeworld alien, right down to the elongated jaw and the mini-mouth that snapped from between his lips toward the microphone clutched in one wired-up fist. The only difference was that the android had eyes where aliens had none, and those same eyes bulged from their sockets at appropriate times during the band's flamboyant performance.

But the music was . . . *intense*, the beats were strong and true, and it didn't take Michael long to lose himself in the massive double set of drums on which a four-armed female android was enthusiastically pounding. Two other androids, one with long hair and spidery silver fingers that skimmed like metallic lightning across the lead guitar strings and another whose tongue ran all the way to the bass strings for voice/note transference, added to the turbulent noise pulsating from the speakers. Before he knew it, Michael was stomping his feet and smacking the arms of his chair in time with the music and the other people around him. In some ways he felt silly to be here, listening to this kind of music at his age, but at least he didn't need any help to enjoy himself like those idiots in the audience who openly guzzled blue vials of jelly. As the Helltones ground out the first song of their set, Michael could barely make out the words. It didn't matter; the vidscreen was a nearly perfect visual representation of the things they sang about—

Violence . . .

and love . . .

and death.

Smiling ruefully, Michael sipped his cup of soda and tapped his feet in time to the music. Violence? Love? Death? Why, he hadn't gotten away from work at all.

Damon brought the small keyboard down on the back of Darcy Vance's neck with enough force to crack the plastic casing and break out the last three keys. She didn't make a sound as she pitched forward and hit the floor, then slowly rolled on her left side. She gave a small groan and for a moment Damon thought Vance was going to get up, that he hadn't hit her hard enough to knock her out; then her eyes, which had still been open enough to give him a glimpse of surprised blue, closed the rest of the way and she was still. Standing over her with the broken keyboard still clutched in one hand, Damon saw a small puddle of blood, shockingly red against the industrial gray floor, begin to spread from somewhere under her chin. Droplets of it were splashed around her head and on her clothes, and bits of plastic and the broken keys were scattered around her.

"Now," Damon said softly, "I will *hear* it." All of it . . . the subtlety, the ambivalence, the *intimacy* that was missing from every other musical kill that Mozart had given him and which Damon had captured on syndiscs—it would all come to pass with this final, ultimate offering, this kill. And yes, Mozart would kill her—he *must.* That was his nature, his life; but this one would not be like the others the alien had destroyed, with their useless battles and struggles to survive pitted against Mozart's vicious victories and superior size and strength. Surely, after all the time and effort that Vance had expended on the alien's part, the attention and crooning, the feeding—surely slaying her would cause the creature pain. After all, she was the only human Mozart had ever known—as much as he was able—and depended upon. Slaughtering her would terminate the only shred of familiarity that existed in his world. The alien would self-inflict the ultimate psychic pain . . . the last, climactic expression of emotion that Damon needed.

Damon bent and grabbed the back of Vance's coat, tugging until he managed to get her into a wobbly sitting-up position. As quickly as he could, he dragged her inside the red square that denoted the area of the feeder cage. From his awkward position behind her he could see the purple and green lump that had risen from the point of impact at the base of her skull, but she was breathing steadily so he was fairly certain she was going to be all right.

Propping her carefully against the door to Mozart's enclosure where she wouldn't stop the feeder cage as it lowered around her, Damon swiftly backed away and pressed the button that lowered the glass booth. For a moment the ramifications of what he was about to do hit him, hard, and his mind began to spin in doubt and fear. I'll tell Brangwen that I wasn't here, he thought irrationally. How hard would it be to believe that she had taken her "communication" experiments too far? After all, she spent every waking moment talking to the alien, charting his progress, putting down hundreds of observations about his behavior, dozens of preposterous speculations on how he might act in hypothetical situations. It would be easy for them to believe she'd gone too far and let herself into the alien's cage to test her theories; and easier to guess that she'd probably thought she had enough time to get back in the feeder cage and close the door. Then all Damon would have to do was concoct a story about how his keyboard got broken—he'd clean it up and claim he dropped it . . . and, of course, why the cage door was locked from the outside. That might be the hardest thing to cover, but he'd think of something, and frankly, those things weren't very important in his world right now. The ultimate in symphony productions was hanging just over his head, and all Damon had to do was turn on the equipment and run with it. And oh, it was going to be *so* beautiful!

Broken keyboards and a locked feeder cage door were inconsequential. Right now all that mattered was Darcy Vance—and Mozart, of course, hunched on the other side of the glass with the snout of his massive, shelled head batting lightly against its surface whenever it sensed Damon walking back and forth. Perhaps it wasn't Damon's movements that attracted it at all, and Damon eyed the creature and gave it a dark smile; for so long now it had seemed to know every move that Vance made. Could it tell right now that she . . . *wasn't* moving?

"Soon, my black-shelled friend," Damon told it as he hurried to the recording console and began adjusting the settings. "Soon you will finally meet your friend in the flesh." He thought he could feel all those doses of royal jelly inside his system, pushing his perceptions once more into overdrive, turning him into a human sound system wired for the ultimate reception.

Lights glowed in readiness on the equipment while inside the enclosure Mozart rose and began to pace the length of the glass in loping strides; the alien's head turned toward the ceiling, neck stretching in anticipation as he felt the electronic pulse of the overhead microphones and knew that soon he would be fed. From where he stood at the console Damon could see the creature's massive mouth and sharp teeth part in expectation, the thick, faintly green saliva thinning as it stretched from upper to lower teeth in glistening strands.

Finally, after what felt like eons, Vance began to stir inside the feeder cage and Damon let himself grin as he pushed the volume slides higher, adjusting them to capture everything—the sound of a drop of blood striking the floor, the sweet tones of Darcy Vance's voice as she screamed, a sound not so long ago that he'd likened to a skillfully played clarinet. The console humming with readiness, Damon got up and strode over to the cage, waiting with his finger pressed against the button for the two-way speaker so he could speak to her when she was fully cognizant.

A few moments later she opened her eyes. Blinking, she steadied herself against the floor with one hand while the other went to the back of her neck and gingerly felt the lump there; when she brought her hand back to her face, it was covered in blood. Then, as Damon shuffled impatiently, she finally realized where she was.

"What hap—my *God!*"

"Now it's your turn, Darcy," Damon said gleefully. He gestured to Mozart, forced to wait patiently at the door to the feeder cage. She couldn't see the alien, of course, but she'd been through this enough times to know where he was. "My grand finale awaits, and I have to hear Mozart sing as he kills his favorite little friend." Damon's mouth was pulled in a smile so wide he could feel spit leaking from the corners, but he didn't care. He was far beyond caring what others thought of him, his appearance, his mental stability;

besides, in five more minutes, this woman would be dead.

Inside the cage, Vance tried to stand but made it only to her knees. "You bastard," she hissed. "You're crazy—a *maniac.* I always knew you couldn't be trusted! You can't do this—it's murder, Eddington. Don't you see what this project, what your jelly, has done to you? *Please*—think about what you're planning to do!"

"Oh, I *have*, believe me. Murder?" Damon tilted his head back and laughed. "We're *all* murderers here, my dear. Do you think because you never personally pushed the feeder cage button that you're any different from me, or Brangwen, or Ahiro? Spare me your moralistic speeches." His hands were cold with excitement and he couldn't help rubbing them together, as much for warmth as from anticipation. She stared at him through the glass, blood leaking down her forehead where it had run across her scalp while she was unconscious, a lovely scarlet splash across her pale skin. "Besides," he continued, "you don't have to die, remember? You have the same chance as everyone else. The second Electrostun rifle that Ahiro gave the last subject is still in there with Mozart, practically right outside the cage door. If you stay calm and move slowly, you can . . . *probably* . . . get to it." Damon grinned again at her dull, disbelieving look. "We all know how Mozart hates those quick moves, don't we?"

"Mr. Eddington—*Damon*—please. Mozart is just an alien. He doesn't think like us, he isn't going to *care* that it's me in there any more than he cared about any of the others. Don't you see that? Me talking to him, observing him all this time—all that was only part of the project, the *experiment*. He's just an alien, and he isn't going to sound any different this time than he did the other times."

Damon laughed again, louder. "Nice try, Vance, but I don't believe it for a minute and I don't think you do, either. Enough screwing around. I think it's time to find out what good friends you two really are." He slid his hand into his pocket and pulled out the last vial of jelly he had; when he felt the warm glass in his palm, his mouth watered in anticipation. As the time had rolled by, the flavor of the jelly for Damon had changed, each dose tasting less like a child's cotton candy fantasy and more like rich port wine, heavy with alcohol and fermented grapes. "Let's see," he rasped at Vance, "how much he likes you. I hope he does." Damon raised the vial and toasted the bioscientist, then drained it, chuckling as Vance slapped angrily at the glass between them in response. Royal jelly flowed over his teeth and tongue, blazing a trail of startling vibrancy along everything it touched, not just inside but along his lips and the roof of his mouth, dribbling down the sharp line of skin along his jaw and collarbone where the drug seeped from the side of his mouth. Bluish splotches of it dotted the deep-cut neckline of his T-shirt.

He tossed the vial aside. "I hope he's in *agony* over killing you," he told her. "I hope it fucking cuts his monster's *heart* out . . . if he has one." His prisoner started to speak but Damon knew exactly what to do to put a swift end to that, and he quickly toggled the speaker switch to OFF. Without another look at Darcy Vance, Damon sidestepped to the wall control, wrapped his hand around the sliding switch that controlled the door leading to Mozart's enclosure inside the feeder cage, and pulled.

The guy in charge of the loading dock in back of Presley Hall was a mope in a blue suit with little experience and less confidence. Barely old enough to legally hold a job, he had thick, youthful brown hair and a thin mustache. The mustache did a poor job of disguising the man's age; leaning over the flunkie's desk, Phillip Rice was close enough to see a light rash of pimples underneath the sparse hair. He could also see the guy sweat, and that was good. He *liked* making people wiggle.

"We can go in with or without you as an escort," he

repeated. "I'm giving you formal notice that this is a search for a highly addictive, controlled substance."

"You n-need a search warrant," the young man stammered. He was trying desperately to look tough and failing miserably. "You c-can't—"

"I can and I will." Rice leaned over the desk farther, until the metal brow of his white helmet was nearly touching the watch supervisor's—what a joke—forehead. In a way he felt sorry for the kid; it was a helluva position to be in. On the other hand, if the guy was going to act like an asshole, he was going to get treated like one. "Look"—Rice's gaze dropped to the plastic name tag on the left front of the guy's suit jacket and he gave it a poke for emphasis—"Higgins. Maybe you aren't familiar with the appropriate city ordinance, maybe you're just stalling for time. It doesn't matter which, because the result is the same. So I'll tell you the way the law reads here in Manhattan, but I'm only using my air to say it once." Higgins started to open his mouth, but Rice held up a warning finger. "Manhattan Substance Abuse Ordinance Number 2021-14.85.4673 says that, and I'm quoting here, so pay attention, 'When an investigation is conducted wherein the target material is the substance commonly known as *royal jelly*, derivatives or materials in connection therewith, no search warrant is required by the conducting officer when a Homeworld creature is used as the mechanism by which the search will be carried out.' End quote." Held more or less firmly in place by Rice's two men, ol' Blue swayed slightly behind Rice, and the MedTech security chief waved a hand in the direction of the creature's face. In response, the alien hissed instinctively and tossed his head. "In other words, Mr. Higgins, these babies either find what we're looking for, or they don't. They don't lie and they can't be bribed, because to them there's no difference between good guys and bad. Now you either call your boss or whoever's got the authority to lead this little tour, or we'll go on our own and leave you to cover your own ass. If we have the misfortune to run into a locked door, we'll laser it open. And trust me when I tell you that we aren't going to pay any bills for damages that Synsound tries to mail us." He gave the gaping young man a sardonic grin. "Do we understand each other, Mr. Higgins?"

Higgins nodded, his jerky movements reminding Rice of an antique string puppet. The young man fumbled with a telephone on the desk—an older model that showed the loading dock didn't rate vidscreens—and pressed a combination of keys. Beneath the low, fairly calm hissing of ol' Blue, Rice could hear not only Higgins's whining voice, but that of the person he'd called.

"Morton here."

"Ch-chief, this is Guard Higgins. Down at the loading dock?" The young guy swiped nervously at the moisture leaking down his forehead, his gaze skittering back and forth from Rice to the alien.

"I know who the hell you are, you moron! What is it?"

"Could you . . . ah . . . come to the loading dock?" Higgins swallowed as Rice and his men grinned back; behind them, the creature continued to rock gently on its haunches between the guidepoles.

"What for?"

Before Higgins could answer, Rice rapped his knuckles sharply on the desktop to make sure he had the guard's attention. "Be very careful what you say on the phone to your supervisor, Mr. Higgins," he said in a quiet, steely voice. "It would be very unfortunate for me to think you're giving someone a tip or anything, now wouldn't it?"

Higgins swallowed more noticeably and Rice saw that the young man's shirt collar was dark with moisture. The sight made his grin widen; God, how he loved getting under people's skin and twisting.

"Higgins, who are you talking to down there?"

"There's a-a situation, sir," Higgins choked out. "You-you should be here."

"Do you need more men?" A note of alarm had crept into the unseen speaker's previously annoyed voice.

Higgins shook his head as though his supervisor could see him, then flushed under Rice's unwavering scrutiny. "No, sir," he said stiffly. "I think you should just come down. Immediately."

There was a cuss word or two, then a final response that was nearly a shout. "*All right, damn it! But if I get there and find out that this is something you could've handled yourself, you're in a world of shit, Higgins!*"

Despite his boss's anger, Higgins looked relieved. "Thank you, sir." The young man hung up the telephone with a defiant *bang*, then looked at Rice and his team wordlessly, his eyes wide, gaze still flicking fearfully to the harnessed and muzzled alien.

Rice smiled at him from beneath the overhang of his helmet, his expression tranquil. "And thank *you*."

A few minutes later—a good thing, too, because at the five-minute mark Rice wasn't going to wait any longer—a red-haired man with a receding hairline and a thick, bristly beard stalked out of the door marked PRESLEY HALL SECURITY PERSONNEL ONLY on the rear wall of the receiving area. His mouth was already on rapid-fire, tone of voice a perfect match for the unpleasant scowl on his face. "Okay, Higgins," he snapped, "what the hell do you . . ." As Rice expected, the sight of ol' Blue put a sudden lag into the sentence, making it end more like a squeaked-out question than a supervisor's demand as the man jerked to a stop at Higgins's desk. ". . . want?"

Rice stepped forward, deciding to spare Higgins the pain of trying to explain. "*I* want you to take us wherever the hell *he* wants to go," he said with a note of finality. He gave enough of a tug on his guidepole to make the alien tense and shift within his bonds.

"This is highly unorthodox," Morton began. "I'll have to get approval—"

"*No.*" Keeping his grip firmly on the guidepole, Rice took a couple of steps forward, closing the distance between himself and Presley Hall's chief of security. Behind him, ol' Blue followed the movement of the guidepole by rising expectantly and taking a single long step. "We both know you can't legally refuse to let us conduct the search, and we both also know that I don't have to wait for anyone's approval or permission. So it comes down to this: We can do this with you leading and unlocking whatever doors need to be opened along the way, or we can go on our own and burn our way through 'em with lasers if they happen to be locked. Take your pick." Rice rearranged his expression into a scowl. "But do it quickly, *Mr.* Morton, because I'm getting tired of wasting my time and having to repeat myself."

"I . . ." Morton's mouth opened and closed helplessly a few times, then he drew his shoulders back with as much dignity as he could manage. "Right this way, gentlemen. Higgins, you come, too." With Morton leading, the group followed him into a small, cramped stairway, and Rice ducked his head and grinned at the quickly disguised look of vindication on Higgins's face as he shoved aside the evening's paperwork to accompany Chief Morton and the team on their search.

I must not pass out.

Darcy had never noticed before how loudly the door to Mozart's cage squealed when it opened. When she had been where Eddington was now, on the outside of the cage and looking in, the sound had been nothing, just another part of the process. Now it was immense, like God's fingernails sliding across the blackboard surface of her sanity and clearing her head of any thoughts of self-indulgent oblivion. And there was Mozart, of course, waiting where he always did when something was in the feeder, directly outside the door to the cage, his blue-black head and shoulders tilted into his normal hunched position. Without the protection of the unbreakable quartz window, his teeth seemed so much larger than before, still bright white with youth, the four rear incisors sparkling with alien mucus along their slim edges. At any second that massive mouth would part and pull a fragile webbing of saliva across the dark, dripping cavern that was beyond the creature's teeth. He was swaying slightly, that same strangely parrotlike movement that made him resemble a bizarre cross between an insect and bird in a mating ritual.

One part of her gut was telling her to run, in any direction as long as it was *away;* the other said that if she just stayed inside the feeder cage and cowered like a little girl hiding under the covers, maybe the monster wouldn't see her, or maybe it would be gone when she finally opened her eyes. Obeying either instinct would mean death; instead Darcy crept forward, fighting her natural impulses with every inch, breathing in short, soundless gasps that matched the beat of her heart in frequency and threatened to make her hyperventilate.

I must not pass out.

Two seconds, then four, and her icy fingers brushed the plastic stock of the Electrostun rifle, warmed by the higher heat of the room enough so that she nearly recoiled at the unexpected fleshlike feel of the soft, textured grip.

Mozart didn't move.

Darcy lifted it slowly and swung it to fit under her right arm. He should be roaring at her, *charging* her. What was Mozart waiting for? Perhaps he *does* know me, she thought desperately. Maybe he can sense who I am. Should I talk to him as I have so many times over these past weeks?

She bit the inside of her cheek hard, letting the pain refocus her thinking and bring her back to sanity. Now was not the time to theorize about the working of alien minds, nor was she willing—despite what Eddington wanted—to be the first human test subject in the realm of possible future Homeworld alien training. Her right forefinger found the stunner's power switch and flicked it on; her reward was the low vibration of energy along the rifle's stock that signaled the weapon was ready. Thank God—if such a being existed—for automatic shutoffs, although the rifle's last user hadn't employed much in the way of the Electrostun's charge.

And, like the four others before him, now he was dead.

Darcy couldn't help the tremble that started beneath the hair on her scalp and swept all the way to her feet. Mozart still hadn't advanced and she could see him in more detail than she'd ever hoped for. Beneath his feet were a jumble of shattered bones and rotting flesh, the remains of the last man and his predecessors, a bottom jaw, a cracked-open skull. The smell hanging in the hot, semitropical air was enough to force a silent retch from her throat, like being made to inhale through an air mask where the supply came from tanks filled with decomposing meat. She tried futilely to breathe through her mouth but it was no good; already coating the inside of her nostrils, the scent was like oil, clogging every pore in her sinuses. Less than two yards away from her, Mozart rocked slightly back and forth, his low, continuous hissing drowning out the quiet thrum of the rifle. What unknown senses did he use to keep track of her location? Scent, of course, but was there something else, a psychic sense that humankind was still unable to admit existed? She thought again that maybe all the time and effort she'd invested in talking to and caring for the creature had been worthwhile; it wasn't inconceivable that a Homeworld life-form could be trained, just imaginative, something that, because of their dangerous nature, no one else had ever considered. Then again—

Darcy's breath locked in her throat as at last the alien's outer mouth slowly opened and allowed the inner one to extend. The disturbing hiss doubled in volume, then tripled as the creature swung into a final, low crouch and flexed his spiky hands. She'd seen the movement enough times, so *many* times, to recognize it: the prelude to a leap.

A final instant of recollection before the confrontation: back in the early days of the project, what were the words she had said to Michael?

"*. . . To pause a moment before it kills you.*"

How ironic that she had been so correct; after so much time invested in him, Mozart truly *had* given her the most she could have hoped for.

Darcy hugged the Electrostun to her cheek, aimed, and squeezed the trigger. Electricity crackled as a white arc of fire surged from the insulated barrel of the weapon and snapped through Mozart, its point of contact the front of his throat directly below the jawline.

Through everything—her terror, the ponderous but rapid beating of her heart, the steamy hissing sound that seemed not so much a vocalization by the alien as a *projection* of him . . . Darcy could still recognize that Mozart screamed as he had never screamed before. Emotions that made no sense whiplashed through her mind: panic, flight, *guilt*. And hate, too, directed at this creature to which she had devoted so much of herself for so long; she didn't blame or condemn it for attacking—certainly its nature could not be denied. But she despised it utterly for giving what she knew must be exactly what Eddington, poised over his recording console in the outer lab, had wanted all along. There was an undercurrent to the alien's shriek that she had never heard before, and surely it was the things the creature felt right now and revealed in that unique and previously secret sound that Eddington had most sought: of anything that had existed in Mozart's limited world, she had been the only thing familiar, and steady, and . . . *trusted*. He was her savage and innocent child, and she had betrayed him.

Darcy caught a glimpse of Eddington hunched at his post beyond the safety of the glass as she scrambled a few feet to her left and prepared to fire again. Fighting for her life, struggling against impossible odds of survival, it was no comfort to see from his deranged expression that the dance of certain death she and Mozart did were giving the musician everything he'd wished for and more.

* * *

"Yes," Damon whispered, "yes, yes, *yes!*" Mozart was screeching, *crying*, the music rippling from deeper within the creature than Damon had ever dreamed possible. Abandoning his position at the glass, Damon sped back to the mixing console and pushed the volume slides up another two notches. Sound thundered through the speakers, making the surface of the equipment vibrate beneath Damon's spasming fingers, rattling the lines of paper still rolled into the dot matrix printers. Blending with the wails of the alien was the bellowslike *whoosh* of Darcy's harsh, labored breathing. Damon's pulse jackhammered in time with the musical sounds of the battle, the alien's screams, Darcy's frenzied panting, the sound of the Electrostun rifle when it fired, like a huge wall of crumpled plastic exploding into flame. Nothing he'd ever experienced in his lifetime could compare to the nearly orgasmic sensations throbbing through his mind and body tonight in absolute synchrony with every exquisite note of Mozart's dark and perfect music.

And, as his hand moved from the volume slide controls to the small gift Ahiro gave him before the final man was put into Mozart's cage, Damon knew that the best of everything was only the push of a button away. What would the Japanese assassin say if he knew the use to which Damon was about to put it? The composer touched Ahiro's gift reverently, then picked it up and hurried back to the glass, holding it high and wishing that Vance had a moment to turn and see what he held. If she had, her own screams of disbelief would doubtless add all but the grandest touch to the great finale of his Symphony of Hate.

Damon pressed himself against the glass, holding the object against the barrier where it could easily be seen, but Vance was intent on her strategy, a series of short, carefully aimed bursts of electricity that were slowly driving Mozart to the right and away from the entrance of the tunnel closest to her. A fine plan, and if only the woman would look at him and see the object in his hand, she could not help but realize that it was only a useless fantasy.

"Time to *die*, Darcy," Damon said aloud. He looked at the object in his hands and tried to focus on it, knowing the wrong choice at this point could destroy everything he'd worked for, bring the project to an untimely and forever incomplete ending.

A small metal box, four modest square buttons below different colored lights, ON, OFF, POWER INCREASE %, POWER DECREASE %. Right now the green light above the On button was glowing steadily and a small red LED display told him that the "power" was set at fifteen percent. Before his forefinger moved to the Off button, Damon touched the raised yellow letters across the top of the small box solemnly and raised his gaze to the woman and the creature battling earnestly six yards away.

ELECTROSTUN REMOTE

22

In the recesses of her mind, Darcy still had hope that she would survive this ordeal.

She was not a drug addict or an alcoholic—she didn't even drink coffee. Nothing she had ingested would chemically cloud her mind or reflexes, the lump on the back of her head notwithstanding. Added to that was the fact that the alien had given her the ghost of an advantage by not immediately attacking, and she had a strategy that seemed to be working.

She was only three feet from the mouth of the tunnel when the Electrostun rifle ran out of power.

Scratch that—it didn't slow down as it would do in the course of normally losing its charge; it simply *quit.* Darcy wasn't stupid and she didn't need more than a millisecond to know that Eddington had shut it off via remote control. He didn't *want* her to survive any more than he'd wanted any of Mozart's other victims to ultimately escape. She, *they*, were all fodder—

meals for the alien, musical fuel for Eddington's madness. With the others he had wanted the game played out for as long as possible and had been furious with Ahiro the one time the ninja had dared to tilt the odds in favor of the alien. Darcy, however, was the one test subject whose death Damon Eddington coveted as surely as he sought that special alien scream for his grand finale.

At nearly the same instant as the rifle died, a monstrous whine of feedback squealed through the speakers above Mozart's enclosure, clawing its way along every nerve ending in Darcy's body and making her teeth involuntarily clench. Mozart felt it, too, and he roared and tossed his massive head in protest, arching his back until he looked like he might bend completely backward. Darcy didn't wait for him to recover; she grabbed the opportunity to scuttle sideways another meter along the wall and damned near got inside the circular entrance to the passageway before the alien swung his dripping mouth back in her direction and double-snapped at her. She twisted out of range—barely—and realized that the time of playing was over: the creature was going to attack. Now that she was defenseless, it would be his final assault. But she would not just stand here and meet death placidly. She would fight to the end, damn it, and instead of waiting or readying herself for the deadly slash of his claws, Darcy took the offensive and charged him, her puny voice boiling out of her lungs in a high, desperate shriek as she flung the useless Electrostun rifle at the alien's eyeless head.

It struck him squarely in the forehead, and, incredibly, Mozart stumbled backward.

Like Pavlov's dog, the life-form had come to associate the Electrostun rifle with raw, electrifying pain, and he had no clue that it would not cause that same agony without the aid of a human hand. Darcy still didn't know how he identified the things in his world—by smell or something else—but she wasn't going to wait for another invitation to make her move. At the same time as the alien recoiled from the weapon, she made a crazed dash for the entry into the closest tunnel; a moment later, Mozart scrambled after her.

Darcy realized immediately that she was at a distinct disadvantage inside the tunnel.

She and Michael had not planned for this, had not factored in the possibility that amid his wanderings in and out of the dual-entranced passageway Mozart would line it so thoroughly with the sticky, moisture-laden resin that was found in such abundance in the nests the creatures had constructed on Homeworld. Who would have thought that Mozart, existing alone, would manage to attach his secretions to the Teflon-coated walls of the passageways, or would successfully twine the entire length of the circular corridor with yard after yard of the gummy brown substance?

Darcy clawed her way frantically along the knobby surface, her hands and clothes tangled in ropy, wet strands of sticky resin. The absurd thought that she was a fly fighting its way along the surface of flypaper was bouncing madly around in her thoughts and Mozart was close behind her and gaining when she rammed facefirst into something hanging from the ceiling. She screamed and instinct tried to make her recoil, but she fought the urge and won, instead wrapped her arms around the cocooned and putrefying corpse of the blond-haired MedTech executive and pulled it free of its gluey hold on the wall. Darcy caught a glimpse of the other Electrostun rifle that was entwined with him but had no time to extract it; she barely managed to duck past as the bloated cadaver spilled onto the rounded floor in a heavy lump, gaining her a precious few seconds to reach the smaller side tunnel the dead man had tried so hard to find but never achieved. Lit from within by a muted purplish glow, it was a tunnel large enough for a human, but far too small for the oversize alien.

She almost made it unscathed.

Half a foot, *six measly inches.* Darcy would have thanked God, again, for getting her to safety and making Mozart's claws have only a tenuous hold on her ankle as she slid headlong down the angled, smaller escape shaft—had the alien not slashed the vulnerable skin of her ankle to the bone before she was out of reach.

Wailing with pain, Darcy pulled herself deeper into the tunnel, far beyond the stretch of Mozart's searching arm and fingers. Out of the creature's physical range at last, Darcy could still look back and see him, her treasured alien prodigy and deadly experiment, as he raged impotently at the mouth of the tunnel, vainly clawing at the titanium-ringed opening. Her foot felt wet—*I'm bleeding, a lot*—but warm and faraway, and as each second dragged past it hurt less as a slow and comforting numbness spread upward from the wound. A bend in the tunnel and she was out of Mozart's sight as well, her fingers fumbling with a recessed catch that Eddington didn't know existed. Ahiro had known but paid little attention to her and Michael—they'd thought—when they had insisted on the last-minute inclusion of this small escape panel in the renovation plans, their faith in the gas that was used to sedate Mozart being less than complete. She heard the manual lock release and pushed weakly with her fingertips—they had purposely constructed the panel so that it could only be opened manually by a human hand—and it finally slid aside.

She barely had the strength to haul herself over the opening and hardly felt the hard landing when she dropped stiffly through and into the small area below floor level. She knew she should slide the overhead door closed but she was so *tired;* a dim but more reasonable portion of her thoughts told her frantically that it was because she was bleeding badly and she needed a tourniquet, but really, the alcove was so small and she had no first aid supplies . . . she could hardly just reach down and fix it, now could she?

Darcy could see the alarm button on the underside of the floor next to the opening. She would be able to reach it easily . . . but later, after Eddington had given her up for dead and left the apiary. Someone would come then, Synsound workers whose job it was to remove Mozart to whatever facility for disposal or further experiment that they no doubt already had planned, and then she would press the button that in turn would trigger an alarm light on nearly every console in the apiary. Then she would be rescued, and they would fix her ankle, and she could take a hot shower to wash away the smell of blood and the stench of Mozart's dead victims.

In the meantime, she would close her eyes and rest awhile.

23

"Any second now." Damon was so excited he was wheezing and dripping with sweat. "Any *moment.* It'll be beautiful, so new and different—"

He could no longer see Mozart or Vance; both had disappeared into the escape tunnel and Damon couldn't help feeling rather proud of her, in a twisted, fatherly sort of way. Besides being the sole woman to face Mozart and a bioscientist with no survival training at all, she had the distinction of being only the second human who'd made it to the tunnels—quite a feat, considering not all of her predecessors were junkies or drunks. When he'd cut the power to her Electrostun rifle, Damon had been convinced the combat would be over immediately. But still she had succeeded, surprising Damon as much as she had startled Mozart by throwing the weapon at the creature and striking it on the head.

But Damon's concern had nothing to do with the

visual aspects of this ultimate of Mozart's kills; he didn't *need* to see Darcy Vance die or watch the alien itself perform the deed. Damon lived for the sound, for the *music*, and now he quickly returned to the mixer console and jammed the volume slides to the maximum to ensure that the slightest, most elusive thing would not escape the microphones so carefully inset within the ceilings of the tunnels. Every bass, midrange and tweeter, all the amplifiers, *everything* went to the limit as Damon held his breath and waited for Mozart to give his most magnificent scream ever—

There was a humming, then a distant, metallic *thud* as the sound system circuit breakers overloaded and tripped. Wired on their own circuits, the medical consoles around the lab kept glowing cheerfully. Only Damon's recording console was thrown into powerless darkness.

A two-second span of utter silence, then—

"*No!*" Damon bellowed. "Damn you to hell and back, not *now!*" He rammed a fist against the console, but of course it did no good; the machine sat there, its power cut, its magical abilities destroyed. Damon spun indecisively, fingers opening and closing so fast they began to cramp. The circuit box—where was it? *Where?* Brangwen had tried to tell him once, and he had waved the older man away impatiently, not wanting to be bothered with such trivial details; now Damon wanted to punch himself for his stupidity. The apiary itself was huge, with miles of metal-coated electrical wires and junction boxes that led to more junction boxes—he'd never identify the proper one on his own. And he couldn't very well call the maintenance department and ask now, could he, with Darcy inside Mozart's enclosure and the object of the alien's less than desirable attentions at any second? What would he say? "*By the way, could you get down here quickly before the alien kills her so I can get the sound on tape?*" The creature's pen was silent now, but undoubtedly Darcy's screams would soon fill its tunnels.

There—on the table next to the plastic dishes and trash still left from their meal, was Brangwen's portable syndisc player/recorder. He'd left it behind, knowing the Presley Hall entrance scanners would pick it up and confiscate it. A crude tool and outdated, too, barely fit to use . . . but unfortunately all that was available. Damon was desperate enough to resort to primitive methods, and there might be enough time to actually pull it off—

Damon raced to the table and snatched up the recorder, checked quickly to make sure the device worked and that there was a disc in place that could be recorded onto. The handheld microphone that Damon used to make vocal notes on his demo discs was dangling off the recording console and he jerked it free and plugged it into the portable recorder, sped to the feeder cage and—

Stopped cold.

The music was there, waiting for him as it had always been; but Damon abruptly realized that the only way to get Brangwen's syndisc recorder inside Mozart's cage to capture those elusive sounds was to . . .

Open it.

He stood outside the glass feeder cage as precious seconds ticked past, staring through the unbreakable panels at the yawning entry to Mozart's realm. It would be so easy to do: just raise the feeder cage, walk to the open door and step inside, hold the recorder and the microphone out, and step back out when it was over, lower the feeder cage, and lock it up.

"So easy," Damon repeated hoarsely, not realizing he was speaking out loud. "I'll just step in and hold out the microphone so it catches the music. He'll be . . . *busy* with Darcy in the tunnels, and I'll . . . I'll hear him screaming, hear him *singing*. He'll never even see me, never know I'm there."

Teetering on the edge of decision, swaying back and forth like the alien occasionally did inside his cage, first one way, then the other. It was dangerous, too dangerous, but . . . this was *him*, after all; Damon *Eddington*. He wasn't like the others, the junkies and drunkards, or even the ignorant MedTech man that Ahiro had brought in for a reason known only to the Japanese man and those to whom he reported. Even Vance was different—she was there for him to use in his project in whatever way was necessary for him to deliver the results he had promised Synsound . . . hence the reason she was in there at Mozart's mercy, and Damon was out here, on the controlling end. In this room, in his situation, Damon Eddington was the controller, the one in charge. The *god*.

Taking a deep breath, Damon carefully pressed the button to raise the glass feeder cage, knowing the well-lubricated hydraulics would raise the cage smoothly and quietly, without the screech of metal that always accompanied the sliding back of the metal door that led directly into the alien's enclosure and separated it from the glass feeder cage. There was a low, nearly soundless hum and Damon stared fearfully through the exposed entryway. Everything was quiet—there was no scrabble of chitinous nails against the slippery, curving tunnel walls that signaled Mozart's advance, no telltale escalating hiss that marked the beast's breathing. Damon let his air out in relief, still mindful of the sound his exhalation would make. A few cautious steps forward and he was bathed in the smell of Mozart's corrupted meals, flesh turned putrid by the pseudo-tropical climate in which aliens were most comfortable. Best not to stay, Damon decided. I'll just tuck the recorder into the corner where the wall and steel door meet, roll the microphone and its wire just past the threshold and into the alien's cage. When the music was finished and Damon closed the door, the metal would sever the wires and then he could safely retrieve the recorder and its precious contents.

Damon was still bending down when Mozart catapulted from the entrance to the tunnel, his mouths snapping in fury, his only sound a hissing more filled with rage than any the alien had ever voiced.

"No!" Damon's voice was hardly more than a drawn-out rasp of denial. He turned to run and his feet slipped, then slipped again, dragging against his weight as though they were glued to the floor and stuck within that gaudy rectangle of red warning tape by a gooey dose of royal jelly. *"Not me—NO!"*

He made it out of Mozart's enclosure and rammed the side of his hand against the button that would lower the feeder cage, then stopped its descent by panicking and slapping at it again, inadvertently toggling it off. The third time got it going and he tried frantically to hasten the descent of the glass enclosure into the locking grooves on the floor, hanging off the side as he used his weight in an idiot attempt to increase the drop speed. It was nearly down when Mozart's terrifying, tooth-filled head filled Damon's vision. Damon instinctively released his grip on the top edge of the feeder box and sprang backward, shouting in terror as Mozart's dark, double-shelled fingers found enough room to slip under the edge of the glass cage before it could settle into the grooves in the floor and lock in place.

The cage, built on an open-close cycle for safety purposes, obligingly switched directions when the creature tried to heft it upward.

"Wait!" Damon screamed. *"Not me, not ME! I'm the musician—"*

He hardly felt it as the alien bounded from beneath the still rising glass box and lifted him until Damon's chest was even with his huge, dripping mouth. Hissing swelled in his ears, his brain, his *heart*, blotting out everything but the thunderous beat of his heart. *"No—"*

Pain then, white-hot and enough to make him scream beyond what he could have ever believed he was capable of, slamming through a rib cage that was nothing more than a fragile lace spiderweb against the teeth that split him from breastbone to gut and twice as deep. Writhing in agony in the grasp of the genius child-beast he had nurtured and hated and loved—

—Damon's last, desperate hope was that the antiquated syndisc recorder still functioned, that its cheap, portable microphone somehow managed to chronicle his final, beautiful death cry.

24

It took damned near half an hour for ol' Blue to sniff his way through a maze of dimly lit staircases and sublevels, but Rice refused to believe his watchdog was taking them on a useless chase. *Something* had the alien's attention, and it wasn't the normal influx of alien pheromones that generally mixed in the air of a place like this. As long as they were far enough away, those scents, diluted, impossibly scrambled, usually succeeded only in making an alien confused and vaguely hyper, unlike the concentrated assault that ol' Blue had launched against the jelly dealer and his customer the last time Rice had taken him on the street. Now that he was inside the Presley Hall Building, ol' Blue was clearly onto a specific scent, and the only indication that the smell was an old one was his tendency to change direction almost ponderously.

Finally, they stood in front of a closed door painted in garish orange and guarded by a keypad that required a security code. Nothing else about the door indicated that it was anything special; the floor-level announcement they had seen on their last elevator ride had said LEVEL 1A in innocuous letters. Rice could see the surprise in his team members' eyes; the men had climbed up and down so many staircases, side-tracked on more than a few elevators, then twisted through so many halls that they had all been convinced they were considerably farther below ground. Now, however, it looked like they were no farther down than a regular basement, but damned if it wasn't a hard place to find. Ol' Blue was getting downright jittery and Rice felt the palms of his hands beginning to dampen around his unyielding grip on the guide-poles; finally, after all this time, he and his team were going to get their hands on the elusive egg thief. Frankly, he wasn't surprised to find it was one of these Synsound slugs . . . he'd suspected Synsound all along, although he still couldn't fathom what the music company would want with an alien or an unhatched egg.

Higgins and Morton stood to either side of the orange door uncertainly, their expressions mirroring each other's indecision. Well, well, well, Rice thought smugly. Special little secrets in here for certain. Aloud he said, "Come on, guys, let's go—open it up. It's way too late to back out now. Besides, you know that MedTech's private investigations rarely result in prosecution. We go in, clean out the jelly, and skedaddle." Rice gave Morton a toothy smile that made the men on his team smirk. "What better service can you get?"

For the first time, Morton looked over at his subordinate for support, but the younger man avoided his boss's gaze, fixing on a spot on the floor somewhere in the vicinity of his right shoe. "I really should check with someone," Morton managed. "This is a highly restricted area. I—I've never been in here before."

With ol' Blue as jumpy as a scared fly, it was a risk for Rice to firm up his grip on the guidepole with one hand and unholster his laser pistol with the other. "My patience with this is about worn out, Chief Morton. If you don't open this fucking door, I'm going to burn it apart and then you and everybody else can explore the other side to your heart's content. This is your last chance; punch in the code or step aside."

Surrendering, Morton angrily jabbed four keys on the pad. Without a sound, the bright orange door slid aside, exposing a short, wide hallway without the benefit of light. From its other end a rectangle of glowing fluorescent light beckoned, and it was in that direction that ol' Blue suddenly began lurching, nearly dragging the team members off their feet in his eagerness to get to whatever was inside.

"Whoa!" McGarrity exclaimed as he fought with the center guidepole of the alien's harness and dodged a reflexive twitch of the creature's tail. It was the first time the Irishman had spoken since their arrival back at the Presley Hall loading dock. "I'd say this ugly son of a bitch is getting right *passionate* about our expedition, Chief."

"I'll give him a mini-squirt," Rice said. His thumb found and pressed the button on the box that controlled the Surgealyn; four more seconds, and the alien's struggles melted away and he stood among the five men, docile and nearly silent as he swayed gently like some huge, hand-trained tropical parrot. God, the Surgealyn was so powerful—

Good thing, too. When they stepped through the brightly lit doorway, it was obvious that sometime in the recent past, the room had been occupied by one of Blue's own kind.

"Well, guys, I think it's safe to surmise that the stolen egg has hatched," Rice commented dryly. Standing with his men and the two Synsound security workers, they all stared at what was left—and it wasn't much—of a dark-haired man lying on the floor next to a shattered electronic keyboard. Most of the man's chest and abdomen were gone and the ragged edges of his broken ribs showed as stained white around the bloody hole in the center of his body; traces of scarlet dribbled down the sides of the nearby keyboard and splattered the floor around the corpse. "Any idea who he was?"

Morton cleared his throat, a sick expression on his face. "I think his name was Damon Eddington. He was a musician, or a composer. Something like that."

"I've heard of him," Higgins piped in. "Seen his picture on the syndisc covers, too. Most people thought his music was kind of . . . weird." No one seemed impressed.

"Looks like somebody's pet got real pissed," Rice said flatly. A blood-splashed empty jelly vial was partially jammed beneath the body and he pointed at it. "And here's why." Rice's keen gaze tracked an intermittent trail of alien saliva away from the corpse until he nodded at another open doorway. "Anyone know where that leads?"

"I used to know this place fairly well when I was working city security," Morez spoke up when neither of the Synsound men seemed inclined to volunteer the information. "The trip down here got me kind of turned around, but I think that might be another way to the stage."

Silence followed Morez's response as the three MedTech specialists considered the possibilities. The air in the large room stank of death, and to their left was a wall of quartz glass that showed an expansive area filled with the remains of humans and animals alike. Cracked human skulls were scattered amid the splintered and picked-over skeletons of larger beasts that could no longer be identified. The creature that had lived in there before tonight had obviously been well fed; taken into consideration with the door and stairs leading to the other levels of Presley Hall, the gaping, unguarded entryway to the enclosure promised more dark events before the night was over.

"Your ticket holders are gonna get a real show tonight," said Rice. He nodded toward the opening. "Put ol' Blue in there and give him a triple dose from the box before you close it up. That'll hold him for a good three hours, until we can come back and pick him up." McGarrity and Morez moved to do as Rice instructed, expertly steering the oversize alien through the waiting entrance.

"What does this mean?" Morton asked Rice as he and Higgins watched the alien being caged. "Are you saying there was an alien in here?"

"Here"—MedTech's chief of security smiled placidly—"let me explain it." He stepped closer and his hands snapped forward. "Dream time," he said simply.

"Wha—hey!" Morton and Higgins both yelped as Rice pricked them simultaneously in the upper arms with lancets of Surgealyn. "What was . . . was . . . wha . . ."

Neither managed a complete sentence before they slid to the floor.

Rice held up the uncapped tips of the anesthetic vials for McGarrity and Morez to see. "They'll be out for hours," he announced. He tossed the used lancets at a nearby trash can, then carefully adjusted his gloves. "Hopefully this won't take longer than that." He motioned to his men to follow him into the waiting stairwell.

"But what if it does?" Morez asked worriedly. "What if ol' Blue comes around? There's no telling what kind of smells are in that enclosure. We didn't even check it."

Rice glanced at the cage's window wall and saw ol' Blue, crouched quietly on the other side, massive head hanging low from the effects of the anesthetic. He shrugged. "Well, the missing alien should be one of ol' Blue's own hive, and besides, Blue's still fully harnessed. If he goes a little crazy, we'll be all right as long as we can get close enough to grab the Surgealyn control." He paused at the bottom of the stairs, listening. From somewhere deep in the building, the three of them could hear the throbbing of a concert in full swing on Presley Hall's main stage.

"I hope you boys are ready to rock and roll," Rice said softly as he grabbed the banister and took his first step. "I got a feeling the time has come to get down to the serious hunting."

25

It had been easy to follow the smattering trail of alien saliva through the disorienting maze of underground hallways and stairwells. Too easy, in fact. Now, of course, the fun times were at an end and Rice, McGarrity, and Morez discovered that the stairs they were climbing ended in a dual choice: more stairs up and to their left, or a bidirectional hallway directly in front of them, and not a gloppy wad of Homeworld alien spit to be found.

"What the hell!" Rice hurried a few paces in one direction, then tried the other. "Did the thing suddenly dry up or what?"

"For all we know, the bastard sprouted wings. This is great," McGarrity said in disgust as the group faltered and stopped. "Which way?"

Rice grimaced and scanned the landing again, but it was useless; he couldn't spot any more droplets of the telltale greenish slime. "Hell, anyone's guess is as good as mine." He glanced around a final time, checking the shadows among the industrial pipes and joints overhead just to be sure, but with no luck. At last he shrugged and pointed at the stairs. "He's been down level so long, maybe he'll keep going up. Let's try that way."

Shifting under the weight of his backpack, Rice turned and began climbing with his men close on his heels.

Michael heard the audience scream louder with delight and looked up from digging into his bag for the last piece of candy to see an alien leap on the stage with the Helltones.

"I'll be damned," he said. Eyes wide, he dropped the empty paper bag on the floor and stood, trying to see around the people in front of him—who were also standing and jumping and craning their necks in an effort to see this surprise addition to the show. Michael's seat was pretty good, but not made to provide visual access when the entire assembly of concert attendees decided to stand. As a result, he could only get a glimpse of what was going on down on the stage now and then through the mass of bodies that seemed to visibly swell with excitement at the sight of the alien.

"Oh, cool!" exclaimed the girl on Michael's left. The dyed pink and yellow mini-braids that went down the center of her otherwise shaven scalp bobbed with approval in time with her gold skull earrings; to Michael, it sounded like she'd said *"Kew-al."* "A 'droid alien!" she continued loudly. "Is this like a rave or what?" Her hand flashed to her face and the glowing blue contents of a vial of jelly disappeared into her mouth.

On the stage beneath his balcony location, Michael saw the alien android take a swipe at the lead singer and thought it was amusing that he was the one the performance manager had programmed the thing to attack; after all, the singing android was a parody of the alien creature itself. The immense vidscreen showed it all as, apparently unconcerned, the

Helltones' lead singer continued to belt out his harsh lyrics beneath the circulating, multicolor laser lights—

"*. . . with each bloody thrust . . .*"

—as the bigger alien android rebounded across the stage and wrapped a huge, clawed hand around his head. "*Drink deep, baby,*" the singer bayed at the microphone, and his voice was still going strong when the alien ripped his mechanical head free of his body and flung the two pieces in different directions.

Michael's gasp was lost as the audience screamed its approval, and he barely made out the alien android's answering cry. Straining to see past the crowd, Michael's heart abruptly began to pound heavily. He knew that sound, had heard it a thousand times, two thousand. It sounded so real, so very much like . . .

Mozart!

The creature on the stage was in a paroxysm of rage as strings of its greenish saliva mixed with the sudden white splash of the demolished android's nutrient and lubrication fluids. Michael had seen the alien fight more times than he cared to remember, but never like this—maddened beyond anything previous, Michael realized there must be dozens of shattered vials of jelly down there, each dropped dose pushing the creature deeper into its battle frenzy. His hands went to his mouth in shock as the band member closest to the alien was the creature's next victim, and for all their gruesome lyrics and dangerous appearances, the singing band members were placid, defenseless concoctions of synthetic flesh and plastic skeletons. Limited cellular programming made the lead guitarist continue his strumming motions despite the crush of jaws that severed its elongated fingers forever. Long hair swinging, the second guitarist was gamely singing the backup lyrics when his chest was torn apart.

Around Michael, the concert attendees were going wild, delighted with this unannounced addition to the Helltones' show. Michael was far too shocked and frightened to share in their enthusiasm; a hellish premonition of what was to come made the swishy combination of candy and soda in his gut abruptly want to boil up. "It-it can't be," he stuttered. He looked around imploringly, but there was no one who looked like an usher or even a vendor, and security in the balcony was generally nonexistent. With mounting horror, he saw dozens of people in the balcony alone intensify their exhilaration with doses of jelly—how many more vials were being opened on the main floor?

Desperate, he turned toward the girl next to him. She was whipping her head from side to side, braids streaming in time to the thinned-out music and not at all bothered by the fact that half of the band was now in a multitude of sloshy pieces across the stage. "Yeah!" the young woman screamed at the stage. "It's about time you guys did something different!"

Unexpected anger made heat rush to his face. God forbid you should get bored, Michael thought with completely out-of-place annoyance. The Helltones have been around for a whole month—what on earth will you want next *week*? "Hey!" he yelled at her, waving his arms to get her attention. "Listen to me—it's not an android! It's real—we should all get out of here!" But she only glanced at him and rolled her eyes before going back to her involvement with the physical beat.

Roaring louder as he destroyed one android after another, Mozart—and Michael was sure it was him—was awash in dripping hues of yellow and red as the light show danced over him and the severed pieces of the band members. Feedback razored through the speakers from the shattered instruments, twisting along Michael's nerves like the feel of biting into aluminum foil, and if the people around him in the balcony were getting into the Helltones' newest performer, those directly in front of the stage were ecstatic. The only person who seemed to have a brain about what the situation really was had been the guy holding the video camera for the giant vidscreen, who had gotten the hell out of there at the first sight of the alien—no fool there; if it wasn't on the program schedule, he wasn't worrying about taping it. No one down there had the sense to connect his abandonment of his post with the alien and the sudden appearance of two dozen security men running toward the stage. Some people, in fact, were shouting a parody of rhythm to Mozart's screams and pushing through the mob toward the stage, waving their arms at the alien and trying to sing along with the fragmented words that were still coming from what was left of the lead singer's head at one side of the floor. Junkies, Brangwen saw in dismay, their opened vials clutched high as they worked their way amid their fellow ticket-holders, all no doubt brethren to the long-dead Ken Petrillo. Every one of them convinced they heard the same righteous wailing of love and music embedded within the alien's screams.

The audience's approval as Mozart annihilated the last of the band members was thunderous, their adulation consummate as the creature finished his presentation by spinning and crushing what remained of the Helltones' lead singer's head—the top half, stuck in a recorded loop of *"My knife of lo—CHIK! My knife of lo—CHIK! My knife of lo—CHIK!"*

Horrified, Michael clutched the edge of the balcony and watched in a daze as Mozart, his work on stage completed with a final, vicious hiss at a microphone before he pulverized it, reared and faced the audience.

Some of the fools were trying to struggle past the throng of shouting security guards and clamber onto the stage itself, reaching happily for what they still thought was an android that wouldn't harm them. The first to die were two of the faux leather-jacketed security men, taken out in a swift flash of teeth and claws that only an unfortunate few were close enough to see—those witnesses were next, slaughtered still in the act of turning tail and trying to flee.

Pandemonium ensued. In the overhanging balcony, Michael found himself screaming uselessly at the people below, beating on the balcony's railing in an effort to make people hear his cries of warning. From up here it looked like people were spontaneously disintegrating in small explosions of blood and body matter seconds after Mozart reached them; Michael's shouts were lost in the chaotic combination of those who were still convinced it was all part of the show and those who'd had a sudden change of heart and decided to get the hell out. Abruptly Michael turned to flee, his choice with the later group; having seen from up close what Mozart could do, the bioengineer had no desire to join the firsthand experience club. Better to be among the survivors who would remember and have nightmares than be one of the mucky puddles of remains.

Mozart was tearing a bloody path through the first three rows when Michael pushed his way to the side aisle and headed for the exit while others in the balcony couldn't make up their minds whether to stay or go. Still babbling at people who wouldn't listen, unable to stop himself, Michael was halfway up the aisle when he passed three men in armored white uniforms that he didn't recognize. The police? Some sort of special army unit? He had no idea, and his thoughts were too disjointed to sort it out right now. One thing he was sure of: Whoever they were, the three guys who were sprinting *into* the fray and headed for the edge of the balcony, pulling out an assortment of weapons as they went, were probably the only hope left for the people on the main floor.

26

"Let's go, people—come on, clear it out!" Rice shouted at the people scrambling around in the balcony aisle. "Let us through, damn it!" He glanced back at McGarrity and Morez. "So much for keeping this quiet!" His words could barely be heard over the yells and screams of the crowd. He had thought the panic was contained on the first floor, but for some reason it had started spreading upstairs, too.

"No kidding, Chief." Morez pointed over the balcony's railing. "Look—there's our hatchling, down on the main floor."

"Where—aw, *crap!*" Thirty feet below the balcony, a full-grown alien was energetically cutting his way through anything soft within reach. Still swearing, the security chief struggled to get the backpack off. He was unzipping it when his men leaned on the railing, their weapons ready.

"Pretty good size for his age," McGarrity said

grimly. He and Morez didn't need to be told to fire on the alien, and a moment later the sound of weapons fire split the commotion caused by the fleeing and screaming crowd; another instant and the noise doubled as the people who hadn't been leaving decided it was time to head for the hills. Finally the ones who still believed it was all part of the show were getting a clue.

Morez cursed as he missed his target. Armed with a LaserFire .385 pistol, his weapon was an excellent choice but the alien's movements were too fast and trying to follow with the laser beam as the creature bounded erratically across the floor invariably left a smoking streak across some hapless man or woman. McGarrity's aim with the scope on his Redsteine .440 was better but still ineffective; the bullets of laser light did little beyond make surface stings on the alien's teeth and carapace that only served to enrage him more. Every time a bullet hit, it seemed like the creature swiped at the spot in fury, then clawed at some poor schmuck as retaliation.

McGarrity's swear words joined his partner's. "Damn it! I wish we could make armor out of whatever it is that makes up his teeth. You better get the grenade popper together quick, Chief—they're dying by the bunch!"

"Almost . . . there," Rice affirmed. He had opened the plastic backpack and was now concentrating on the contents spread on the littered floor at his feet. He pulled out a number of items and swiftly screwed them together. "Just . . . a few more . . . seconds—" A firm turn of his wrist and the final weapon was loaded.

"Ready."

His men automatically moved back as Rice leaned one elbow on the balcony railing to steady his arm. With a flick of his hand, he plugged in the visual sight that ran from the launcher to his helmet. When his point of view found the alien, the carnage around the creature made him grimace. Mozart had just finished crushing the head of an unfortunate man in a suit who would be lucky to be identified later on. "Time to say good night," Rice said under his breath as the creature flung the man aside like a broken doll. Rice's forefinger sought the trigger, then fell comfortably into position. The sight from the eyepiece of his helmet showed the long silver barrel stretching in front of him; he moved it slightly to the right and the alien's form filled the target. In another second he'd locked on, the visor showing him a bloodred spot centered on the alien's chest.

"There's plenty more where you came from, pal."

Rice fired.

There was a sound like a mini-rocket launching as the explosive-filled red and green grenade shot from the launcher. Before the smell of the acrid smoke left in its wake could sink into their sinuses, the streak of fire found its mark and plunged into the alien's chest cavity, biting easily through the protective rib cage. A millisecond later, in time with Mozart's blistering death scream, the grenade exploded. The sound of the blast made everyone in the concert hall, Rice and his men included, instinctively duck.

Sometimes, Rice thought as he struggled back to his feet and leaned over the railing to stare below, the cure could be as bad as the illness. This situation was a classic example, as the concertgoers with the misfortune to be within splashing distance who weren't hit by flying pieces of shrapnel and jagged chunks of alien carcass and carapace were showered with globules of the creature's acid blood. Wails of agony joined the feedback still blaring from the speakers and the shrieks of those caught between panic and flight. With an abruptness that left a hollow ringing in their ears, all sound from the speakers stopped—somebody in the control room, finally pulling the master switch. From somewhere outside, carrying through the layers of the building by flung-open doors, they heard a multitude of sirens screaming toward the concert hall.

McGarrity and Morez joined Rice at the railing, peering over to make sure the battle was finished. Bodies littered the floor amid the smoking puddles of alien blood, too many tangled limbs to count from their positions. "What do you think?" McGarrity said. "Should we help clean it up?"

"Hell, no. We've done what we could, and more than the Synsound bastards deserved." Rice stood and swung the grenade launcher over one shoulder, then bent to pick up the backpack. "They made the mess, let them straighten it out." He looked at his men with a grim expression on his dark face. "Now it's time to go get ol' Blue and find out what the hell this was all about."

27

Amid the chaos, no one saw Ahiro and his best two men slip into Presley Hall through one of the many back entrances and swiftly make their way down to the apiary. They'd received the alert via Morton's silent signal, and while Ahiro didn't know the details of what the situation was, Presley Hall's chief of security hadn't been ordered to carry a satellite beeper linked to Ahiro so he could call the Japanese man for trivial matters. The summons could mean only one thing: Something was endangering the apiary, and Ahiro could not allow that to happen.

When they glided silently through the main entrance to the secret laboratory, however, what they found brought all three to a halt.

Then Ahiro strode to where Michael Brangwen stood, staring down at the mangled remains of Damon Eddington. "What happened here?" Ahiro demanded, looking from the dead man to the alien squatting complacently within the holding area. "How did—wait! That is not the same beast!" Dismayed, he stared at the thing on the other side of the glass.

"No," Michael agreed, "it's not." There was no question about it; the creature in Mozart's cage was bigger and older, with a darker cast to his carapace that made it more midnight-blue than Mozart's black color. Behind the bracket of some kind of muzzle, its teeth were long and yellowed with age, and its sinewy arms were held firmly at its sides by a series of mesh sheets that connected in a sort of harness. Three long poles were connected to the harness at various points, and a thin tube made of steel and plastic fibers was embedded deep into the rear of the alien's lower jaw; at its opposite end, the tube terminated in a small gray box with a bright red button on it. Except for his steady hissing, the alien, which had a more elongated and scarred shell covering its huge head, was strangely calm.

Ahiro hooked a finger onto the material of Brangwen's coat and pulled the bioengineer to face him. "Then where is Mr. Eddington's alien?" he asked. Thoughts spun in his head: the need to find the alien, not for Eddington but for Yoriku; the mystery of how they would return the creature to its cage, since Ahiro knew only how to kill them, not capture. Most of all, a sense of burgeoning shame at his failure to keep safe one of the possessions that Yoriku treasured so highly. He had thought Eddington was through with his musical project now that the last of the five men had been sacrificed to Mozart. What insane thing had the artist tried to do that had brought about this destruction?

"I think Mozart's upstairs," Michael told him. The older man's face was pale and covered with perspiration, lined with the ravages of fear and shock. He waved his hands at the composer's mutilated corpse. "I don't know how it got out—Eddington must have done that, but I don't know *why.* I can't even find Darcy. But the alien was upstairs in the concert hall, Ahiro—just . . . *slaughtering* everyone in its way. It was terrible, death everywhere, people screaming and dying. I-I ran, but I didn't know where else to go except back down here to see what happened. When I was leaving the balcony, there were three men just going in—"

At the sound of clattering footsteps behind them, Ahiro and his men automatically whirled and raised their swords. He heard only part of Michael's next words—"Yes, those three!"—before he dismissed the presence of the older bioengineer from his mind. Three against three, he thought clearly. But as Ahiro and his men dropped instinctively into a fighting stance and began to move forward to close the forty-foot distance between them and their targets, he also knew they would never win.

"My life for you, Yoriku," Ahiro whispered. "My destiny, for my friend, and my savior."

Sacrifice time.

"Hold it right there," Rice ordered coldly. "Don't move a muscle." There were three of them, dressed in historical ninja garb and holding wicked-looking swords. Rice didn't know whether to be afraid or to laugh now that he was actually seeing them . . . *ninjas?* What kind of a corporate covert security team was that? Then again, he *had* heard that Synsound's CEO was a traditional kind of guy who still held to centuries-old Japanese customs. Never underestimate, he reminded himself as he remembered the dead alien watchdogs back in the secret lab at MedTech; these guys were probably handpicked killers. Come to think of it, their swords were just the thing to succeed against one of the Homeworld creatures. Slice and dice on those arm and leg joints and a man could dance a jig around an alien, so long as he stayed out of range of that nasty double-mouthed head.

Still, swords against firepower left a lot of room for failure.

In spite of Rice's warning, the three ninjas began a soft, fleet-footed advance, knees bent and swords upraised. Rice wasn't about to let them get *too* close—

and the combination of a trained martial arts leap and the full-armed swing of a hand bearing a sword meant they had about . . . oh, eighteen inches leeway.

"I'm only going to tell you this one time. I am not fucking around," Rice warned again. "Halt or we'll fire." He dropped the grenade launcher—reloaded on the way back here—into position from its strap on his shoulder but their three opponents kept coming, the two in the rear following at the heels of their hard-headed leader. Their stubborn silence was eerie; was it just in the antique movies that ninjas made those screaming noises when they attacked? As the leader took another step and tensed to leap, Rice decided not to find out.

McGarrity and Morez had learned through the years to follow Rice's body language, and their shots were nearly simultaneous with their chief's. With just under twenty feet separating the two groups, the swords were no competition for the MedTech team's heavy firepower; had the laser beam and bullets not found their marks—and they did—Rice's grenade would have finished the Japanese trio anyway.

A four-second burst of light and noise, and the distinctly one-sided battle was over.

"Now there's a waste of your life," Morez said in disgust as he lowered his LaserFire pistol. "What the hell did they fight for? We would've let 'em go."

"Bah—who knows how those weirdos think?" McGarrity pushed the edge of one of the dropped swords to the side with the barrel of his Redsteine. "They're living in the wrong time period, and still trying to fight the same way."

Rice snorted. "You see how much good it did them. Technology wins again and they bite the big one for nothing." He flicked the power switch on the grenade launcher to OFF and didn't bother to load it again, then his gaze swept the room. It was full of dead bodies—the three fools who had tried to attack them, the other man several feet away by the entrance to the cage that they'd put ol' Blue into. Given the choice, Rice thought he would have preferred to die the way the ninjas had—it actually looked more merciful. The dark-haired guy on the floor resembled a rag doll that had been turned inside out.

Standing silently a few feet away was someone Rice and his men hadn't seen before, an older man with thick white hair and a neatly trimmed mustache. Dressed in clothes that seemed too young for him, his glassy, shocked eyes were wide above the grim line of his mouth. It was doubtful the guy had simply wandered in here, so he must know something about what was going on—who the dead men on the floor were, why this place had been constructed, and who had engineered it, *who had stolen MedTech's egg.* Why, this man was the answer to a whole slew of questions that had been eating at Rice for quite some time.

As the man finally seemed to regain the ability to focus on his surroundings, Rice met his gaze and found himself beginning to smile.

28

"I'm Chief Phillip Rice, MedTech Security. I think we need to have a little conversation," the security officer said. His teeth were very white and in perfect, enviable condition as he smiled. There was nothing friendly about the expression. "And there are some minor matters that need to be cleared up, Mr.—" He looked at Michael pointedly.

In Presley Hall, the thundering of the weapons discharging as Michael had fled had been swallowed up by the crowd, simply more big noises amid the screams. There the weapons of the white-suited men had sounded like airhammers and the whine of the laser bullets ricocheting off the walls had made Michael's teeth ache until he'd escaped the frenzy and fled back here.

But the nightmare wasn't over; now it faced him in the form of this brawny black man with the commanding voice who was wearing what Michael ultimately recognized as the power uniform of MedTech's Elite Security Force.

"Brangwen," Michael finally managed to choke out.

"Brangwen." The smile was already gone, replaced by a look that would have frozen boiling water. "We can start with the identity of the person who stole the alien egg."

Michael wasn't going to be senseless enough to pretend he didn't know what the man was talking about; instead, he decided to try a different tactic. "Do you have jurisdiction here?" he asked uncertainly. "You're from MedTech, not the metro police—"

"Anything involving an alien—from the egg to the jelly to the creature itself—is considered a drug investigation and falls within our purview. So you can answer our questions here or . . . let's just say I can make life really miserable for you. *If* I decide to let you live." The flashing smile reappeared, then dropped off his face again with alarming swiftness. "I'm getting pretty fucking tired of all these games. It's your choice, old man," he said frostily. "What'll it be?"

When Michael looked at him helplessly, the man nodded and folded his arms. "I thought so. I'll keep it simple and to the point." Suddenly the MedTech security officer was right in his face, and Michael could hear suppressed fury in the man's voice as his hot, heavy breath washed over the bioengineer's face. A few feet behind their chief, the other two men looked absurdly amused.

"Who stole the egg, damn it?"

Michael started to point at Damon Eddington, then realized that doing so wouldn't be entirely truthful. If he lied now, he would be as guilty as any of the dead men, and it wasn't his fault that the egg had been stolen; he was just a Synsound employee, one more flunkie worker in the hive. When the assignment to work on this project had come to his desk, he had packed up his materials and gone, the age-old employer/employee connection automatically coming into play: *You want me to jump? How high?* As far as he was concerned, the egg had been "procured."

"He—they did," he finally answered, his damning finger moving from the direction of Eddington's corpse to the blasted remains of Ahiro and his ninjas. "They were the ones who brought it here, anyway."

Rice's gaze flicked from Ahiro to Eddington. "And who *wanted* it? Him?"

Michael nodded. "He was going to make music from its screams—a symphony. He—"

Rice waved his hand impatiently in the air and Michael shut up. Apparently this man didn't care about the details, and who could blame him? With nearly everyone dead, the information Michael could fill in was limited anyway. The chain of command pretty much ended here with Ahiro; above him was Keene, but Michael would bet that slippery son of a bitch would simply point right back at the dead Japanese man and say that personally he'd known nothing about it. Any paper or computer trail would be obliterated—hell, it probably already had been.

"And what about those people? Who were they?"

Michael jumped, then flushed deeply when he realized that Rice was standing at the window to the alien enclosure, staring past the new alien to the scattering of bones inside. There was no disguising the fact that many . . . well, *most* . . . of the bones that were still recognizable were human. It was strange to see a Homeworld life-form sitting so quietly, not the slightest bit interested in its surroundings; Michael hadn't realized they could be controlled like that. "I-I don't know," he said truthfully. "The first man was a jelly cultist who volunteered to hatch the egg. I was told the rest were drifters and addicts, people like that. I didn't like it, but there was nothing I could do. I'm just an employee . . ." Michael heard himself starting to whine and closed his mouth abruptly. There remained the question of the identity of the man who Michael clearly remembered had claimed to be a MedTech executive, but what good would revealing that do now? The project had already blown up in Synsound's corporate face and the responsible parties, most of them at least, were dead. Who was left to prosecute for being involved in this—and there was no doubt that MedTech would prosecute if it discovered that one of its own employees had literally been fed to Mozart in some secret Synsound laboratory—besides him? Darcy perhaps, but he made himself believe that she was probably at home and knew nothing about what had happened here tonight. Anyway, why should the two bioengineers, the grunts of the whole project, take the fall for the high-powered businessmen? On the other hand, if the man questioning Michael found out later that he had lied . . .

"Interesting," Rice muttered. His eyes glittered as he looked at Michael, then back to the grisly contents of the cage. The older man's heart thudded painfully. "It could be anyone in there. Maybe we should—"

"Maybe we should give ol' Blue in there another dose of dope if we're going to stick around here much longer," one of the other MedTech men suggested. "Before he starts to come out of it."

Rice glanced at the alien thoughtfully, then turned away from the glass with a shake of his head. "Nah—forget it. Let's just pack him up and head back to MedTech. Listen to me carefully, old man." He pointed emphatically at Michael, then at the dead men at their feet. "See what fucking around with MedTech and its property got these fools?" His hand went to his helmet and he pulled down a dark blue visor that covered half his face, but Michael could still see a hint of his dangerous gaze. "You tell Synsound not to try this kind of shit again unless it wants a full-fledged war. If they do, I'll be happy to oblige."

Rice and his men were gone quickly, after less than three minutes of grappling with the guidepoles on the harness that was strapped around their alien. Now the apiary lab was empty and silent, the only sound the quiet hum of the computers that were never powered down and the fainter noise of the air circulation units. It had been a long time since this place was this hushed, without even the sound of alien hissing to cut through the stuffy room.

Where *was* Darcy, anyway? Michael had speculated earlier that she'd gone home, but that couldn't be—they were still under orders not to leave Presley Hall. A scarier, sadder possibility was that between Damon's madness and her fixation with the alien's behavior, she might be one of the butchered lumps of flesh within Mozart's now-empty enclosure that Michael couldn't bring himself to examine more closely. It was a cruel end for a young woman, and she didn't deserve to die for being, like himself, another of Synsound's foolish, dedicated puppets. Wandering from one piece of equipment to another, loath to stay but afraid to leave, Michael's mind craftily filled in the voices that were missing from the room, *all* of them—from Damon Eddington, Ken Petrillo and the other dead subjects, to Darcy's and that of the overbearing MedTech Security Chief who had just left. Payback on this project was going to be heavy, and this was a room full of ghosts; among the guilty, he was the only survivor.

Michael wasn't sure, but he thought the next step was to call Keene, but he decided to leave that mess to the two Presley Hall security men, who were still alive when he checked them. They could handle that end of things when they came around—no doubt Rice and his men had injected them with something to keep them out of the way. Pacing around the room and going from body to body with a sort of undeniable morbid fascination, Michael stopped by Ahiro's corpse and stared down at the Japanese man. Alive, Ahiro had worn a perpetual slight frown that had accentuated the scar across his eyebrow and made him look continually ominous and unapproachable, definitely someone you didn't want holding a grudge against you. In death, his face was smooth and surprisingly unlined, as if he'd had little to worry about during his lifetime beyond whatever orders were issued by . . . who? Michael couldn't see Mr. Keene as having that kind of hold over this man who had been simultaneously unconcerned about Keene but passionate about fulfilling Eddington's every wish, and he still remembered Eddington's puzzled look when he and Darcy had first mentioned Ahiro. Obviously, Ahiro had acted on the orders of someone much more elevated in the Synsound hierarchy; Yoriku, perhaps, but at this point, Michael would probably never be sure. He thought briefly of going through the man's pockets on the auspices of looking for the name of someone to call, and even started to bend and gingerly pat the side pockets of Ahiro's black slacks. Abruptly Michael dismissed the idea; doing so would obligate him to do the same for Eddington, and frankly, that was Synsound's job. They'd gotten themselves into this situation; they could handle the dirty work of notifying family members themselves. Before he straightened, however, Michael saw something white clipped to the inside of the right pocket of the dead man's pants, a plastic card that would have been invisible when Ahiro was walking around. Curiosity wouldn't let Michael ignore it, and a closer inspection showed it to be a computer keycard with a MedTech logo on it. Across the bottom in Ahiro's spiky writing—Michael recognized it from the signatures on a hundred work orders and disbursements—was the name "Eddie McGarrity." The name sounded familiar—had he seen it somewhere recently?—but he couldn't tie it into anything. Perhaps among the blameworthy in this death-soaked project, there were even those at MedTech.

It was time to leave this place. Surely the orders to stay on the grounds were moot now that the project had been destroyed. The smell of blood crawled up his nose like wet metal and permeated the room, and Michael decided he might as well get out of here before it settled into his clothes and forced him to carry this ordeal home. He was still hearing voices in his head, whispers of blame as he remembered himself not, perhaps, protesting enough when all those men were fed to Mozart as part of Eddington's experiment. As he gathered up the few personal items he'd brought in, he thought he could hear Darcy's voice, too, unaccountably louder than the accusing murmurs in his own head. It wasn't until he'd swept his belongings into a bag and stopped for a final look around that he began to think it *wasn't* his imagination after all. Standing suddenly still and silent in the center of the bloodied lab, clutching his paper bag by its edges to halt the sound of crumpling paper, there was no mistaking it—

"Help . . ."

Faint, but there—*somewhere.*

When the cry came again, Michael dropped the bag and ran through the gaping entrance to the alien enclosure, his heart suddenly pounding painfully inside his chest. Was it Darcy? It sounded like her, but it was so faint it was hard to tell, and he didn't trust his overactive imagination not to lie when it told him that it was his companion bioengineer. Stepping into Mozart's cage was like stepping into a portion of hell and the smell of decomposing flesh made Michael gag outright, temporarily blotting out the nearly inaudible call. It was little comfort knowing that the slowly disintegrating piles of . . . *meat* around him could never have talked; he was half-afraid that any one of them—or *all* of them—would sit up and grab at his ankle as he scurried past.

"Please . . ."

He hesitated at the mouth of the escape tunnel, fighting a sudden bout of claustrophobia. The voice was definitely feminine—it *had* to be Darcy. But how on earth had she gotten in here? If she'd gone in after the alien was freed, there would be no reason for her to be trapped. The only other way Michael could think of for her to end up inside the enclosure was—

Eddington!

Heart thudding, the older bioengineer scrambled into the tunnel, gritting his teeth against a concentrated smell that was ten times worse than it was in the larger outer chamber. He was shocked to see the walls of the tunnel encrusted with dark, gooey resin in deep, circular ridges that were clearly the instinctive setup for future nesting. Climbing over a corpse with sticky locks of blond hair showing above the whitish strands of cocoon material was like seeing a nightmare with his eyes wide open, and Michael hoped to God he found the source of the cry for help soon—

"Here . . ."

—because he really didn't think the overloaded heart in his aging, pudgy body could take much more of this.

Finally, the side tunnel; too small for Mozart but Michael could fit—barely—and he inched his way along the steel-gray length, bruising his knees and elbows, banging his head too many times to count as he realized he was following a trail of sticky blood. He could see the other end of the tunnel where, true to Eddington's cruel nature, it intersected the larger tunnel that had easily accommodated Mozart's oversize body. The opening was clear, which meant that only one place could've held Darcy undetected for this long: the small escape hatch that Michael had nearly forgotten about. When he finally pulled himself to its edge and peered over, his mouth dropped open. Darcy was there, all right, her face pale and bloodless and seeming to float in the darkness below. He reached for her instinctively, finding her hands and wrapping his fingers around hers; her skin was moist, waxy, and frigid, the fingernails blue. "Darcy," he managed, "are you hurt? Can you climb out?"

"Can't," she whispered, "he . . . got my ankle." Her eyes were dull and barely open. "Listen to . . . me. Have to . . . tell you." She fought to keep going, her voice fading in and out like the poor reception of an antique transistor radio. "I was . . . right about . . . establishing a . . . *bond*, Michael. Remember? What I told you . . . before . . . what we talked about? Mozart, he . . . hesitated. Just for . . . a moment."

Her voice dropped away and Michael reached for her, frantically checking for a pulse. He found one, but it was erratic and thready, and he didn't dare try to drag her out of the tunnels by himself. Clambering his way down to the opening at the opposite end, intent on the telephone in the outer lab of the apiary, he couldn't help but marvel about the fixation that still existed in Darcy's heart for this project. Lying there, too weak to reach the alarm and nearly dead, perhaps not expecting to survive as she forced herself to tell him about it . . .

Michael could have sworn she was *smiling.*

29

"Come on in." Ricky Morez beamed at them from the doorway to his flat. "I'm really glad you both could come. You're just in time—the nightly news is about to start and they're supposed to show the piece about the Presley Hall attack."

Rice stepped to the side to let Tobi go inside first, secretly impressed with Morez's manners and flawless invitation. Rice had mentioned earlier on the phone that he was bringing a guest but he hadn't said who, and if Morez had been surprised to see Tobi Roenick, nothing had shown on his face. Layered against the damp spring weather, Rice could feel perspiration building beneath the collar of the shirt he wore under a brightly colored sweater. Leaving his jacket in the front hall closet with Tobi's didn't help a bit, and Rice was beginning to wish he'd come alone or not at all. Losing a hundred credits to Morez was nothing compared to what Tobi would do to him if she ever got a hint that this date could be traced back to a bet made on an alien egg hunt. While he really had suggested this as their first date as a way of diffusing the strain of a one-on-one evening, Rice knew he would have a terrible time convincing her of that if the business about the wager ever came to light. Morez was okay, but McGarrity—that asshole couldn't keep a secret if his mother's life depended on it.

"Hey, Phil!" Eddie McGarrity's voice boomed from one end of the couch in the living room as Rice and Tobi walked in. "Hi ya, Tobi. Come on over and meet my friend, Belinda." A cooling flash of relief—*safe!*—swept through Rice as he saw the pretty young woman with auburn hair and gray eyes sitting next to McGarrity. If the Irishman was stupid enough to mention the bet now, it'd be a self-imposed social suicide for both of them. Thus far McGarrity hadn't said anything rude or made a big deal out of Tobi's unexpected appearance. The truth was, Rice would just as soon forget the damned wager had ever been made and let Morez keep his money. McGarrity might bitch about it, but it was a small price to pay to keep Morez quiet. For all Rice knew, that might have been the plan all along.

Introductions were quickly made as Tessa Morez brought in a tray bearing six wine goblets and a couple of straw-wrapped bottles of Chianti that had already been uncorked. Ricky was still pouring when they heard the familiar jingle that signaled the beginning of the six o'clock broadcast.

"*Good evening from Manhattan's Channel One,*" said the newsman gravely, "*your First Choice in News. Still running as one of our top stories this evening, we can now bring you complete coverage on the massive slaughter that took place last week at Presley Hall.*" On his face was an expression that was appropriately grim. "*As we previously reported when we first began coverage of the story, a Homeworld alien ran rampant through the first-floor crowd gathered at Synsound's famous Presley Hall to hear a performance by the wildly popular group, the Helltones.*

While details were at first sketchy, today the final death count rests at seventeen with injuries totaling thirty-two more, four of whom remain in critical condition. New details include this footage—"

Here the anchorman's face winked out in favor of a panoramic but suspiciously fuzzy shot of the carnage at Presley Hall showing sprawled bodies, both human and android. Bits and pieces of the alien were splattered across the floor, leaving acidic puddles of smoking residue amid the lurid crimson stains of human blood and milky android nutrient fluid.

"*—shot after the alien was destroyed by this man—*"

A new image showed a gaunt-faced man with a heavy black mustache. The dusky coloring of his face was nearly obscured by a large, dark-tinted eye shield coming out of a helmet painted olive-drab to match his military-type uniform. Something like a radio microphone fed from his helmet to his mouth, and resting on one padded shoulder was a type of mini-rocket launcher manufactured a decade ago and now used primarily by mercenary guerrillas.

"*—presumed to be either an illicit weapons or drug dealer. His identity and whereabouts remain unknown at this time.*"

Rice and all of his companions except Belinda were listening with rapt attention and the more the story unfolded, the more absurd it became to them. The shot on the television changed again, this time to a grainy close-up of the alien when it had still been alive, presumably edited from the tape in one of the high-mounted security cameras surrounding the stage. The creature's snout was covered with blood and filled with immense, spearlike teeth that made Belinda and Tessa wince. Ribbons of alien saliva and pieces of shredded flesh dangled from its jaws. Of the women, only Tobi maintained a calm, unchanging expression. Jesus, Rice thought admiringly, nothing ruffles her.

On the screen, the newscaster's face rearranged itself, trying to project more compassion as he began to recite the casualties. "*The families of the dead and the survivors and their families have each been personally invited by Mayor Kroschel to attend counseling sponsored by HeartWeb, the city's newest emotional trauma counseling center and the fifty-third of its kind to open since the mayor's term began."* On cue, the man's expression went from sympathetic to solemn. *"The creature that was destroyed is believed to be one of an infestation found in the city's sewer system. A search and destroy team exterminated the other seven aliens found there earlier today, and the Health and Safety Commissioner has assured the city that there will be no further incidents."*

Sewer system, my happy little ass, Rice thought in disgust. He saw a flicker of a frown pass across Tobi's eyes and knew she felt the same. The rest of the account was sufficient considering it was a hurriedly fabricated yarn to cover up the public deaths although they were pushing it a bit on the low death count, but . . . *sewer system?* That was the part Rice and his men had protested, but clearly some muckity-muck in the MedTech hierarchy had overruled his suggestion that they find somewhere else to place the blame. Stupid, *stupid*; the whole concept of underground tunnels was too easily distorted by the viewers that MedTech was foolishly assuming were inattentive. Their chief of security didn't have to stretch much to imagine the questions and essays that would pepper the newspapers for weeks to come, column after column of hysterical speculation every time some half-dead drunk or jelly junkie thought he saw an oversize rat anywhere near a manhole cover. The first of many such questions Rice predicted would land his way, in fact, was being vocalized in this very room by McGarrity's date. A perfect example of the conclusions to which people were *always* inclined to jump.

"Gee," Belinda said with a shake of auburn curls. "The sewer? That's under the whole city . . . isn't that an awfully large amount of ground to cover? How can the police be sure they got them all?"

Bingo, Rice thought. This time he lucked out and didn't have to answer; McGarrity beat him to it. "Motion scanners," Eddie told her. "The men and women wear them around their wrists while they walk through the pipeways."

Belinda frowned at her date and McGarrity had the good grace to look slightly ashamed. Her pretty, pixie-shaped face had taken on a look that was half disbelief, half irritation at being fed a line of bullshit. "No way, Eddie. I always heard those creatures basically hibernate until they have a reason to come out of it. I wouldn't think a man just walking around would be enough to bring them out. It certainly didn't do it on Homeworld—if you remember, we lost over a thousand people before we had a decent idea what we were up against."

"You're right, of course," Rice said, joining the discussion to redeem McGarrity as the newscaster spiraled into something else with an inane smile and Tessa silenced the screen with a flick of the remote. Down-to-earth McGarrity didn't have the best imagination and he could easily sour the entire evening by continuing to treat his new girlfriend like the undereducated bubblehead she clearly *wasn't.* Time to save his unimaginative butt. "But the army has scouting dogs that the tactical units send ahead. They're a lot like the canines taught to find bombs and drugs, except these animals are trained to detect hibernating aliens and sound an alarm. The aliens usually wake up when they hear the dogs, the motion detectors pick up the movement, and the crew knows where to go to kill them." There were a thousand holes in his quick story, but he thought he could get away with it as is. Part of it was actually true, but he had a strong hunch Belinda wouldn't appreciate the knowledge that the scout dogs had an average life span of a single mission; rarely did a dog flee fast enough to avoid being killed by the revived aliens.

"Really," was all Belinda said. She was still frowning, but Tessa and her husband smoothly turned the conversation in the direction of the coming meal and the spaghetti with meat sauce that had been promised to McGarrity. A good thing, too; in less than a week, Rice had answered enough questions about the Presley Hall farce to last him a year and he could feel unintentional impatience starting to taint his mood. Suffice to say that an appropriate amount of money had changed hands and ended up in certain well-connected pockets within the media; thus the right people had been . . . *persuaded* as to the content of the "real" story of the terrible tragedy at Synsound's Presley Hall. Overall, Rice was pleased at the final results: It had taken longer than anticipated to locate, but the hatched alien had been destroyed, Synsound had shuddered a bit on its corporate foundation, and the silence of the press would ensure the continued secrecy of MedTech's high security team and private research nest. This problem was over, and life, all in all, was a good thing again.

Now if he only knew how the hell Ahiro, the dead ninja, had gotten into MedTech's underground lab to begin with.

Three months had passed.

Spring had a tentative hold on Manhattan, trying valiantly to push out a few weak green buds along the spindly branches of the rare tree that still tried to grow in the inner city. In the full grip of summer, only the park areas—Central Park in particular, under careful supervision and who knew what kind of chemical experimentation by MedTech—could be said to be lush; right now, however, those trees and the grass were engaged in the yearly struggle to renew as much as any of their more unfortunate inner city brethren. Still, partly because of warmer than usual weather and a steady diet of gentle rainfall, leaves were finally starting to make tiny appearances here and there.

At Presley Hall, the Helltones were back in all their original, mutated glory, grinding out their most popular tunes amid a music system reengineered to be capable of sounds never before exploited in the music industry. The lead singer and his troupe looked and sounded the same, although inside the workings and movements were constructed more economically, and the number of programmed commands and range of response was considerably smaller. The aim here was disposability.

There was a first performance, with predictable songs and physical gyrations that defied visual explanation, even for mutadroids—all of which most of the people in the audience had seen a hundred times on videos or during prior performances. The second show had always been the best in the past, because that was when the people in the front rows could shout out requests for an encore and the 'droids would process the requests and randomly select a set of three or four songs to perform. As a tangible expense item, the Helltones were significantly cheaper now that the programming and microprocessors necessary to function at that level of memory and custom response could be eliminated. After all, none of the group would ever make it to the encore portion of the performance again.

The Manhattan ordinances that regulated live and electronic performances required Synsound to prominently warn the public of the nature of the group's act. The corporation chose to do it via the splashy lights and moving displays on the marquees that jutted from the outside of the building at five locations:

RETURN OF THE HELLTONES! NIGHT OF DEATH! THE FABLED PRESLEY HALL SLAUGHTERNIGHT RE-CREATED!

Inside, every detail had been painstakingly recreated from the footage in the security cameras, starting with the alarmingly life-size android re-creation of the alien that leaped onto the stage from an unseen perch above the platform. True to the memories of those among the gore-loving audience who had been there on the original bloody night, the Helltones' band members were the first to be destroyed, the fragments of their music—

"My knife of lo—CHIK! My knife of lo—CHIK! My knife of lo—CHIK!"

—rolling from the speakers as the immense vidscreen showed the carnage in close, panoramic shots that had been impossible on the original night. Its destruction on stage achieved, the oversize android alien moved into the crowd, systematically butchering some twenty-odd selected fans and jelly junkies in the first ten rows—androids all—as it followed its meticulously programmed instructions. Not a drop of human blood was spilled, not a single living soul was endangered, and the viewers and listeners, including those who now considered themselves fortunate to have been there for the genuine thing, adored it.

There had been a few lawsuits, but they were trivial against the deep pockets of the company that controlled the world's music. They were settled quickly and out of court, although Synsound wouldn't have cared otherwise. Court battles gave the lawyers in their legal department busywork and provided wonderful media exposure, especially if things got heated. The marketing division had used its creativity to turn the massacre into the biggest moneymaker the company had ever stumbled across, and the best part of it was that no live actor had to be paid an advance or royalties—ever. Now Synsound already had scriptwriters and composers laboring over fresh ideas combining concerts and what they now called the mutadroid audience participants in their acts: *performing androids.* An entire new department had been created to house several dozen eager artists and mechanical architects; now they were enthusiastically designing formerly undreamed of "alien" monsters to be included in future acts.

As always, the concert's ultimate moment was when the grenade split the alien android's carapace and the creature exploded. There was no acid alien blood to rain down upon the audience, no melting flesh or warm and sticky human blood—no real pain or mortal fear for anyone. Only the sound so lovingly engineered and coveted but never heard by Damon

Eddington, captured three months ago with faithful accuracy by Synsound's patented recording microphones despite the wails of the injured and dying . . .

The alien's death scream.

Soaring with dark and invisible wings above the heads of the concert hall's roaring multitude until the mob's own screams of delight swallowed it up.

31

Two blocks away, the late-evening crowd gathered at Gorasmi Recital House for the premiere of Damon Eddington's "Rage Symphony" was an altogether different one.

Peering between heavy maroon curtains, Michael Brangwen thought he knew what it felt like to be one of those small, insignificant spots of life staring into the face of the vast world that awaited.

Gorasmi was small, what the advertising department at Synsound liked to call *intimate*. Essentially that meant it could seat two hundred comfortably; beyond that number, the ticket holders would close down and simply shut the doors. Black-gray upholstered seats lined the small room until they disappeared into the shadows at its rear, and the best description of the stage was a forty-by-twenty slab of concrete under carpet. This was no concert-sized, standing-room-only hall reserved for Synsound's best moneymakers; rather, it was in rooms like these that

Damon Eddington had made his living for most of his musical career. If nothing else good could be said about the place, at least the sound system was top of the line, with a row of appropriately sized speakers placed strategically along the stage and a state-of-the-art music control console at the stage's center point.

Slipping back into the safe darkness behind the stage curtain, Michael brushed his hair back nervously, then eased out the rear stage door and made his way to the front entrance. Even the ticket taker didn't know him and he had to show his Synsound employee identification card to go inside without buying a ticket. The feeling of anonymity was frightening and nearly suffocating—that impression of being a tree bud returned—and again Michael thought of Eddington and how he had deteriorated so badly toward the end of his life. If things had been this lonely and overwhelming for the deceased composer, no wonder the man had gone insane.

The show wasn't due to start for another twenty minutes and there were no more preparations that Michael could think of to fiddle with. In less than a half hour, it would be a do-or-die situation, and he hadn't gone through the ordeal of the Eddington project and Mozart, followed by the last three months of painstaking work, to turn coward and abandon it all. Right now he just wanted to . . . mingle, blend in with the crowd, such as it was, and hear what they were saying, feel what he hoped was an air of anticipation. Among the small gathering of fans, he recognized a few of the faces in the sparse audience as local critics and his mouth turned down. Already he could tell by their expressions that they would not be kind, and Michael thought caustically that even in death, they continued to haunt Eddington, to condemn him before they ever heard the music. He set his shoulders and dismissed them as he continued on his way; as long as he stayed away from the reserved front row, no one would recognize him.

There wasn't much to hear. Fewer than twenty-five of the seats were taken and so much empty space lent the room an echoing quality that Michael found appealing although he wondered how it was going to affect the presentation. Most of the people were silent as they waited; others murmured to each other so quietly that Michael couldn't catch their words as he drifted down the side aisle toward the steps that led to the rear of the stage at the right side. Only one group of three were seated close enough to the end of a row for Michael to understand their preconcert conversation. The few sentences he caught brought a sad smile to his face.

"I heard he died instantly in a skiing accident," said the young black man in an expensive blue turtleneck who sat at the end of the row. "Massive head injuries—they had to have a closed funeral service."

In the middle of the three was a woman about the same age as her companion but with eyes the color of swimming-pool water and blunt-cut golden hair. An expensive necklace of amethysts adorned her neck and the matching earrings sparkled prettily as she tilted her head, puzzled. "I didn't know Eddington skied."

"He didn't," said the final member of the threesome as he studied his program.

As he passed out of earshot, Michael thought that the shaggy-cut hair and fashionably worn shirt of the final speaker seemed far more in keeping with the listeners Damon Eddington had spent his life trying to reach.

Yoriku saw Jarlath Keene and his escort for the evening in their seats as soon as he entered the recital hall. Engrossed in the woman seated beside him, his vice president didn't look up until Yoriku and his companion were standing in front of the seats that had been reserved for them.

"Jarlath," Yoriku said silkily. He extended a hand when Keene jumped to his feet with a wide, obviously practiced smile. They shook, Yoriku squeezing slightly harder than he should have, the most minute show of power that the other man didn't dare try to outdo. Yoriku knew it would eat at Keene to be bettered in so small a thing . . . just like he knew about the little games that Keene so often played and thought were such well-kept secrets. While it had provided some immense entertainment, in the end Keene's latest and greatest diversion had cost more than Yoriku had anticipated. Some things were irreplaceable, and tonight he would bring all those little amusements to a crumbling halt, annihilate the shaking foundation on which Keene had so stupidly based his existence. And tomorrow for Jarlath . . . ah.

Life was good, and Yoriku was always the victor.

"It's so good to see you, Yoriku." Jarlath beamed at them and indicated the woman at his side with a nod of his head. "This is Rilette." Keene's brunette date nodded and gave them a tight smile, eyeing Yoriku's companion suspiciously.

Yoriku looked past them to where Darcy Vance struggled to position her crutches so she could stand. Before she could succeed, he stepped forward and touched her arm. "Please, Ms. Vance," he said, "don't trouble yourself. It is good to see you up and about. You had us all quite concerned."

"I-I—thank you," she managed, her expression relieved. She looked considerably different from when he'd studied the video in her personnel file four or five months ago; now she was thin to the point of wasted and her eyes seemed overly large, sunken into her face above puffy, bruised skin. Some of that might be attributable to her injury, but her hair had changed, too—she had shaved it almost to fuzz on the sides and back, and left a flat-topped crown of gel-combed curls going up at least two inches. The style looked too radical for the restrained young woman he'd handpicked for the project; maybe it was her association with Eddington that had done it, a dose of his strange, so-called artistic influence and musical "genius" permeating her personality.

Or perhaps, Yoriku mused, in another year Darcy would end up just like the dead composer, an addict obsessed with a creature she could never control; a shame, really, because Yoriku had always known that Damon was destined to die for his art, but Darcy had always struck him as the sort of woman who lived, rather than died, for her work. Decades of this business had taught Yoriku that musicians and artists were weak people, so very malleable. How easy it had been to have Ahiro slip that vial of jelly into Ken Petrillo's pocket in such a way that it was guaranteed to roll out, how predictable that Damon Eddington would be unable to resist its lure, how downright *laughable* that Jarlath had thought *he* had invented and manipulated more than a sliver of the entire project. And Eddington . . . no doubt the composer had spent hours justifying his jelly dependence and absolving himself of any wrongdoing by reason of his imagined mastery. Given those factors, for Eddington to become an addict was nearly preordained, as was his death in the name of his music. No matter what the critics said, the success of Eddington's "Rage Symphony," as Michael Brangwen had elected to rename it, was clinched the moment Synsound's press release had hit the NewsVids and papers. Carefully engineered advertising and promotion programs would ride the swells of popularity and see to it that the same waves were continually well fed. All those complicated things about which Keene knew nothing beyond the fulfillment of some piddling revenge trip, and one not even successfully carried through to its ending. In truth, dead musicians were so much more popular, so *identified* with, that Synsound's expensive promo push on Eddington's behalf would be more than worthwhile; how ironic that Eddington's music would finally have the support that could have made the man a success in his life.

Darcy, Jarlath, and—what was it?—Rilette were looking at him expectantly and Yoriku allowed himself a final, brief moment of satisfaction before turning to the woman whose delicate hand was now so warmly tucked into the bend of his elbow. Never before had he bothered to socialize with Jarlath or introduce the man to anyone among his inner circle, another thing that he was positive played a major part in Keene's continuous plans to undermine and embarrass him. Yoriku's lady friend was wearing an outfit sewn from virtually nothing but a multitude of black scarves inset with glittering bits of gold-tinted cubic zirconia, an ensemble that sent a mixed message of mourning and affluence. Such an odd thing to wear to the world premiere of Damon Eddington's Symphony of Hate, and no doubt Keene was assuming that Yoriku was accompanied by a new mistress.

Keene couldn't have been more wrong.

Yoriku steered his companion carefully forward and she began gracefully pulling aside the sparkling material obscuring her face. While he smiled graciously at all of them, his eyes were trained on Keene's face as the man's smug expression began to falter. "This is my companion," Yoriku said. He kept his voice mild but took great pains to make the words as formal as possible. "She has recently returned after a short business assignment and comes to hear the 'Rage Symphony' in the midst of mourning for her brother, who died to help make it possible. You remember him, of course—Ahiro?" Yoriku's gaze was bright and sharp in the low light of the recital hall as Keene nodded woodenly. Beside him, Darcy had perked up considerably as she listened.

Next to Yoriku, his companion had pulled away the last of the scarves and now stood regally at his side. One look at the exquisite oriental woman had made Rilette turn her face sullenly toward the stage; her expression was so rigid that a tap on the cheekbone might have shattered it. Yoriku's next words certainly didn't help matters. "Jarlath, I believe you and my lady friend have met."

Keene's brain was screaming at him—*danger! danger! danger!*—

—long before the face beneath the gauzy black fabric was fully revealed. Yoriku's chuckle seemed to come from an immense distance as the woman locked gazes with him. For an instant Keene was enveloped in flash memories of black glitter in a starless room; then he was sure that someone had stolen the air from his lungs and covered his head in a suffocating plastic pillowcase as Yoriku serenely continued with the remainder of his dignified introduction.

Had the older man said *business assignment*? Sweet Jesus, Yoriku had *known* about Keene's plans the entire time, had probably masterminded more than Keene could comprehend—

"Of course you know Jarlath Keene, my dear," Yoriku said silkily. "Jarlath, this is . . .

"Mina."

Returning behind the curtain, Michael risked one final peek through its dusty folds and wondered if Eddington would have appreciated the presence of the people who sat in the front row. Already seated was Jarlath Keene and his companion, a woman who had to be less than half his age and who hung on his arm like a tenacious vine to a windowsill. On his other side, grasping a set of crutches that jutted above her seat, was Darcy Vance. Of course she would be here after nearly dying because of the project, how could she miss what the program book announced as *The World Premiere of Damon Eddington's Rage Symphony as completed by Michael Brangwen?* He hadn't been sure about calling her and offering her the complimentary pass, but she hadn't been shocked or offended. Rather, she had made it clear that she was *delighted* that Michael had finished the composition. Her presence here tonight and eager expression were proof that she'd been telling the truth.

Right before the lights dimmed, Michael was surprised to see the three in the front row joined by two more, none other than Synsound's esteemed chief operating officer himself. At his side, moving so smoothly she seemed more a fragile butterfly than a human being, was a woman swathed in black chiffon sprinkled with faint, glittering specks of gold. He was too far away to hear the introductions that were made, but he did see the woman's delicate fingers reach gracefully to the black folds hiding her face and draw them aside. Suddenly it didn't matter that he was yards away; Michael could tell that she was easily the most beautiful woman he'd ever seen, outshining and outclassing the instantly jealous lady Keene had chosen to escort this evening. Inexplicably, Keene's face drained of color as he stared at her; then the lights dimmed and the Synsound party sat back down.

Okay, Michael thought with a deep breath, here it is—the final work for which Damon Eddington, Ken Fasta Petrillo—and, yes, even Ahiro—had died to see created. Fingers resting on the controls as a single, shining yellow spotlight suddenly bathed his station, Michael closed his eyes for a second, then pressed the first of the keys that would fill the small recital hall with music and alien fury.

Sometime toward the end of the recital, his ears ringing with the screams of an alien dead a quarter year, Michael dared a glance at the audience. What he saw was a mixed blessing—the rapt enjoyment of the fans, the smug and self-assured expression on Yoriku's face, a puzzling, vague terror on Keene's. What drew him most was the distaste and disdain on the faces of those few reviewers sitting in the audience, notepads in hand with pens wielded like bloody-edged razors. Frustration, stronger than any he'd ever known, welled so sudden and fierce inside him that Brangwen's fingers almost stumbled on the arrangement. Outwardly calm, his movements deceptively smooth and precise, his thoughts were raging at their premature dismissal. All that work, the sacrificing of lives, the crippling of a lovely young woman, the *blood*—and look how little Eddington or he received in return for their efforts! Sneers and snide remarks, biting words that would be plastered in the columns of newspapers across the city for everyone to see.

Michael couldn't help the film of tears that slid across his vision. To be rejected like this, so thoroughly and in utter disregard for the humble offering by Eddington and himself of *everything*, was unforgivable, the ultimate accomplishment of human cruelty. Nothing that Eddington or Darcy or himself had ever done could equal or deserve such treatment.

So much rejection, the belittling of self-esteem that had haunted Eddington was too monumental for Michael to contemplate. Enough, though, to make him at last understand the true depth of the feelings that had lived in Eddington's dark and thwarted soul. Dawning comprehension at last, in perfect timing with the final sound for which the original composer had searched so diligently . . .

The ultimate scream, a resonance from the heart, soul, and death of Damon Eddington.

Epilogue

Spring, 2125

The warmth of the changing seasons and the promise of spring had done nothing to relieve the chilly interior of the building that sheltered The Church of the Queen Mother. The old wood that was haphazardly nailed across its broken windows and yawning doorways absorbed the dampness rather than the weak sunshine, drew the gray drizzle into itself and tried to squeeze it through the cracks to the molding walls on the inside. The street grates embedded in the sidewalks in front of the church rattled now and then as the surge of runoff in the sewers below swelled and ebbed with the spring rains, and in the filthy tides that moved below the metal covers the jelly junkies heard the sweet songs of their craving.

Inside, huddled together for warmth on the floor along the walls, the addicts waited dully for the next scheduled fix, their eyes trained on the door from which the preacher always came; at one time or another every one of them had surreptitiously tested its strength, only to discover that the barrier that looked like worn wood was really painted steel. Now, halfway into the first week of May, they dressed as warmly as they could, their clothes foraged from the trash bins and charity houses, their body's temperature gauge reversed by the jelly's strange biological influence.

With no clean place to sit, other junkies, more carefully clothed in their business suits and expensive designer dresses, milled about in the center of the well-lit room. They kept their heads down, intentionally avoiding the gazes of others like themselves for fear someone would recognize them—or worse, they would recognize someone whom they knew or cared about. Shuffling quietly, sidestepping the mutated cockroaches that darted between their shoes and grimacing as the more ill-fated people snatched at them for food, they stared vacantly into the darker shadows where the rats darted along the rotting baseboards and slipped in and out of the holes in the exposed plaster.

All this was home to the woman who had once been Darcy Vance.

She had been all right until the night Michael had gone through his presentation of Damon Eddington's "Rage Symphony." Recuperating at home with her school and medical expenses paid by Synsound and full disability as well, her life had been acceptable if not exactly fulfilled. She had thought that interest in the real world and all its normal affairs—eating and sleeping, among them—would return now that the alien portion of the Eddington project was over, but she'd been wrong. She ate enough to quell the hunger pains but that was all, and she slept only as long as her mind allowed; neither function was anything more than a necessity. With the recital's music ringing in her mind, the rest of the world slipped out of focus, like an outdated vidscreen that no one watched anymore.

Darcy had been up and around again a week after the recital, finally, dragging herself on errands and planning without any enthusiasm her return to work in Synsound's android repair lab the following Monday. She was still on crutches but not as dependent on the props when a man on the street said something bizarre to her—

"I know what you need and where to find it."

Such a strange, simple line . . . with so many *possibilities.*

Shabbily dressed below a bony face and long, wispy red hair, the man reminded her uncomfortably of Ken Petrillo, the addict who had sacrificed himself so that Mozart could be created.

Mozart . . .

Having the dead alien's screams fill her ears again at the hands of Michael Brangwen had sent longing through her, fierce, unforgettable, nearly unendurable. Mozart stalked her thoughts relentlessly, memories of his long, blue-black fingers reaching to meet hers on the other side of the glass, his loping gait around the enclosure as he attacked, the way his head had tipped sideways when she'd been thrust into the cage with him. Her job with Synsound had at its peak been intriguing, her life interesting, her hours alone at home limited only to time needed for personal hygiene and clean clothes. Compared to the hellish nothing that had come before it, the time she'd spent with Eddington, Michael, Ahiro, and Mozart had been an excellent existence, the pinnacle of her life so far.

Following the stranger could mean literally tossing that same life carelessly into the hands of the unknown, exposing herself to the whims of a stranger, possibly to a madman. But she had done all that before and survived, and now . . .

Now, again, she was left with nothing.

"I know what you need and where to find it."

At first Darcy had thought he was a jelly dealer, but her heart was tied to the aliens in a way that could never be satisfied by the drug, and she had no desire to end up like Ken Petrillo or Damon Eddington. No, she wanted to be alive and aware—*sharp* when the right opportunities, whatever they might be, came around again. Something had steered her in this direction . . . but what? Fate? Chance? Or some*one*? Desperation made her shove her doubts to the background when the slender man had led her up to the front of the room close to the altar, then guided her into the line of addicts filing toward the preacher and the rations he so carefully gave out.

"*In nomine Matri Regina.*"

When her turn came, she balanced on her crutches in front of him but did not hold out her hand, shook her head at the vial he proffered anyway. "That's not what I want," she said in a voice soft enough so that only he could hear. "I was told you could give me . . . something else."

Up so close to the preacher she could see the shrewd glint in his clear eyes and the softness of his well-cared-for skin; nothing about him seemed truly suited to this place, this self-proclaimed church for the masses of dirty, destitute junkies. Caught in their own hellish desire, the others in line would never notice the details, the fine capped teeth behind his smile, the hair painstakingly cut to look perpetually tousled.

"Yes," he said. His voice was a smooth, rich baritone, cultured and mesmerizing, trained for things of which his motley parish members would never envision or resist. "I believe I can do exactly that." He indicated the carefully camouflaged door with a tilt of his head. "If you will wait for me there, I will talk with you immediately after the service." In that soothing, singsong voice, the preacher's gaze went to the person behind her and the ceremony continued as if they had never spoken.

"*In nomine Matri Regina.*"

And give her something he did, and thus began the death of Darcy Vance—

—and the birth of Jariah, the first female preacher in the Manhattan branch of The Church of the Queen Mother.

Behind the locked steel doors Darcy née Jariah found fulfillment. She neither knew nor cared who her benefactor was, only that he or it or they somehow, in ways that were never quite clear and became increasingly nebulous as the weeks went by, fulfilled the longing in her for the sounds of alien screams. She found hope and a future, even if she had no clear vision of what that future held or what it was she truly hoped *for*. Training as a church disciple, she let everything in her old life go, right *then*, simply . . . left it and never returned. The junkies who surrounded her accepted her constant presence and learned to trust her, calling her by the new name or, more reverently, *The Limping Woman.* She often heard them whispering among themselves about the ragged patch of scar tissue that ringed her ankle below a dark, circular tattoo that looked oddly like teeth, inventing far-fetched tales that were closer to the truth than any of them dreamed.

At night in her simple room, her duties for each day completed and her heart serene, MedTech's newest trainee burned incense to the image of the queen mother and dreamed dark and impossibly musical dreams about a long-dead creature called Mozart.

ABOUT THE AUTHOR

YVONNE NAVARRO is a dark fantasy writer and illustrator who lives in a western suburb of Chicago. Her first short story appeared in *The Horror Show* in 1984, and since then her short fiction and illustrations have appeared in over forty anthologies and small press magazines. She has also authored a reference book called *The First Name Reverse Dictionary* for writers and parents to be. She has written three previous novels for Bantam, *AfterAge*, *Species* and *deadrush*, and has recently completed her next one, *Final Impact*.

Be sure to visit her website:
http://www.sff.net/people/y.navarro/
for updates, covers and excerpts from all Yvonne Navarro's novels.